Hailey,
I hope you enjoy!
[illegible]
Ps. 46:10

A Matter of Control

J.E. Solinski

Copyright © 2015 Jody Eileen Solinski.

All rights reserved. No part of this book may be used or reproduced by
any means, graphic, electronic, or mechanical, including photocopying,
recording, taping or by any information storage retrieval system
without the written permission of the publisher except in the case
of brief quotations embodied in critical articles and reviews.

All verses in this book are from the New American Standard Bible except the verses on the following pages: the page following the dedication, page 225, John 3:16 on page 296, and page 303. These four verses are from the New International Version.

Scripture quotations taken from the New American Standard Bible®,
Copyright © 1960, 1962, 1963, 1968, 1971, 1972, 1973, 1975, 1977, 1995
by The Lockman Foundation. Used by permission. (www.Lockman.org)

Scripture taken from the Holy Bible, NEW INTERNATIONAL VERSION®.
Copyright © 1973, 1978, 1984 by Biblica, Inc. All rights reserved worldwide.
Used by permission. NEW INTERNATIONAL VERSION® and NIV® are
registered trademarks of Biblica, Inc. Use of either trademark for the offering
of goods or services requires the prior written consent of Biblica US, Inc.

WestBow Press books may be ordered through booksellers or by contacting:

WestBow Press
A Division of Thomas Nelson & Zondervan
1663 Liberty Drive
Bloomington, IN 47403
www.westbowpress.com
1 (866) 928-1240

Because of the dynamic nature of the Internet, any web addresses or
links contained in this book may have changed since publication and
may no longer be valid. The views expressed in this work are solely those
of the author and do not necessarily reflect the views of the publisher,
and the publisher hereby disclaims any responsibility for them.

Any people depicted in stock imagery provided by Thinkstock are models,
and such images are being used for illustrative purposes only.
Certain stock imagery © Thinkstock.

ISBN: 978-1-4908-6496-9 (sc)
ISBN: 978-1-4908-6497-6 (hc)
ISBN: 978-1-4908-6495-2 (e)

Library of Congress Control Number: 2015900203

Printed in the United States of America.

WestBow Press rev. date: 1/28/2015

To my sister Pamela, whose initiative, encouragement, and artistic talent made this book a reality.

Then they will know that I am the Sovereign Lord.
(Ezekiel 29:16)

Chapter 1

Martha Richards snaked her way through the potholed streets that were steaming in the mid-August afternoon heat and eyed the world outside her closed car windows with a sense of despondency.

Young men, in their twenties perhaps, sat in the shadows of dilapidated doorways taking sips of Coors from cans held languidly from two fingers. They eyed her suspiciously as she drove slowly by. Teenage boys moved adroitly to the sounds screaming out of their anachronistic ghetto blasters, doing twenty-first-century versions of breaking, moonwalking, and "popping." They, too, watched her without missing a beat. A couple of boys leaned against a wall peppered with graffiti; each had one leg propped up behind him as they casually smoked cigarettes and followed the progress of her car behind the anonymity of mirrored Ray-Bans.

Down the street, small girls skipped rope on a sidewalk that looked like a jackhammer had been taken to it while a cluster of young boys squealed in the refreshing drenching that a broken water main afforded. On the corner, three young women clad in tight knit skirts, too-small tank tops, and three-inch heels swayed and strutted in a five-foot circle like wary tigers as they glared at Martha's car contemptuously.

A stooped figure with a dingy, wool winter coat—despite the ninety-plus heat—and wearing black rubber boots and a bright orange and white scarf that sported the letters "IGAN" worked her way through this montage of youth, managing to maneuver a full shopping cart through the masses without drawing any attention whatsoever.

As she did every year, Martha reevaluated her decision to drive through this section of Detroit, but she took this annual pilgrimage to remind herself of what needed to be done, what lives needed to be touched, and how she could best help. But instead, she was drenched in a heaviness that was more oppressive than the Detroit humidity as she gazed at the squalor, the apathy, and the anger staring back at her.

"Don't they realize they don't have to stay in this sty?" she muttered under her breath as she watched the seedy young men openly leering at the seductive young women who crossed their path. "They could get out. It's only a matter of having a little discipline."

She had escaped, and she was as black as any of them. Still, their eyes followed her suspiciously. Her new Basque Red Pearl Honda Civic was a definite anomaly on this street where huge, vintage black Cadillacs and ancient Lincolns lined the chipped curbs.

Martha felt like a foreigner even though she herself had been raised only a few blocks from here amid the drugs and gangs. She empathized with the young children who were laughing and playing with carefree abandon. How long would their innocence remain? How long before they recognized the filth that surrounded them … or had it already laid claim to their minds and souls? Would they be like frogs boiled alive because they never felt the gradual increase of heat? Tired of what she saw, she pushed the pedal and accelerated up the street, the eyes still following her intently.

The last four blocks held the same view. Neglected tenements connected by strings of laundry looking like miles of old, discarded

Christmas garland. Toothless, shirtless men loitered about the doorways; unkempt children ran in between abandoned cars and into the street without warning; and big, soft women hung loosely out of windows, fanning themselves apathetically.

Nothing changed. Children played in the potholed street, men lounged lazily in the doorways, young women flaunted their bodies, and all curiously watched the progress of the little red car making its way down the street.

At the next intersection, Martha turned right and after two more blocks, a huge brick building, looking like an early twentieth-century factory, complete with sordid horror stories about child labor abuse, rose off to her left. She turned into the empty parking lot that was surrounded by barbed wire and cyclone fencing, and stopped in front of the building. Martha glanced at her watch. One fifteen. Mr. Jackson, the veteran school custodian, had offered to open the door for her at one thirty. She decided to put off her afternoon sweat bath and left the car running while she waited.

Soon, the nearby door opened and an aged little black man with snowy white hair and a stooped back stepped out and put his hand up to shield his eyes from the afternoon sun. Spotting her car, his face broke into a wide toothless grin, and he waved her in. Martha turned off the car and stepped out. A huge blast of stagnant, heavy, hot air assaulted her, and she gasped as she tried to catch her breath. Even a lifetime of living in Detroit had not accustomed her to the hot and humid conditions.

"Hello, Mr. Jackson," she called out cheerfully, still trying to regain her breath. "Let me just grab a few things and I'll be right with you."

He nodded and then propped the door open and shuffled over to help her.

"My, you hab a ca full dere now don' you?" he said, more as a statement than a question. "Why don' ah gib you a hand and we'll get it all inside da do, and den ah'll get a dolly, an' we'll truck it on up to yo room. You still up on de thud flo?"

Martha nodded and smiled. Each year followed the same routine. Emmet Jackson would open the door early for her, offer to "truck" her supplies up to her room and then shake his head sadly when he learned she was still delegated to the third floor. But she didn't mind. She thrived on routine.

"Don' know why dey don' move you closer to de office. You have seniority now, don' you?" he asked.

Martha nodded to the last question and then just shook her head to the situation as a whole while Emmet clucked sadly. If the truth be known, she had no desire to be nearer the office. Too much commotion, too many distractions, and too much close scrutiny. The third floor suited her just fine.

They boarded the ancient elevator used for maintenance purposes only and creaked their way up two floors. With effort, Emmet pulled back the iron grating, which at one time might have boasted of a rich, glossy black coat, but now looked as though acid rain had eaten away at it. He shuffled down the hall to room 312, pushing the loaded dolly ahead of him.

"You don' got yo keys yet, do you?" he said when they reached the room.

"Not till Friday," she answered, silently wondering why the obsolete bureaucratic red tape that prohibited teachers from having access to the premises until the day before school started was still on the books. *What are they afraid we'll do that the kids haven't done already?* she wondered.

She held her breath as Emmet opened the door. At the end of each school year, she left her room immaculate, and each year after summer school—or Montgomery's version of it—it was destroyed.

The door swung open and Martha's heart sank. Besides the oppressive heat and stagnant air, piles of papers littered the teacher's desk and the floor. Jars of dirty water and empty clay pots lined the cabinets. Student desks were turned over with clumps of gum stuck to the bottom of most. Those still upright were covered with graffiti and carvings. Cobwebs hung in every corner, and a layer of dust covered every flat surface. The sun, though shining brightly outside, was diffused by a greasy film on the windows.

Martha just stood there and felt her heart sink lower and lower.

"Guess the boys habn' made it up here yet," Emmet said with little concern. "Yo can leeb yo stuff here and come back Friday if yo like. Might be ready by then." Martha gave him a knowing look, and he withered beneath her stare.

"Awright, awright," he said, quickly leading the way out of the room and down the hall. "I'll open the janitor's closet for yo, but's not yo job, yo know. Dey'll get to it by the end of the week if you can wait."

"Well, I can't, Emmet, and you know that," she replied, and the little man nodded.

"I unnerstan." He opened up a small room that held a sink and a host of janitorial supplies that Martha suspected had seldom been used.

"I'll jes leeb dis do open and yo can use whateba yo need. Jes lock it up when yo leeb."

Martha thanked the little man and watched him shuffle away down the hall to do whatever it was he did. She found a broom, dustpan, and a box of large garbage bags and went back to do the first round of clean-up. The empty lockers that lined the hallway gaped openly at her, revealing all sorts of private and perverted messages on their inner walls. Even after twenty years of teaching, she still blushed.

When she returned to her room, she made a final reconnaissance of the nuclear disaster before her, mentally formed her plan of attack, and headed for the back corner. She would work her way to the door. A sharp whistle blast from outside caught her attention. Martha wiped a small circle clean in the greasy window and looked down to the field below.

Despite the oppressive heat, some sixty football hopefuls in shorts, helmets, and shoulder pads ran patterns on the field beneath her. She watched the quarterback pull back, set up, and then throw toward the sideline. His receiver, at the cut, turned right instead of left, and the ball whistled toward no one. The quarterback dropped his head in disgust; the coach threw his arms up in a rage and headed for the receiver, berating him in pantomime. Martha felt a sudden pang of pity for the receiver, who had obviously misread the play. She turned back to the job before her.

"Thus begins another school year," she said softly and began throwing handfuls of papers into the bag.

"Ready. Set." The whistle blasted, and Alex pushed off the line and sprinted twenty yards downfield. At the hash mark, he feinted a move to his left and then cut right, leaving his defender a good two steps behind. He looked up for the ball, but instead of being right in his hands, there was nothing. He slowed to a halt, and out of the corner of his eye saw a brown object careening off the sideline.

"*Kowalski! What do you think you're doing?*" Alex's mistake became clear to him, and he jogged dejectedly back toward the line of scrimmage, but Coach Bauer wasn't through with him just yet. He grabbed Alex's face mask and jerked his head toward him until Alex was staring straight into his eyes.

"When the play is called "stadium left" that means go to your left. Makes sense, doesn't it, Kowalski?" he yelled with more than a hint of sarcasm. Coach Bauer's face was only inches from Alex's, and his breath was hot and stale, but there was nowhere for Alex to go. Coach had a firm grip on his face mask.

"Yes, sir," he replied, trying hard not to breathe.

"Or don't you know your left from your right, Kowalski?" And he jerked his helmet back the other way as he released him. "Brighten up, Kowalski, if you expect to play varsity football!"

Humiliated, Alex trotted back to the end of the line.

"C'mon, man, get your head together," came a voice to his left, and he looked up to see Richard, his best friend, staring at him strangely. "I haven't seen you make that mistake since the beginning of last season. What gives?"

Alex just shook his head and turned away. It was too tough to explain. How did you tell your best buddy that Coach was right, that he *was* a dummy, that he *didn't* know his left from his right, that *that* was half of the reason he was almost seventeen and only a sophomore.

He watched Richard step up to the line and explode at the whistle. His muscular, long brown legs outstriding his defender within twenty yards, his smooth cut losing the guy completely, and his long fingers pulling in the ball before he fluidly turned downfield.

Alex marveled at Richard's skill—Jerry Rice reincarnated. And bright, too. Richard was a junior and headed for college. Between all his honors classes and athletic talent, he was bound to get a scholarship or two from somewhere. Why Richard had ever befriended him was still a mystery to Alex, but the liaison had formed years before when they were both in grammar school and in the same grade. Even when Alex was held back, Richard was always there.

Richard came trotting back grinning and flipped the ball to an assistant coach. Alex stepped out of line and slapped him on the back.

"Nice catch, Rice cake."

"Now let's see you match it." The challenge came flying back.

Alex bent down and untied the shoestring on his right shoe, wrapped it once around the toe and then retied it.

"Ring—right," he told himself. Last year he had actually worn a ring on his right hand to help him remember his directions, but a spring and summer of weight lifting had made his fingers too big. He hoped the shoestring would be enough of a help. When it was his turn again, he stepped up to the line, his heart pounding so hard in his chest he almost didn't hear the cadence.

"Red 24–left," called the coach. "Ready. Set …" Alex checked his shoes. *The other way,* he thought. The whistle blasted and he shot off the line, made a slight move to the right, cut left for five yards, and then turned back downfield. This time when he looked up toward the sideline, the ball was there but too high. He took a couple of more steps and then left his feet, his arms stretching for the ball, never taking his eyes off of it.

He felt the rough leather touch his outstretched fingers, and he pulled it toward him until he clutched it possessively next to his chest. By this time, all forward momentum had ceased and gravity took effect. Alex landed on the ground with a thud, but the football remained securely in his grasp. He picked himself up and jogged back to the line, flipping the ball to Coach Bauer as he passed by.

"Better, Kowalski," was his only comment, but Richard met him in line for a high five, followed by a reverse low five, and then an elbow crash.

"Yea, my man. That's the Polish Piston we're used to seeing."

Alex grinned and fell back into line. Polish Piston was a nickname Richard had started way back in the third grade when Alex had beaten most of the black boys in sprints. "Legs like pistons," Richard had said, which was more than appropriate for a white boy raised in Detroit, whose father worked the line at the Dodge Hamtramck plant. The name stuck, and Alex kind of liked it.

Practice wore on, and the heat and humidity intensified. Receiving patterns were followed by footwork drills, then blocking drills, and finally sprints. By four o'clock, Alex's lungs screamed for air, his muscles ached, and his body dripped in sweat. He and Richard walked silently to the locker room.

The shower washed away the layers of turf and salt but did little to refresh him. The Detroit humidity seeped through the porous walls, and even after toweling off, he was just as wet as before his shower. Alex sat limply on the bench, dredging up enough energy to comb his wet hair.

"You get your schedule in the mail?" he asked Richard.

"Shore did. Got every class I wanted too, even old Baxter for chemistry. The guy may have one foot in the grave, but he knoooows his chemistry." Richard laughed. "How 'bout you? Whadya get?"

Alex pulled a slip out of his shirt pocket and tossed it casually to Richard.

"See for yourself."

Richard caught the paper in midair and glanced down the list before letting out a slow whistle.

"What's the matter?" Alex asked.

"You've got crazy Manheim for geometry. That little dude is a disaster waiting to happen, with a sense of humor as dry as the Gobi Desert and a vocabulary half Hebrew. Man, *I* didn't even know what he was sayin' half the time."

Richard pulled in his full lips till they formed a tight pucker, somehow metamorphosed his six-three, one-eighty frame to take on the appearance of a five-five weakling and crossed his eyes. He placed his hands before him with fingertips touching just under his chin, glanced down at his mismatched socks, and then said in a high, nasal twang, "I guess I am not congruent."

Alex burst out laughing, and Richard stood up straight. "And that was one of his *good* jokes. I can remember copying down an Algebra II problem that was half a mile long, and when he got to the end, you know, where the answer's supposed to be," Richard rolled his dark brown eyes melodramatically, "he stands up and looks at his work and says, 'I made a mistake somewhere' and then proceeds to erase the entire north wall. I tell you, Polish, you are in for a year of heartburn with Manny."

Alex just grinned. With Richard already conceding he'd need help, it would be much easier to get it from him. "What do you think about the rest of my schedule?" he asked, and Richard looked back at the piece of paper.

"Not bad, not bad. First, Jackson for history. He's cool. Won't tax that porous brain of yours. Second …" he paused. "Richards for English." He looked down at Alex. "She's tough, man. No nonsense, but you'll learn something."

He went through the rest of the schedule while Alex half listened. Richards for English meant problems. Most of the teachers had given up on him, but she had a reputation for staying on a guy. He sighed deeply.

"Ahhhh," Richard concluded. "Then you finish up with the silver tongue himself, Coach Bauer, for good ole weight training. But at least you and I will have *one* class together." He handed Alex back his schedule and shut his locker.

Alex took the paper and looked at it carefully. Little did Richard know how much he wanted to have other classes with him as well—to take chemistry, and calculus, and the harder classes. When they talked, the subjects thrilled him, and he actually caught on quickly and retained just about everything Richard said.

He glanced back at the paper in his hand. But that would never be. Not when even the little symbols on his schedule made no sense to him. Not when sometimes he couldn't even recognize his own name if it was in a different handwriting. Not when he didn't know his left from his right.

Discouraged, he stuffed the paper into his pocket. Manipulation had gotten him through school this far. Already, without even being able to read a letter on the page, he had his schedule memorized, first by having his mother look it over and then asking her strategic questions, and now with Richard. He shut his locker and followed Richard out into the oppressive air.

Sometimes he felt he knew more than anyone else, that he understood concepts the other kids couldn't grasp, but that didn't make sense. There was something drastically wrong with a guy who was almost seventeen but couldn't read, yet tried so hard to; who didn't know his left from his right even though he worked on it year after year. Coach Bauer was right. He *was* just a dummy.

Chapter 2

Reba slid the two new, unsharpened Dixon pencils and one blue, medium-point Bic pen into the plastic pouch and then zipped it up and ran her hand over the cool plastic, smoothing it out. Before closing her new slant-ring binder, she checked to make sure there was an even amount of paper behind each colored divider: English, Introduction to Physical Science, World History, Geometry, and Drama. It was doubtful that she would need paper for PE, but she included some after a sixth tab just in case. She rechecked to make sure her schedule was taped securely to the inside cover of her binder and then satisfied all was in place, she closed it and set it on the bed.

She took the remaining box of pencils and the package of pens and went to the dresser, opened the top drawer—*her* drawer—and carefully placed them under a pile of neatly folded blouses. After closing the drawer, Reba retrieved the binder off her bed and took it over to a homemade bookshelf nailed to the opposite wall and placed it up next to the small collection of books.

As always, Reba glanced at the titles, each immediately evoking a pleasant memory. They were arranged according to height, starting with Dr. Suess's *Horton Hears a Who!* and *Green Eggs and Ham*. She reached up and tenderly pulled down the next book, *The Velveteen Rabbit*, flipping through its tattered pages. It had gone through four children already, and now her mother was reading it to three-year-old Chris.

Reba placed it back on the shelf and smiled wanly. She could hardly believe she was already a freshman in high school. It seemed like only yesterday that Mamma was "reading" her that book—after a fashion—for in those days, her mother couldn't read. She had only purchased the book because Reba, her oldest and only two years old at the time, had reached for the big book with the picture of the motley rabbit on the front every time they walked by the bookstore.

Mrs. Washington had brought it home, propped Reba up on her knee, and, going by the clues supplied by the pictures, created a story that was remarkably close to the one in print. Mr. Washington, listening from his chair, would have been glad to help, but he couldn't read either.

By attending Head Start and watching *Sesame Street* on an old Motorola television set, Reba learned to read by the middle of kindergarten. Suddenly, she realized that the words on the pages of *The Velveteen Rabbit* were not the ones her mother had been saying all these years.

"Why do you tell the story different?" Reba had asked one day.

Her mother didn't hesitate to state the truth. "Because I can't read the story they tell with the words," she had admitted matter-of-factly.

The confession had had little effect on the tiny five-year-old, who replied as matter-of-factly as her mother, "Well, I know how to read, so I can teach you." And she did. As a five-year-old, each evening she would sit between her parents on the worn sofa with two-year-old Willie on her father's lap and go through the sounds and letter combinations and words that she herself had just learned that day, until sure enough, her parents, as well as little Willie, did learn to read. When Jake was born, Reba decided to start early, so

The Velveteen Rabbit and the Dr. Suess stories were read to the baby as he lay on the floor.

By the time Jocelyn came along, Reba was ten, and her small collection of books had grown. The adventures of Henry Huggins and Ramona Quimby had been added. The poems of Paul Laurence Dunbar were read or recited to the troops as well as excerpts from *Jane Eyre* and *Anne of Green Gables.* In their little bedroom, she would pull in the kitchen chairs and the footstool and set up a school of her own, mercilessly putting her charges through their tasks of writing their names and reciting verses from the Bible as well as creating stories of their own.

But they adored their older sister, and so while Reba would sit at the kitchen table each night doing her homework, the little ones would pick up some work of their own and join her—even the youngest who was just big enough to grab his coloring book.

Reba straightened the other books and then checked to make sure the rest of the room was in order, which was why her mother had sent her in there in the first place. She glanced around the bedroom. Two sets of bunk beds—one iron, carefully painted white; and the other wood, chipped from years of use but still highly polished—stood opposite each other. Between them and beneath the one window in the room on the north wall was the four-drawer dresser, one drawer for each child.

The bookshelf was on the south wall next to the door that led out to the kitchen-living area. A threadbare throw rug lay in the space between the two beds. Besides the ceiling lamp, there was nothing else in the room. To say the least, it was meagerly furnished but meticulously kept.

The remainder of the small apartment was the same way. The second bedroom housed a double bed for her parents, a small roll-away for little Chris, and another dresser. The main room had a small alcove that served as the kitchen. A long wooden table with eight chairs around it—seven for the family and one for company—divided the kitchen from the living area, which was determined by another large, threadbare throw rug surrounded by the same sofa and Motorola television set of Reba's youth. Two secondhand easy chairs and a reading lamp rounded out the decor.

All the windows in the house (one in each room) were tightly closed, desperately trying to shut out the ninety-degree heat and 99 percent humidity. However, in the living room, her father had devised a crude air conditioner, having secured two augers to a small table, which held a huge block of ice over a Rubbermaid tub. Behind it a small fan blew, melting the ice and sending the cool air into the small room in a narrow, steady stream.

It was all Reba had ever known. Money had always been scarce. Her father had worked at the Dodge plant, but as the technology increased and his illiteracy was discovered, he was released because he couldn't keep up. He picked up whatever odd jobs he could, and once he learned to read, he started back to school too, trying to bring himself back into the job market.

Mrs. Washington baked. One of the local cafés bought a dozen pies each Saturday. Between the two parents, they had always managed to pull in just slightly less income a month than they could have received through welfare. And after their fifth child was born, the gap grew even greater, but they refused to give in. A proud man, Mr. Washington vowed to support his family through his own efforts, and Mrs. Washington met his determination with her own.

This was Reba's home. Her family valued work, and they were not afraid to admit to a deficiency and then work to correct it. Education was a privilege and a way out of the poverty that had plagued them all their lives, and Reba, like her parents, believed it.

She loved school—especially reading—and would lose herself in the strange and novel worlds of her heroines, dreaming what it would be like to live in England or on Prince Edward Island or to cross the prairie with the Ingalls.

"Reba, are you finished?" her mother called from the other room. "It's time to take the children for their ice cream."

Reba glanced at the Timex on her wrist, an eighth-grade

graduation present from her parents and one of her few extravagances. Two o'clock. They should have been gone by now.

Despite their relative poverty, the Washingtons were not without indulging their children with special treats. Each Friday, all summer, Reba would pack up her four younger siblings and take them three blocks to the ice cream parlor for two scoops of their favorite flavors. Then the remainder of the afternoon would be spent at the park. The Friday ritual not only gave the kids something to look forward to, but it allowed Mrs. Washington a brief respite from her baking and children.

Reba gathered up little Chris while Willie ran to get his basketball. Though it was doubtful that family genetics would ever let him grow much past six feet, Willie was determined to be the next pro basketball player to rise out of the local ghettos of Detroit and play for the Pistons.

The five left the relative coolness of their tiny apartment and worked their way down the three flights of stairs to the streets below. The suffocating heat and stench of the closed hallways was unbearable, even after a lifetime of living there, and they ran down the stairs as quickly as possible.

Once outside, only the acrid smell of sweating bodies disappeared; the oppressive humidity, the yelling, the heat were all still there. Despite the glare of the sun off the pavement, the sky had a hazy texture to it, indicative of an industrial city where the smoke that spews heavenward eventually filters back down with every particle of air. The primary color was gray; the primary mood, except for the children playing, sullen.

But Reba noticed little of it. This was her home, and she accepted the conditions of it without question, the way children in New England accept snow in January; children in LA, morning fog in June; and children in Portland, Oregon, rain in any month.

Reba led her siblings past the stoops, crowded with loiterers, and down the street. Halfway up the block, she was silently joined by a well-built black boy, a year or two older, wearing the nondescript jeans, T-shirt, and mirrored Ray-Bans of the neighborhood. He fell into step with her and little Chris, while the others followed. Willie dribbled the ball back and forth between his legs, Jocelyn silently avoided all cracks, and Jake enviously eyed the boys enjoying the spray of the broken water main.

"Hi, Travis," Reba said, looking straight ahead, never visually acknowledging his presence.

"Reba," was his only reply.

"Get your schedule?" she asked.

"Yup."

"Everything you wanted?"

"Yup."

"If you're busy, we'll be fine," she said.

"Not busy."

The conversation ceased, and the remaining two blocks were covered in silence. At the drugstore, Reba herded the children inside and then hesitated before entering, looking at Travis.

"I'll wait for you here," he said and propped himself up against the wall, his face carrying the same stony facade it had for the last three blocks.

Reba still hesitated, wanting to invite Travis in to share her ice cream, but knowing he would refuse. His presence was not a social gesture nor a budding, romantic one. He was here out of some sense of duty and protection, and Reba both knew and appreciated it. It was not Reba who needed protecting, but Willie, for at eleven, he was at the age when gang recruitment was heaviest. He would be a prime mule; old enough to have some street sense; young enough to avoid prosecution if caught.

Perhaps it was ironic that Travis was acting as bodyguard, for Travis, though only sixteen, had already worked his way up his gang's—the Marauders—organizational chart and into a position of leadership in the complex drug market that pervaded Detroit's underground culture. But the Washingtons, and Reba especially, were friends—friends of a different breed who desired to live by a different set of standards than the ones prescribed by the Detroit slums, and Travis openly admired that and ferociously protected it.

Inside, Reba followed the ordering and then paid Mr. Porter the exact amount. Then each head, from Chris's little pile of tight curls to Willie's shaved sides, bowed silently and offered a silent prayer of thanks. Reba inwardly thanked God for his kindness and protection and then as always, she interceded for Travis, a boy who, as his name suggested, was at the crossroads of life. He had established himself as their protector, and she prayed that God would reveal himself to Travis and let him know there was someone standing by who wanted to do the same for him.

Earlier

Travis took a long, succulent draw on his Marlboro and relished the thick, pungent smoke that filled his mouth. He lowered his arm, slowly exhaled through his nose, then automatically flicked the burning ashes onto the pavement next to his feet and, without moving his head, took a quick survey of the street's activity. Mona and Charlene were setting up tricks on the corner; Quincy was bragging about last night's "take"; the kids were playing in the streets, seemingly oblivious to the activities around them, except that every now and then one would separate himself from his peers, meet on the corner with an older youth, take something, and disappear.

To an innocent bystander, of which there were none in this section of Detroit, the street conveyed an air of listless apathy mixed with childish frivolity. But to Travis, trained in reading the lines of this neighborhood and every other ghetto neighborhood, each move was calculated, each look planned, every meeting purposeful.

Even though just sixteen, Travis had the reputation of being one of Detroit's most successful gang leaders, and he carried that responsibility with calm assurance, having been shot twice already, and having killed a competitive drug lord without shedding a tear, flinching a muscle, or showing any sign of remorse. He had earned the nickname "Stone-bone."

He took another long draw on his cigarette and glanced at his watch, a $2,000 Rolex, the only visible extravagance he wore. While LA gangs might still be wearing colors and flashing their wealth, the Detroit gangs had abandoned such practices long ago. Such exhibitionism only drew attention to the members and made them an easy target for the police, who had decided a crackdown was in order. So the Detroit gangs had discarded the showiness of the rest of the nation's gangs and moved underground and become more organized, and more lethal, though the Detroit police would have one believe that they no longer existed.

Travis glanced at his watch again. One fifty. Reba was late. He tossed his cigarette away and glanced down the street where a group of the Marauders had congregated. Tanisha was moving seductively among the guys, teasing them. Travis watched without emotion. For him, the traditions of the gang life had lost their appeal long ago.

He glanced at his watch again. One fifty-five. Where was she? He glanced quickly to his left to see if anyone had exited the building. No one. He pulled out another cigarette, started to light it, and then stopped. Reba hated cigarettes. He'd wait. Travis thought about what he would do tonight if he didn't hang with the others at the warehouse, partying. He couldn't go home—well, he could, but he didn't want to, not till late.

Home was not much different than the gang party. His mother was an addict herself, willing to bed down with any guy able to give her five grams. Come home before twelve, and you were greeted by animalistic moanings coming from the bedroom, partitioned only by a flimsy blanket. When he was seven or eight, right after his father just up and disappeared, he was drawn to the room and would sit in the dark, late at night, the blanket ever so slightly pulled back, trying to get a peek at what was going on. When his eyes finally adjusted, he was repulsed by what he saw.

Travis had hit the streets soon after. Not merely because of his mother's nightly adventures but also because the tiny apartment reeked of sweat and urine and three-day-old diapers, and there wasn't any food. The middle of seven children, he had never thought about what the older three did or where they went. He just knew that they didn't spend much time at home. Now he knew why.

He became a runner, taking drugs from dealer to buyer, slipping in and out of shadows, faithfully bringing back all the money. As his reputation grew, so did his responsibility, and by the time he was ten, he was moved to the white sectors, the more affluent black areas, downtown, and to the college campuses, all of which had a rich history of buying drugs. Unfortunately, those turfs were not Marauder drug territory, and the reigning gangs did not appreciate his being there.

It was on one of these runs that he was first shot, through the left shoulder, by an unexpected single-shot rifle. The bullet hadn't come close to any vital organs, but the burning pain seared through him, and though he thought he was going to die, he never let out a cry and refused to fall. Travis ran the entire two miles back to safe ground, holding his bleeding shoulder and biting his lower lip. When he finally made it to the old abandoned warehouse used for gang meetings, one of the members fixed him up. The bullet had gone clean through. In a week, he was back on the street.

Travis was fourteen when he was shot the second time, but this time he wasn't so lucky. Determined to prove himself a leader, he rallied a group around him to take over one of the disputed drug turfs, and armed with his own AK-47, he hired a driver, and the foursome headed out. He had expected to scare off some of the mules but never expected to see the kingpin himself.

But as they rounded the corner, there he was, right in Travis's sight. Not wanting to miss, Travis slid the van door wide open so that nothing would obstruct his view or aim, and even though the driver gunned it twenty yards before the hit, one of the opposing force was able to get off a round of his own, peppering Travis with a series of bullets right in the abdomen.

With Travis bleeding profusely, the van rushed toward the nearest hospital and then just dumped him in the emergency room parking lot. Not until he was released a week later did he learn that *his* shots had also hit their mark—fatally. He immediately moved up the "corporate" ladder and earned that stoic nickname of Stone-bone.

Travis glanced at his watch again: five after. He let out an impatient sigh. Where was she? He stood up just as the familiar figure exited the apartment complex door with three-year-old Chris in tow. Immediately he resumed his earlier position, not wanting her to see his impatience. The little entourage approached him, and he seemed not to notice, but when they came even with him, he smoothly pivoted and joined them, never looking, never acknowledging. Reba knew the game and played along, but even though she was willing not to look at him, she could not refrain from talking to him. He answered her in monosyllables.

He wasn't sure what had driven him to be bodyguard to this quintet. He had no physical attraction to Reba, not even in the crudest sense of the term. Two years his younger, she was not pretty. Her nose was flat with flaring nostrils; her lips, large and thick on her round billiard-ball face, were not large enough to hide her slightly bucked teeth; and her eyes were big with too much white around them. She had tried to straighten her hair, but that had only succeeded in causing it to stand perpendicular to her head if she didn't tie it down or back or something, like she did now.

Reba was scrawny, barely five feet, with somewhat bowed legs. She was a poor cross between Cicely Tyson and Whoopie Goldberg. She was the Washingtons' firstborn, and it was as if God had been experimenting to see just how ugly he could make someone. When he thought he had succeeded, he tried it again on a boy: Willie. Willie was the spitting image of his older sister, only he shaved off most of his hair instead of trying to straighten it.

Travis stared straight ahead and could hear the rhythmic dribble of Willie's basketball and the plodding of young Jake, but he could also pick up the silence, and he knew that silence was Jocelyn. In spite of himself, Travis felt himself smile a bit. Little four-year-old Jocelyn was God's apology to the Washingtons. She was beautiful, with thin lips, light-brown skin, aquiline nose, and soft brown eyes with long lashes. Her hair seemed to naturally brush straight, and Travis had a feeling that this is what Whitney Houston looked like as a four-year-old.

Little Chris worked hard to keep up with his big sister. Chris, like Jake, was a cross: a little too much of the Reba side, but at least enough of Jocelyn's good looks to save him from ridicule later on.

Travis escorted the five down the street, not worrying about his motives. Reba, he knew, had nothing to fear. Her size and looks were assurance that no gang would try to bring her in. Besides, girls weren't usually recruited but joined of their own free will, and he knew that Reba would not join. No, his first concern was Willie. Though Travis held a prominent role in the Marauders, he was not in charge of recruitment, a necessary and ongoing process. Willie was perfect both in size and age, and Jake wasn't too far behind. Only Travis's presence would keep the dogs at bay. And he wanted to keep them at bay, to protect this family.

The Washingtons were the only people who evoked some feeling in him. He and Reba had become "friends" in grammar school when Mrs. Washington had elicited the help of seven-year-old Travis to walk kindergartner Reba to and from school. He had accepted out of ignorance, but the payback had been a weekly meal at their home, and there was something about this family that spoke to him, that made his heart yearn.

Perhaps it was the quietness or cleanliness of their home—two things he was not accustomed to—or perhaps it was the simple pride of Mr. Washington, the obvious love of Mrs. Washington, or Reba's overt determination and candor. Travis didn't know. He had not openly responded to any of it, never letting them know he appreciated them or their home, but that had never stopped them from sharing their lives with him or from him coming back week after week.

Today as they arrived at the drugstore, he casually took a position against the wall, his mirrored eyes staring at the building across the street. Reba glanced at him, but before she could say anything, he spoke.

"I'll wait for you here," he said. He saw her hesitate before entering and then she disappeared. He released his pent-up breath. He wouldn't have minded having some ice cream, and certainly could afford it a lot more than they could, but he knew they were going to pray, the way they did in their home before each meal. That was why he had finally stopped accepting their invitations. He couldn't buy it.

How could a person believe in a God who made everything if this part of Detroit was part of that creation? A God who saw what he made and said it was good. What was good about this neighborhood where drug dealing, prostitution, murder, and rape were common occurrences? Where forty-year-old men going on eighty wallowed in their own poverty, liquor, and urine? Where the local flower was opium; the tree, marijuana; and the candy, crack?

No, it made no sense, and more than anything else in the world, Travis desperately wanted this family and what they had to make sense.

Chapter 3

The Montgomery High School library teemed with the sights and sounds and smells of the opening of school. Teachers were back after a summer of second jobs, required college courses to keep their credentials current, tedious planning for new classes, and then frantic last-minute planning because those courses were changed. They milled about, each migrating to his or her appointed clique—comparing, complaining.

The voices that mingled in the open air were a mixture of the boisterous laughter and locker-room stories of the male coaches, the disgruntled grumbling of the burnouts, the excited chatter of friends who hadn't seen each other in almost three months, and the anxious concerns of the new teachers.

Wafting its way between all of this was the rich aroma of fresh coffee, the steam from the cups rising like little volcanic spews. Also permeating the room was the acrid, heavy smell of cigarette smoke, which, though restricted to the teachers' lounge, had found its way into the library and had most of the teachers coughing and unconsciously fanning it out of their faces.

Martha Richards walked in and quickly surveyed the scene. She caught the eye of head football coach Lennis Bauer and gave him a wry grin, which he returned with a casual salute. In the twenty years that both had been at Montgomery, they had definitely had their differences of opinions, but as the years passed, the two had learned to respect, admire, and depend on each other.

She stopped and talked quietly with the cluster of new teachers who looked like gun-shy recruits on the eve of their first battle. She wished them her best and gave them her room number should they have any problems or questions. They, in return, smiled gratefully. It was only then that her eyes fell on a short, curly haired brunette who smiled broadly and waved her over with both arms.

"Martha! Martha! We've been wondering where you've been. You just about missed the sweet rolls. Another two minutes and those coaches would have helped themselves to fifths!"

Martha suppressed a laugh but let a smile escape. Clarice Mulholland had exaggerated the situation just a bit because everything about Clarice was exaggerated. If any sweet rolls were in danger, it was from Clarice's sweet tooth, not the coaches.

Clarice stood only four eleven but weighed a portly 150 pounds. A broad smile and high, full cheekbones took up most of her round face. Her eyes would take turns between hiding in the folds of her flesh when she smiled and opening to full moons in utter amazement. She spoke with her hands, her arms, her eyes, and her mouth, and she taught with the same vivacity. Any student who wound up with Clarice Mulholland for French came out of that class with an enthusiasm and knowledge of the language, the people, and Miss Mulholland.

This enthusiasm was what had first attracted Martha to the other woman when Clarice arrived at Montgomery five years ago. Here was another teacher who didn't water down her classes because the students "weren't as bright," or "had too many problems at home," or "weren't doing anything," or "didn't like French."

When you took French from Clarice Mulholland, you signed up for the whole nine yards: irregular verbs, subjunctive case, imperfect forms—everything! It was an intense saturation into the language and culture, and if you didn't swim, you sank. But Clarice managed to keep most of her little crew afloat, and year by year her classes grew, refuting all theories that "these kids" really didn't want to be challenged.

"Testing. One. Two. Testing."

The voice of Principal Bob Smith crackled over the portable sound system as he and Emmet worked with the controls to get the static out. Though Bob Smith tried to appear casual in jeans and a golf shirt, he still looked like a principal: ineffectual and nondescript. Thin, blond hair on a balding scalp, poker face to please all yet none, and a thin smile that assured even the most veteran of teachers that he always had one up his sleeve so don't even try.

"Testing. One. Two."

A loud screech erupted, and hands rushed to protect sensitive ears. Principal Smith smiled apologetically, while Emmet frantically turned knobs and flipped switches until the screeching and crackling vanished.

"All right, ladies and gentlemen. If we could have all of you find a seat, we will begin."

The volume of the conversations diminished, but the conversations themselves did not as the various groups moved to the center of the library where rows of chairs had been set up.

"Thank you. If we could have some of you move to the front." A twitter of laughter floated through the room. Teachers were no better than kids.

"There are some empty chairs up front," Principal Smith encouraged to those men who had decided to stand in the back. "Everyone gets a seat," and he motioned them to move forward. Begrudgingly they shuffled to the front.

"Thataway, Jimmy," a fellow coach taunted. "Take a front seat." Jim Crowell turned and stuck his tongue out at the perpetrator, and the coaches' corner roared. Martha smiled and shook her head. Fifteen years ago she would have found such behavior juvenile, but time had taught her that levity was one of the basic necessities of the teaching profession. It helped insure longevity.

Principal Smith smiled in spite of himself. "Thank you, Jimmy." He turned to face the rest of the faculty. "It's good to see all of you back and to welcome the new teachers to our staff," he said, directing his last comment to the four who had voluntarily chosen front seats and sat ready to take notes. "I know we're all looking forward to a successful and rewarding year here at Montgomery High—"

"Hummmph!" snorted Phil Clark from the back row, interrupting Principal Smith's welcome. Right then Martha knew the school year had officially begun.

Alex finished his shower, feeling the soreness of his muscles, but he didn't mind. It was Friday and there was only one practice today due to the teachers' meetings. He grinned contentedly. With the teachers strolling around, it was beginning to feel like school again, and even though he struggled every year, he honestly had to admit he liked school.

He combed his wet hair back into place. Then he buttoned his shirt and tucked it in, making sure it was neat and snug in the back. He stepped back and looked himself over in the mirror and smiled ruefully. He looked okay, but he was definitely looking more Polish all the time.

Alex had high cheekbones with that splash of red to them and small eyes in a rather full face. His blond hair was straight, but not too long. Football saw to that. He had that Polish build too. At five ten and 185, he was built for power and speed. He would be the first great Polish receiver. There had been linemen and linebackers and even a pro quarterback, but the blacks with their excess of gray muscle fibers, which physiologists said supplied a person with quickness, jumping ability, and bursts of power, still had the market on the running back and wide receiver positions. Most white guys had to settle for tight ends and fullback positions, where lumbering brute force was the call. But he would change all that. His smile broadened as his mind drifted off toward the future.

"Hey, Piston. Got a girl on your mind?"

Alex's mind returned abruptly to the present.

"What?" He looked up to see Richard standing there, grinning at him.

"You have a smile half a mile long. You've been primping before that mirror for, gee"—he glanced at his watch—"all of twenty minutes now." Richard shrugged. "Has to be a girl."

Alex felt a rush of blood go to his already ruddy cheeks and cursed his pale skin. A second reason it would be nice to be black. Richard's grin broadened, and Alex knew his embarrassment was apparent.

"No—no girl," he replied.

Richard's eyes shot open in disbelief. "Well then, where was that little pea brain of yours?"

Even though he knew Richard was only joking, Alex grimaced at the mention of his substandard mental ability. That humorous reminder popped the bubble of the dream he was carrying in his head. He would never make it to college, and if a guy didn't go to college, what chance did he ever have of getting a pro career? No, his lot was going to be like his dad's: twenty-five years on the assembly line of one of the big three. If they lasted that long. The way the economy and the layoffs were headed, by the time he graduated from school, American cars could be obsolete.

He felt the blood drain from his cheeks, replaced by pale reality, but he countered Richard's joke as he always had, with a little humor of his own. "It wasn't just *one* girl I was thinking about," he said with a grin. "I was admiring what *all* of them were missing." Richard gave him a "get real" look and then slapped him on the head.

"Now I know you've got a screw loose, Polish," he said and grabbed Alex around the neck in a headlock and pulled him toward the door.

Martha pulled the class lists out of her box and gradually looked over the list of names. Though many were unfamiliar, after twenty years of teaching, there were a lot of duplicates. Some she had heard only through dangerous lunchtime gossip. Others she knew all too well: *John Carpenter. Possibly Sarah and Gary's brother. Another Pike? Heavens. Thought we had graduated the last Pike last year. Don't tell me there are more coming. … Stuart. Please, Lord, if this one is related to Martin and Priscilla, may she be the kind of student Martin was and Priscilla was not.* Her drama classes offered a lot of repeats since it was a class students could take more than once for credit.

She looked at her numbers. Thirty-five in first period Freshman College Prep English. Twenty-five in sophomore remedial. Now that was a nice change. Were the counselors really trying to keep the numbers down or was this a fluke on the part of the computers? Martha had taught long enough to know not to celebrate too soon what, on paper, looked like a small class. They had a way of filling up rapidly.

Third period junior English had thirty-two. Fourth period was prep. Then lunch. After lunch came drama: fifth period beginning drama sat at a whopping forty, and Martha knew that as large as that seemed now, it too would grow. Drama became the dumping ground for counselors who still thought of it as a nothing class. But sixth period—her advanced drama class—rested easy at thirty. And what a thirty they were. Many had the potential for going on and pursuing some dramatic career. Others had gained self-respect and poise from their years of work. It was a wonderful way to end the day.

She shuffled the papers in her hands, glancing at the names quickly, and then she closed her eyes in her traditional beginning-of-the-school-year prayer. *Lord,* she prayed while around her the bustle of pre-school activities continued. *I pray for each of these students whom you have placed in my care this year. Only you know what their personal and academic needs are, but I pray that you make me a willing listener, an avid encourager and exhorter, and a fruitful teacher. May I follow your example as the great teacher, recognizing where my students are, where they need to be, and how to get them there. May I not expect less of them or myself. Give me the strength and wisdom to meet each of their needs. Amen.*

She opened her eyes and straightened her papers on the attendance counter before heading for her room.

Chapter 4

Travis chewed on the end of the pencil stub he held in his hand and rethought what he had just written. His eyes narrowed. Then he extracted the pencil from his mouth, erased what he had just written, and frantically replaced it with something else. The pencil returned to his mouth as he thought over his new line. Finally, he nodded and let a small smile escape around the pencil. He liked what he saw.

He glanced at his watch. Nine thirty. At this time of the morning, the house was quiet—relatively speaking. His mother snored loudly from the next room, sleeping off the booze and dope of the evening before; she wouldn't wake up for another hour at the earliest. Tyrone, now fourteen, along with twelve-year-old Byron were already running routes for some of the older boys. Ten-year-old Jasmine had left more than an hour ago to escape to the refuge of the street and a jump roping line. It had been months since the older ones had even been near the house. Most had been in and out of jail numerous times already.

Travis relished this time he, for the most part, had to himself each morning. It was the closest thing to privacy he had ever experienced. He worked the eraser around in his mouth and gazed out the window, turning the next line over in his mind, mentally trying and discarding word after word. After minutes of thought, he wrote something down, scrutinized it, pursed his lips, and then circled one of the words. It wasn't the best, but for now it would have to do. He would come back later and improve it.

The process continued for another thirty minutes until the ancient clock on the wall released ten mournful moans, causing his mother to stir in the next room. Travis quickly folded his piece of paper and slid down the couch to the end table, opened the door, and picked up the huge Bible that lay underneath the pile of magazines.

He stared at it momentarily, as he always did, incredulous that such a book would even be in their house. Where it had come from, he had no idea as it carried no signatures or anything. How it had managed to stay around was the second miracle. His guess was that no one remembered it even existed. All he knew was that it was the safest place in the house to hide something, for it would never be opened.

Travis slid the folded paper between two of the pages and then replaced the Bible back under the pile of magazines and closed the door. He stood up and glanced again at his watch. Five after. He headed for the room he shared with his brothers and reached into the back of the closet and pulled out a clean white shirt, pulled off his T-shirt, and slipped the other one on, carefully buttoning it. He unbuttoned his pants, but before tucking his shirt in, he checked the waistband of his Levis. An extra strip of material had been deftly sewn into the waistband so that it didn't show. He carefully unfolded it and made sure the ten tiny packets of fine, white rock were securely in place, then lowered the band, tucked his shirt in, and rebuttoned his pants. He checked his image in the mirror and then his Rolex: ten fifteen. Right on time.

He left the apartment and headed down to the street, oblivious of those who lived in the small world of the tenement. He had closed his senses and his heart to it years ago. It was merely a place to exist until a person could escape, and he meant to escape. His drug dealings had brought him plenty of money, but unlike the others, he was neither a user nor abuser. He may sell it, but he wasn't stupid enough to use it.

A person lost control when he used dope. And if there was one thing Travis Johnson wanted, it was control. Besides, he had better uses for his money than to eat it all up supporting some dirty habit that would fry his brain and eventually kill him. He saw what the stuff had done to his mom.

He also had no use for the extravagances the other dealers tended to favor: cars, booze, parties, girls, and the other amenities to "fancy living." Most of his money, all that he could safely keep from the use of the gang, was stashed carefully away—in hundreds—in that forgotten Bible for later use.

Once on the street, Travis carefully surveyed the scene—typical activity. He turned and walked in the opposite direction. One thing he had learned early as a dealer: you always varied your routes. He walked a couple of blocks and then caught the bus heading into the hub of the city. Freeways crisscrossed above him; houses and apartments passed by his window. He watched little of it.

Travis exited at the Renaissance Center, walked a few blocks to the financial district, and then caught the People Mover at the corner of Larned and Griswold. At Park and Bagley, he got off and then walked back to Woodward, and finally covered the one and a half miles up to Warren and Wayne State University. Before crossing at the corner, he paused and his eyes ran across the buildings of the university before him, and an unaccustomed thrill coursed through his veins.

Wayne State, Detroit's major academic institution, spread out before him. Travis crossed the street. After one block, he came to the Biological Sciences Building on Gullen Mall and turned into the heart of the campus. Though Labor Day, school had already been in session for a week, so some students were milling around or relaxing on a bench, enjoying the shade of a tree.

Strolling down the mall, Travis enjoyed the refreshing greenery of the mature trees and shrubs, a striking contrast to what he lived with daily. Used to taking in a lot without being noticed, he furtively sucked in every detail around him. He mentally recorded each book title being read and picked up on bits and pieces of numerous conversations. Within minutes, he arrived at the Student Center and stepped inside.

He smiled in satisfaction. Today, because of the holiday, the cafeteria was almost empty. There would be few people to notice anything out of the ordinary.

Travis went upstairs and stood at the far end of the mezzanine and looked down at the couples talking below. It wouldn't be hard to spot his buyer in this crowd. The deal was a relatively large one. Ten grams of crack, in ten individual packages. He checked his watch and waited, hoping the buyer would be on time. Standing alone in an empty room for more than a couple of minutes could look suspicious. He glanced down at the ground floor just as a security guard entered the far door.

Reba clenched the spoon firmly between her teeth and began her half run, half walk toward the line of waiting people fifty feet away.

"Come on, Reba! Faster!" someone yelled, and she tried to pick up her pace. Though she kept her eyes on the egg bobbing precariously in the bowl of the spoon clenched tightly in her teeth, out of the corner of her right eye she could see Geraldine Sayer just about even with her. Out of her left eye she could see no one. The line of people was only a blur, and her eyes, crossed from staring at the wobbling egg, hurt.

"Come on, Reba! Hurry!"

This time she could distinguish Willie's voice from the others as he waited anxiously to receive the egg. She reached him and then deftly slid the egg into his spoon. He took off without a second's delay. She relaxed her aching jaw and stressed eyes. Willie had already expanded her meager lead by another two yards over Peter Sayer. Seven-year-old Jake was across the field awaiting his turn.

Reba took in a deep, contented sigh. Next to Christmas, Labor Day was her favorite holiday. Family tradition ruled heavy on a day like today. First there was shopping for school clothes. Once Washington children started school, their parents would purchase them two new sets of clothes. The younger ones, not to feel left out, would receive one new set.

Now that she was entering high school, her parents had been more lenient with her, giving her the seventy-five dollars and the freedom to make her own selections. While it took only an hour for Willie and Jake's purchases to be made, Reba had taken more than two hours, carefully looking over the selections, comparing prices, quality, and colors. Willie and Jake pleaded for their sister to hurry but were quickly silenced by their parents and then ushered over to the toy department to window-shop until she was ready. They would not hurry their daughter. Today's lesson was as valuable for Reba as any she would learn in school this year.

When all was said and done, Reba left Kohl's with three blouses, two skirts, four pairs of socks, a purse, two pairs of nylons, and three dollars left over. She slipped the nylons into her basket, praying her parents wouldn't object—after all, she was fourteen. But her mother and father never said a word as they reviewed her purchases, merely praising her for her selections. Reba glowed with pleasure.

"How'd you buy all that stuff with only seventy-five dollars?" Willie wanted to know.

Reba beamed.

"She took her time and put her math to good use," her father answered, "instead of grabbing the first pair of sneakers off the table because everybody else has a pair like that." Willie pouted at the reference to his demand that he have the Nike cross trainers.

"I'd say she showed good money management today. We might just have to put her in charge of the household finances."

"Here, here," Mrs. Washington said. "I'm all for that." Reba felt lightheaded.

"Does she get to keep the extra money?" Willie asked, his brow furrowed into a deep wrinkle. Reba turned toward her father, slightly embarrassed. She hadn't even offered to return it.

"I don't see why not," he said. "She squeezed more out of that money than we would have. That deserves some kind of reward, I reckon."

"When do I get to do my own shopping?" Willie prompted. The thought of pocket cash was enticing.

"When you get to high school. Just like Reba."

"Man, when I get to go shopping, I'll just wear my old clothes and then buy some video games," he exclaimed.

Mr. Washington zeroed in on his eldest son. "Then you might not see that seventy-five dollars for some time to come. That money's for school clothes."

Willie shut his mouth, realizing the grave error of his comment. Next time he would keep his thoughts to himself.

"Well, I want to have a fashion show when we get home," interrupted Mrs. Washington, hoping to put an end to the confrontation, "and see how all of you look in your new clothes."

"Aw, you already got to see how we all look," resisted Willie. "Just make Reba."

"Fair enough," she answered and looked at her daughter. "Would you mind modeling your clothes for us after dinner tonight?"

Reba shook her head. She wouldn't mind at all.

"Come on, Jake! You've got 'em beat!"

Reba encouraged her younger brother toward the line where her father waited, spoon clenched firmly in his teeth, legs flexed and ready. Reba loved the annual Labor Day Picnic that the First Neighborhood Church of West Detroit held each year. She especially enjoyed the games. Most, like this egg relay, pitted family against family and required a parent to participate—in this case, to run anchor. A few, like the car hunt (an Easter egg–like setup, only searching for Matchbox cars—a Detroit original), were reserved only for the youngest. And some, like the water balloon fight, which concluded the day's activities, pitted the children against the parents and ended with shrieks and squeals of laughter.

It was a day of fun and fellowship, beginning at eleven with a softball game, followed by a potluck lunch, which usually featured plenty of fried chicken, potato salad, and homemade ice cream. Then there was a time of devotion and singing while the food digested, and finally, the games.

The Washingtons had never won the egg race, but this year, Willie swore they had a chance. Jake was now big enough to hold his own, and Reba's coordination had improved. Reba slugged him for that one. Just 'cause she had tripped over a sprinkler head last year, he'd been calling her Queen Klutz.

But he did seem to be right. After two legs of the relay, they were in first place, and Jake, his eyes crossed in concentration as he focused on the wobbling egg, still had a two-yard lead on his nearest rival.

"C'mon, Jake!" Mrs. Washington screamed as she massaged her waiting husband's shoulders. "Now remember, William," she whispered in his ear, "you have to run smoothly or that egg will be history. Remember what happened two years ago." He nodded in acknowledgment.

"And watch out for that sprinkler about halfway down." Again he nodded.

"Use those legs and—" He cast a harried look her way.

"Okay, okay, I'll shut up."

He turned back to focus on his middle son's progress, and Mrs. Washington commenced to rubbing his shoulders again. Reba warmed inside. How many parents would take a church egg relay race with such seriousness? She looked at her father's taut face as he lowered his six-three frame so it would be level with eight-year-old Jake's when it came time to hand off. Her mother had started whispering instructions again.

The handoff between Jake and Mr. Washington passed without incident. Reba, Jake, and Mrs. Washington yelled encouragement at the bow-legged form ambling rapidly toward the finish line. Willie, the lone Washington at the other end, had his hands on his knees and his pink mouth wide open, yelling at his father.

As the row of men neared the finish line, a hush fell over the crowd. Reba held her breath and waited. In a flash of an instant, Willie jumped into the air and wrapped his arms around his father, sending the egg flying. Reba and her mother screamed in delight and hugged each other, and Jake sprinted back across the field toward his father and brother to join the celebration. The Washingtons had just won their *first* Labor Day Picnic trophy. What better omen than that for the beginning of her high school career.

Chapter 5

The security guard ambled slowly toward the center of the student eating area, his eyes sweeping left, then right, checking out the various tables that might hold something of interest. His gaze would pause momentarily on a couple or on the one foursome that sat toward the rear. Then his gaze swept upward to the mezzanine, checking to make sure all was in order.

From his vantage point half hidden by one of the pillars, Travis watched him carefully. The guard stepped methodically toward the turnstiles that led to the darkened cafeteria, his eyes only stopping briefly to carefully note any movement. Travis shifted his weight, and the guard's eyes picked it up. He hesitated for a brief second as he caught a glimpse of Travis's white shirt. Then he continued his surveillance, never increasing his pace or changing his demeanor. At the far end, he pulled his flashlight from his belt and aimed the beam through the metal grating and into the darkness, letting it rest on the serving counters, racks of chips, and soda machine.

Satisfied, he clicked it off, slid it back into its holder, and then turned slowly and began his methodical retreat back through the maze of sparsely occupied tables, never again looking up to where

Travis was standing. But when he reached the end of the room, instead of leaving, he turned left and headed for the stairs leading to the mezzanine above.

"You got the stuff?"

Travis stood coolly and looked the security guard over from behind his mirrored sunglasses. He hated impatience.

"Would I be here if I didn't?" he asked.

The guard, a young man in his late twenties, didn't care for the tone of this young, black punk. "Then let's see it," he demanded.

Travis stared at him in stony silence. This guy had a lot to learn if he expected to do business with him. "In good time," he said smugly.

"I don't have a lot of *good* time," the guard seethed.

"Let's walk," said Travis taking control, knowing what was going through the mind of the guard. "It might look a little suspicious if you, a nice white security guard, spent too much time just talking with a punk black kid like me, now wouldn't it?" He made no effort to hide the bitterness in his voice. "It would make a whole lot more sense for you to be escorting this black punk out of the building."

The guard glared at him. "This campus is filled with black students. What difference would it make?" Travis shrugged but was satisfied that he had the guy's goat and attention.

"Just a precaution." He cast a furtive glance about the mezzanine to assure himself that they were alone. "You got your share?"

"Yeah."

"Let's see it."

"Let's see the crack first."

Travis looked at him with disdain. "Don't say that," he said as though talking to a child, "unless you want the entire world to know what we're doing up here. Show me your contribution first. I don't even know you."

The guard grumbled and then pulled out an envelope filled with bills. Travis took it and flipped through the money. Once satisfied, he smoothly pulled the string of pouches from his waistband as they walked and handed it to the man.

"Nice even trade," he said smiling, his cold, calculating eyes still hidden behind his glasses.

The guard opened one of the packets, tested the substance between his fingers, and then tasted it. Travis watched him angrily.

"Put that stuff away," he seethed. "I don't give bad stuff, and all that's going to do is draw attention to us."

The guard grinned, glad to have a little leverage of his own. "Relax, little guy. I don't know you either."

Travis tried to maintain his anger. He wasn't sure he wanted to deal with this guy. Too many uncertainties. But he had the Wayne State turf because of his own choosing. Still, he didn't like *this* setup one bit.

Martha slid the last few books into the bookshelf and stood up, placed her hands on her hips, and leaned backward, stretching her tight and tired back muscles. Her eyes swept across the classroom, liking what she saw. Though late in the afternoon, the windows sparkled from the recent wash she had given them. The janitorial staff never did make it to the third floor.

The desks, though still defaced with years of graffiti, were free of gum and stood neatly in their rows. She wished she could be more creative with the arrangements and allow students a little breathing space, but when you needed forty desks, there was little you could do but pack them in.

She looked over the host of books, her personal collection, now neatly placed in the bookshelves her husband, Graydon, had built for her. This was her subversive move to infiltrate the minds of the apathetic by providing them with good literature without their knowing. Oh, she had the big three up there—J. K. Rowling, Steven

King, and John Grisham—but she had slid in a few Newberry Award winners among them like S. E. Hinton, Paula Danziger, Paul Zindel, and Bette Greene.

She had even purchased some science fiction, though she wasn't an avid sci-fi reader. Still, many of the kids were, and along with Asimov and Clark, she had managed to find some of the more current, popular authors. Anything to get them started on reading.

Hidden among these were the classics: John Steinbeck's *Of Mice and Men*, *The Pearl*, and even *The Grapes of Wrath* for the more adventurous. Dickens, London, Caldwell, Heller, Twain, Stowe, Austen, and black authors like Wright, Angelou, and Morrison were on the shelves as well.

Then mingling with these was her Christian literature. Though separation of church and state prohibited her from openly sharing her faith during class time, there was no law that said she couldn't make good Christian literature available to her students if they wished to read it. She searched for her favorites: C. S. Lewis, Thoene, Oke, Wright, McDonald, Rosenberg, LaHaye, and Jenkins.

She moved slowly to the front of the room, passing the counter and cupboards that housed her textbooks. Montgomery had long ago given up the idea of a central textbook room, and instead opted for teachers caring for and sharing the books on their own. For the most part, the sharing worked, but occasionally there would be an extremely protective teacher who just couldn't part with a book.

On the counters were plants and atlases, colored pens, tape, glue, rulers, dictionaries and thesauruses, books of quotations and poetry, many of which she had purchased with her own money. She had learned long ago that what she needed and what the school could or would provide were two very different things.

When she reached her desk, she turned and took a final look over her room, her eyes shining. Posters sporting words of encouragement and classic works of art tastefully covered the holes and paint-chipped walls. The room was neat, clean, and nicely decorated, and exuded learning. She felt a twinge of excitement and nervousness.

Tomorrow those desks would be filled with budding adolescents: some expectant, wanting to learn; some wary, afraid of failing or being criticized; and some downright belligerent, daring her to teach them anything.

Martha breathed in deeply and gathered her roll book and a copy of her first day's activities. It was the kind of challenge she relished. Helping young people learn to think and discriminate on their own—to decipher, to criticize, to defend. She closed her briefcase, walked to the door, and reached for the switch to turn the lights off. Tomorrow she would hopefully begin turning minds on.

Alex carefully smoothed out any latent wrinkles in his khaki slacks and laid them neatly over his desk chair. Then he selected four complementary shirts and held each one next to the pants, evaluating his choices with a critical eye. Finally, he decided on a simple plaid of navy blue and forest green with a touch of burgundy on a tan background. His mother had always liked the shirt, saying that the blues and greens pulled out the color in his eyes while the tan softened his ruddy complexion. Who knew what the burgundy did.

Alex was a fastidious dresser and a meticulous housekeeper. His mother often teased him that he would make some woman a great wife. Either that or drive her insane.

He hung up his shirt and then opened his sock drawer and pulled out a pair of tan socks and set them on top of his Rockports. The shoes were a birthday present, an expensive one, and he carefully brushed off any loose dust. While most of the kids would opt for jeans and Nikes on the first day—and every day thereafter, for that matter—Alex wouldn't. He prided himself in being his own person, and how he dressed was one way of expressing that.

His attire for the next day chosen and ready, he turned toward his desk where his binder—dividers in place, pen and mechanical pencil on top—sat ready for the first day of school. A sinking feeling met his building excitement. It just didn't seem fair that a guy who liked school so much would have so much trouble.

He glanced at his clock and saw that it was ten o'clock. He should be in bed, but he didn't feel the least bit sleepy. He rarely slept the night before school started. Too much adrenaline. Alex rechecked his alarm to make sure it was set for five thirty. Plenty of time to have his devotions before taking his shower.

He sat in the dilapidated easy chair he had inherited from his father, a tangible sign of his surfacing manhood and a definite anomaly in his otherwise spotless room, and he pulled his Bible off the nightstand and began fingering the gold lettering of his name tenderly. Then he flipped off the light. He couldn't read the words in it anyway.

"Lord," he prayed softly, his fingers caressing the cool leather. "I know I ask this every year, but please make this the year when everything finally makes sense. Please change me. Don't keep me a dummy. I really do want to learn, more than anything in the world."

In the black stillness of the room, no one in all of Detroit could hear his plea, and Alex wasn't sure God had either.

Chapter 6

Travis slid in beside Reba as she walked to school. As usual he said nothing, and she upheld his silence. He wore a Detroit Lions baseball cap, a white T-shirt, black jeans, and a pair of Nikes.

Reba looks nice today, he thought as he admired her full white skirt, which made her look like she actually had hips and hid her skinny legs at the same time. The bright watermelon blouse added a glow to her cheeks, and her feet were almost silent in a pair of white sandals.

"New purse?" he asked, and Reba almost stumbled in surprise. He *never* spoke to her. At least not in public.

"Yes," she answered.

"Nice," he said and then fell back into silence. He wasn't sure what had driven him to say anything. He just felt the need to. She looked so—mature.

His walk was casual and normal enough until Montgomery High came into sight. Then he began to add a little rap bounce to his step, gradually increasing it until, as they turned up the main sidewalk, he was into a full-blown rhythmic rapper strut, shoulders swinging, legs bending.

Attitude, he thought approvingly, *like that cocky tennis player Agassi used to say, is everything.* Especially here, on the neutral turf of the school where five different gangs converged. He usually carried a .357 Magnum inside his pants, strapped to his right calf, but undoubtedly they would have the metal detectors out for a blanket search on the first day of school. The administration would want to get off to a clean start this year, he was sure. Still, if a guy wasn't ready, he could be retired *permanently,* and once things had settled down into a pattern, he would be toting the weapon again.

He could feel Reba's sideways glance, and he felt himself warm. *She would never understand,* he thought. *She didn't know how gangs worked, so why even try to explain.* He pushed all thoughts of Reba out of his mind and denied to himself that he would much rather walk straight into the building, deposit his books in his locker, and head to class. But he couldn't, so what was the point of dwelling on it. It was dangerous enough being *in* the gang. It was a nightmare trying to get out.

As they neared the steps to the main doors, Travis slowed down, letting Reba walk through the throngs of people alone. Probably a little selfish, he thought, but he didn't need people thinking this was his girlfriend or anything like that. He could do better than Reba. Still, he watched her pass through what he knew were small clumps of gang members. She either didn't know or wasn't worried in the least because she confidently strode right past them. But his heart didn't slow its hurried beating until she was safely inside. Only then did he head toward the small knot of guys clustered at the north end of the steps.

Martha stood at the door and welcomed each student to class. Some beamed in response, others grunted a reply, and a few chose to ignore her completely. After twenty years of teaching, she had learned not to take any of it personally, but still her heart sank a few inches. This was her *college prep* English class. She had hoped to see a little more enthusiasm from *this* group.

The tardy bell rang, and she scanned the hall for any laggers. They were out there in force, but none were heading her way. She closed the door behind her and walked to the front of the room, her heart fluttering in her chest. Why after all these years did she still get nervous? She turned toward the students and smiled in greeting. Thirty faces eyed her expectantly. A few others were busy checking out the room. Only a couple slouched apathetically in their seats. *A challenge,* she thought and warmed to her task.

"Good morning," she said brightly. A weak "good morning" twittered across the room.

"We can do better than that," she said and repeated her greeting a little louder, leaning toward her charges. Her eyes shone bright and intense, her smile broad.

"Good morning!" they repeated in a much healthier fashion. Only the two slouchers abstained from taking part.

"Much better," she said and relaxed. "Welcome to room 372—Freshman *College Prep* English." She emphasized the middle two words. "Is everyone in the right place?" Her eyes swept the room. "Good." She started walking between the rows of students, and their eyes and bodies twisted to follow her progress.

"I'm Mrs. Richards, and you are in for a year of hard work." She paused. Someone groaned good-naturedly, and the class laughed. Martha smiled. "Good times," she continued, "if you like hard work." More smiles. "And a year of surprising discoveries."

She paused midway in the third row and rested her hand on a student's desk. "Are you with me?" Heads nodded. "Hands up from all those with me."

Thirty-three hands raised enthusiastically. The two slouchers scanned the room, then reluctantly raised their hands weakly with a little support from their desktops. Martha looked each directly in the eye, first one and then the other, a small smile playing on her lips. Both tried to avert their gazes, but she held steady until each looked back in turn.

"Good," she said firmly, a look of commitment in her eyes. She turned and walked back to the front of the room.

"Now, I need to get to know you, and you need to get to know each other. It's a big school, so I doubt everyone knows everyone else in here. Here's how we'll do it. … Who knows what the word *alliteration* means?"

She strode to the board, grabbed a piece of chalk, and wrote the word in large letters, then turned and glanced around the room. A few hands wanted to raise but were tentative. She reworded the question.

"How many of you have heard that word before but are a little unsure of what it means?" Now two-thirds of the hands took the air. The others, not wanting to look ignorant, joined them.

So most of them do know it, she thought. *They're just afraid to be wrong. Well, we'll need to get over that.*

"Let me give you a hint," she continued. "It has to do with the first letter of words."

Confidence regained, four hands bolted excitedly into the air. She settled on a black girl wearing watermelon and white in the front row—rather bony and surprisingly homely.

"It's when words have the same sound—consonant sound," she corrected, "at the beginning of the word."

"Exactly," agreed Martha and returned to the board to write the definition. Notebooks whipped open, and the word and its definition were hurriedly scrawled inside. "Now, can anyone give us an example of alliteration?"

A pale black boy with light hazel eyes raised his hand. She nodded toward him.

"Peter Piper picked a peck of pickled peppers," he answered, grinning.

Martha laughed in appreciation. "Perfect!" she exclaimed, emphasizing the *P*, and the boy's grin widened into a smug smile.

"Tongue twisters exist solely because of the attraction of alliteration. In that tongue twister, what sound was alliterated?"

One of the boys in the back who hadn't raised his hand yet, waved it wildly. Her eyebrows rose in recognition.

"P," he answered with satisfaction.

"Exactly," she replied. "Now. What we are going to do is introduce ourselves to one another by saying our name preceded by—" She stopped abruptly. "*Preceded* means what?"

"To come before," came the answer from a student by the windows.

"Right. Preceded by an alliterative adjective that best describes us." Puzzled faces appeared before her.

"What's an adjective?" Martha asked.

Feeling a little safer now, a few more took a stab at the definition. If they were wrong, she informed them gently. Again, it was the homely girl in the watermelon blouse who finally came up with the correct answer.

"A word that describes a noun," she said, "which is a person, place, or thing—like dog, house, or idea."

Martha smiled and nodded in appreciation. That extra explanation saved some time.

"For instance," Martha explained. "I'll start." She placed her hand on her chin, her forefinger tapping her pursed lips, and gazed up at the ceiling in thought. "I'm Rowdy Richards."

The class laughed.

"Really," she affirmed. "You don't know it yet, but wait and see. I would love to be 'Rich Richards' but …" She smiled and shrugged her shoulders, and the class laughed again. "What sound is alliterated in my name?"

"R!" the class responded.

"What adjective did I use to describe myself?"

"Rowdy!" they shouted again.

"Everyone got the idea?"

Heads nodded enthusiastically, and even the slouchers took a little more interest and straightened up. *Aha! I gotcha!* she thought triumphantly. *At least for the moment.*

"There is a twist to this exercise," she said, and the room quieted down. "It's important you listen very carefully to each person's name because you will be asked to repeat the name of everyone who precedes you." A loud groan filled the room, but some eyes shone with the challenge.

"So who would like to be first?"

A multitude of hands pierced the air, all fully realizing that being last meant memorizing thirty-five names—thirty-six counting Mrs. Richards. She decided on sloucher number two, who threw a satisfied smile around the room and raised both arms in victory. The losers groaned.

"Oh, yes," she said almost as an afterthought. "I forgot to tell you. When we've gone completely around the room, the first person must repeat them all." The class roared with approval while disbelief registered on sloucher number two's face. "Go ahead and begin," she instructed.

He looked at her intently. "You're Rowdy Richards, and I'm …" He paused momentarily as his eyes focused on hers, a wry smile spreading across his face. "And I'm Sucker Sam."

Alex found a seat next to the window and opened his notebook to an empty page as he watched the other students filter into class. He really had no intention of writing anything even though he would like to, but he kept it open just in case. He had found that teachers were more lenient with you if you at least looked like you were trying.

History had never been one of his strong subjects. Too much reading. He had learned to file away a lot of the facts as they were presented in class in the lectures, but there was always so much that came just from the textbook, and *that* he could never grasp. As a result, he had always been assigned to remedial history, which had its ups and downs. The ups were you didn't cover as much material, and they didn't expect as much out of you. The downs were …

He paused as he watched his classmates enter the room. Most came in making crude comments loud enough for everyone's edification. A few were busy kissing or petting each other right in front of the whole class. Only one other student besides Alex seemed to have any paper with him. These were the downs. The people he would have to spend the next 180 days with. Given the choice, he would rather take his chances in the regular sections with the other students. A D in there might mean a whole lot more learning than an A in here, and definitely a lot less stress.

Mr. Jackson walked into the room only a minute before the bell rang. "Welcome back to Montgomery High," he said with little enthusiasm. The boys twirled their hats on their hands and waved him off, booing loudly. The girls chewed their gum loudly and laughed. Alex just slid down in his seat and sighed.

"I know a lot of you have signed up for this class because you already draw on your own," Mrs. Ramirez said, "and I don't want to discourage you. But I do need to warn you that we will be spending a lot of time learning about technique and texture and color. So if you were hoping just to step in here and have a free period to sketch, then you will need to rethink taking this class. You are all untapped, and for the most part, undisciplined artists, and I am here to help you tap into and discipline all of your potential."

Travis sat slouched in the back row, giving the impression of disinterest, but he was listening to every word Mrs. Ramirez said. He had always loved drawing, but most of his sketches were of muscled warriors. He had tried to sketch other things, but they always turned out lame looking.

"What this means," continued Mrs. Ramirez, "is that I may ask you to draw some things that you don't want to draw or that may seem to you to have no purpose." She paused and a smile broke out across her chubby face. "But trust me. They do."

Out of habit, Travis took careful inventory of Mrs. Ramirez. She was a plump woman of about fifty, with a full face that smiled everywhere: her large, brown eyes that squinted into slits smiled; her cheeks, flushed from the heat, smiled; and of course, her mouth, filled with large white teeth, constantly smiled.

I would like to paint her, Travis thought. *To capture her friendliness, her energy.* Period one, he chalked up in his mental first-day evaluation, was going to be okay.

Chapter 7

Martha sat with the other teachers in the lunchroom, reviewing the morning so far.

"I can't believe I have Johnny Avery again," moaned Doris Chapman, one of the math teachers. "You'd think in a school this large they would place him with another teacher. You know, give the kid a chance … Heck, give *me* a chance."

Gail Lytle, the home economics teacher, just smiled. "But no one knows him as well as you do," she said.

"Well, then someone else should have that golden opportunity," Doris suggested. Everyone laughed and raised their hands in a defensive "no thank you" posture.

"Yeah, right," Doris said. "Some friends you guys are."

"Friendship has its limits," said Carol Stefanski, one of the PE teachers, from the far end of the table. This deep philosophical insight was met with ten approving nods, and "Hear, hear," and one despairing groan.

"Besides," said Martha. "How do you know we *don't* have him and just want to make sure you're sharing *our* misery with us?"

"Do you have him?" she asked eagerly.

"Well, no," Martha said, and everyone laughed, "at the present, but we all know that that's not to say he won't end up in my class at some point during the year. Johnny has a habit of making the rounds." Her words of truth had a sobering effect on the group, and they moved on to other topics.

"My feet are killing me," Doris complained. "It's been three months since I've been in heels, let alone stand three hours in them."

"Yesterday, I was ready for school. Today, I'm ready for vacation," added Gail.

"Don't worry. Only 179 and a half days until summer."

"How long till the weekend?"

"Too long."

"Is this what is meant by critical thinking? Reviewing your career choice?"

Martha sat back and enjoyed the banter. She knew that most, at least at this table, loved teaching as much as she did—even with all its headaches and problems. There was something energizing about being in a classroom and working with young minds. They were still impressionable. Of course, there was something frustrating and fatiguing about it at the same time. Decisions, whether trivial or major, had to be made in a moment. It was a pressure job. You could prepare for the lessons, but not for the kids on any given day nor the interaction in the classroom.

Teaching had a chemistry that other professions lacked, giving them a sterile quality. It had a chemistry between students, a chemistry between teacher and students, and a chemistry between subject and students and teacher. It was all so tenuous. A teacher could teach the same subject, the same level, all day and yet never have the same experience.

Teaching was like looking for gold at the bottom of a pool. You took a deep breath in the morning, searched and worked and finally around noon, you came up for air. Then you took another deep breath and dove in again until the final bell sounded. Some days issued tremendous finds, while others seemed completely fruitless.

Martha sipped her coffee as she thought back over the morning. It had gone well, though she was glad to be through with alliterative adjectives. She had different plans for her drama classes. But on the whole, she was pleased.

The bell ending lunch rang out, and a single, unified groan rose from the faculty dining room as chairs squeaked and cards were put away till tomorrow. Martha shuffled her mail together and rose. If it weren't for the hunger pangs that hit precisely at eleven each morning, she would prefer not to take any breaks. It was so difficult to gear back up for the afternoon classes. The momentum was lost—on both sides of the desk. She did have it easier than most teachers, though, in that her afternoon classes were activity oriented. The kids needed to move around as much as she did.

Martha opened her roll book to fifth period and glanced down the list of names. Forty stared back at her. She wondered how many of them actually signed up for the class and how many of them were dumped there because nothing else "fit" into their schedule. Well, she was about to find out.

Reba's heart pounded like a bass drum in her small chest, occasionally skipping a beat completely. She looked around the large room filled with what would qualify as strangers. No one from her neighborhood, nor any of her immediate friends had signed up for drama. She carefully studied the other students in the class.

Quite a few were good-looking, which made sense since most of your actors were beautiful people. Reba rubbed her cheek unconsciously as her eyes took in one particularly beautiful caramel-colored black girl whose skin was rich and smooth looking. She had a petite nose that some black girls dreamed of, and her teeth sparkled white and fit perfectly in a mouth outlined with thin, delicate lips. Reba's heart beat louder till she feared she would break an eardrum. She forced herself to pull her eyes away.

The students who did not fall into the "beautiful" category were outgoing, already clowning around with each other and talking it up. She felt her normal self-confidence wane and questioned her decision to sign up for the class. On the streets and in her neighborhood, where most people would feel intimidated, she felt confident, able to handle anything. But then, those areas and people were familiar to her. This was all new.

Her hands shook slightly. Mrs. Richards was busy at the back of the room signing in even more kids.

Since first period, when she had Mrs. Richards for freshman English, she had been enamored with the woman. She seemed so together, so intelligent. She was everything Reba wanted to be: controlled and in charge. She even got Jesse involved, and everyone in there knew Jesse *never* got involved. She had been fun, demanding, inquisitive, and each time she had stopped by Reba's desk, she would rest her hand gently on the edge, and Reba would feel a tingle course through her body. Mrs. Richards had even called on her to answer a question—two, in fact—and there were a lot of other hands raised.

Reba wanted to please this woman, to gain her approval, to impress her. Maybe that was why she was questioning her decision to join drama. After looking around the room, Reba felt that she didn't really fit the drama type, but for as long as she could remember, she had wanted to be an actress. She had lived hundreds of different lives in her books. Now Reba wanted to live them onstage and then on the screen. In the movies, she could be a hundred different people, thousands even: rich doctors, world travelers, anyone instead of just a black girl who lives in a ghetto.

A rustle at the back of the room indicated Mrs. Richards had completed the housekeeping tasks and was ready to begin class. Just her purposeful movement to the front of the room quieted everyone down, and Reba sat in awe of this woman's power and presence.

"It's good to see *all* of you here," she said distinctly, "and some of you twice." She smiled to a couple of students and then at Reba. Reba's heart beat double time. Mrs. Richards had recognized her. "If you have had me earlier," she continued, "don't panic if you think you're in for another hour of alliterative adjectives." Some laughed.

"It's more important that this group gets to feel comfortable with each other, even perhaps, before we learn each other's name. So we're going to spend this week and perhaps next loosening up. Today we're going to play a little game. One that will demand cleverness and deceit, quickness and keen observation." Mrs. Richards' facial expressions matched each of the words, and Reba watched her carefully. "I want everyone to push the desks back against the walls and then sit in a circle on the floor."

Her instructions were followed immediately, and Reba found herself between two boys and straight across from the beautiful caramel-colored girl. Then Mrs. Richards surprised them all and sat down with them.

"The name of this game is 'wink.'" She paused while some kids murmured their familiarity with the game and their approval.

"If you've played the game before, then just relax while I tell the others the instructions." The murmuring quieted down. "In a moment, I will wink at an individual. That person will be it," she explained. "From that point on, whomever he or she winks at will die, providing the person sees the wink. If someone else in the circle sees 'it' wink at somebody, then 'it' is dead, and the person who caught him or her is now 'it.' If 'it' can make it all the way through without being detected, then he or she wins."

She paused. "Everyone understand?" A few didn't, and Mrs. Richards ran through the directions again, and then again, until everyone was clear on what would happen.

"All right, let's start."

The room became intensely quiet while students' eyes darted from person to person, long enough to catch the winker, but quick enough to avoid being killed. Reba's entire body grew tense. She loved challenges. She was going to win this game. Her eyes flitted around the room looking for the winker, hoping to catch him right away and impress Mrs. Richards with her alertness. She moved her eyes quickly around the circle of students and then she saw it and her heart stopped. Mrs. Richards had winked at her.

Alex whistled as he dressed for football practice. The day had gone exceptionally well, he surmised. Not one bit of writing all day, not even in English. In fact, he had impressed Mrs. Richards and the rest of the class with being able to recite every name and those adjective things without a hitch. Of course, he had a natural knack for memorization. It had been his saving grace in most classes. But he could still see her wide smile and that look of pleasant surprise. Perhaps he was now on her good side, and she would be lenient with his assignments. Hey, it had worked before.

Geometry had intrigued him. The book scared him to death, but just the few concepts they had talked about today made his blood rush. Mechanical engineers, Mr. Manheim had said, use geometry daily. He would have to look into that line of work.

History was a bomb with all the delinquents, but earth science seemed okay, and weight training. Whew, Bauer wasn't going to let them slide for a minute. Day one and already a complete circuit training day.

He stripped his sweaty PE shirt from his soaked body and pulled on a dry one. He would love to take a shower just to freshen up, but that would be a waste. Five minutes of football practice would end that.

Alex pulled on his pads, pants, and shoes, then after a moment's hesitation, he carefully made sure that he wrapped the shoestring of his right shoe around the toe. There was no need to ruin this day with some careless mistake.

Chapter 8

Martha took deep breaths as she strode purposefully down Seventh Avenue, her head up, chest out, and arms pumping rhythmically. The sun was just coming up in the east. She glanced at her watch without breaking her stride: six thirty. She looked at the approaching street sign that read Seventh and Hallmark.

Even though she was a little ahead of schedule, she didn't slow her pace. Power walking had been a part of her routine for over four years now. She was a religious walker, exercising four times a week. It kept her muscles toned, her pulse low, and her spirits high. Plus, it gave her a chance to be outside, and she loved the outdoors.

Her long, thin legs powered her around the corner, and she took in a deep breath of the freshly cut lawn. *Ah, life is just wonderful,* she thought. Since *her* life was in order, everything in its place and running smoothly, then the world was in order. Unlike many of her peers, whose moods vacillated with the stock market or the international political situation, Martha lived in a much smaller and manageable world. As long as God ruled her world, everything was going to be all right.

She turned right once more and saw the large elm that stood in her front yard in the distance. Fall was just beginning to play with its colors. A few of the neighbors were already up and in their yards puttering. They waved hello, and Martha waved in return. Most knew better than to interrupt her now. They could talk later, after the walk. There was plenty of day left.

Martha turned into her front yard at exactly 6:45, and she smiled. She was right on schedule.

Travis walked casually up the walk toward the Wayne State bookstore. Saturdays were not busy days on campus. Most of the students commuted, but a few lived close by in school-owned apartments or houses. As was his custom, he checked his watch, saw he had an hour to spare, and opened the bookstore doors. The smell of paper rushed past him, and he unconsciously smiled. He took some pleasure in strolling up and down the aisles, gazing at the various titles, wondering what was so important to say that the author just had to write it down.

No one paid much attention to him. He looked old enough to be a student and had been in the store on a regular basis, so most of the workers thought he was enrolled. Even if they didn't, they wouldn't question him. Wayne State was used to the public browsing through their collection.

He casually made his way down the literature section, surveying the selections, and reading an occasional jacket flap. He stopped at Richard Wright's *Black Boy*, checked the synopsis on the back, and kept it. He looked through various books on poetry until his eyes fell on a volume of black poets: Langston Hughes, Paul Laurence Dunbar, Maya Angelou. He thumbed through the pages and then slid it under his arm. Had to look credible.

Travis checked his watch again. Time to go. He was due to meet up with the security guard in ten minutes. It would not do to be late. This little business alone was providing him with a comfortable five hundred a week.

He paid for his purchases, slid them under his arm, and then shoved his hands in his pockets. As October knocked on the door, the humidity had died down and the weather had cooled off considerably. The first hint of crispness was in the air.

His mind traveled from the books to school, and for a brief moment he forgot about the drop at hand, so he didn't see the young black man, not much older than he, follow him out of the bookstore and watch his progress through the mall and toward the student union. Not until Travis moved out of sight did the young man follow him, always keeping a safe distance so as not to be seen.

When Travis entered the student union, the young man followed, and when the security guard passed by Travis, the young man caught the slight nod the security guard gave him. The young black man's brow was beaded with sweat, and he ran a pink tongue across his dark lips in a nervous reaction. The security guard circled the mezzanine nonchalantly, then descended to the bottom floor, pausing casually by a stack of magazines as though checking out the selections.

Near the bottom of the stack, he slid in an envelope and then walked on. Less than a minute later, Travis settled himself comfortably next to the magazines and began reading one after another. After the third selection, he reached for the *Time* that was slightly askew, pulled it out, opened it, and slid the envelope into his jacket pocket, all the while keeping a casual but perceptive eye on those around him. When he was sure it was safe, he slid a second envelope into the magazine, continued looking through it, and then replaced it in the stack and left.

"One!" *Slap, slap, slap.* "Two!" *Slap, slap, slap.* "Three!" *Slap, slap, slap.*

The Montgomery High football team ran through their warm-up routine with precision synchronization. Alex felt the adrenaline pumping viciously through his body. He wished the game would start so he could pound a few heads, anything to release some of this nervousness bottled up inside him.

The late September sky was a hazy, pastel blue with a scent of fall in the air. Alex would have preferred to play on a Friday night under the lights, but those games were abandoned three years before he entered high school. The darkness invited gang activities, and the violence around and in the stadium had forced the city and the administration to move all games to Saturday afternoon.

They had also done away with all preseason games. Why push the fates? What that meant, though, was that the Montgomery Panthers faced the Jefferson Jaguars, the defending league champions, in the first game of the season, and Alex was so nervous, he wasn't sure he could move if he had to.

The sun eased its way through the Richards' front window and fell upon the stack of handwritten papers Martha had been working on. A look of concern crossed her face, and she pursed her lips. She had just completed second period's first theme assignment and hadn't remembered reading Alex Kowalski's.

Normally, she wouldn't think twice about an initial writing assignment from the remedial class not being turned in on time, but Alex's she had expected, even looked forward to. He had seemed to have such a good handle on the discussion of the story "The Scarlet Ibis." He had picked up on the symbolism of the exotic bird driven from its natural habitat by a force greater than itself, and he had made the connection almost immediately to the young boy Doodle.

Alex had explained his opinion so eloquently in class that even the slackers and the jokers had sat up and listened. And when she had assigned the theme, asking them to pick a person they knew, or knew of, who was being forced out of a place where he or she was comfortable and into a new environment, his eyes lit up.

Then, as she always did with the remedial students, she had given them the class period to write it, knowing that a paper assignment taken home was rarely returned. She had seen him working hard over his piece of paper. She couldn't understand it not being in the pile.

She rechecked her briefcase and the stack of papers. No theme. She opened her grade book to check his other grades. Four blanks and two D's on his two multiple-choice quizzes after four weeks of class. Something wasn't right here. Something didn't make sense. It might if he didn't appear so eager to learn, to participate. Then she might chalk it up to lack of motivation. But Alex seemed genuinely interested in his education. No. It had to be something else then. She wrote herself a note on a Post-it and stuck it to the roll sheet for second period: "Observe Alex Kowalski."

"*Hut! Hut!*"

The ball snapped into the quarterback's hands, and there was a clash of bodies, grunting, grinding, powering to drive each other off the line of scrimmage. It was the opposite of a tug-of-war but with the same objective. Alex took the five yards the defensive end granted him and then cut inside. The defender cut with him and bumped him—hard—hoping to break his stride, his rhythm, but the months of weight training coupled with his innate sense of balance kept him on his feet and in stride.

He bumped back, pushed, and then spun a one-eighty away from the linebacker and sprinted for the sideline. Though it only took a second for his defender to recover from his mistake, it gave Alex the two-yard lead he needed. Five yards from the sideline he looked up, and there was the ball, already en route, spiraling toward him.

He waited till the last moment to reach out, not wanting to alert his defender that the ball was only seconds away. The ball, perfectly thrown, fell right into his hands, and without breaking stride, Alex pulled it in and turned downfield, running within six inches of the right sideline. He heard the heavy breathing and pounding footsteps of his pursuers, but *he* knew they knew they couldn't catch him. He was the white Calvin Johnson of Montgomery High. Fast, fleet, and sure of hands.

From the corner of his eye he could see the free safety bearing down on him. He glanced ahead. Thirty yards from the free safety. Thirty yards to the goal line. The adrenaline surged through his body, and his legs pumped faster. The safety had the angle on him and could stop him just shy of the goal line. *But he won't,* vowed Alex, and he braced himself for the hit.

He was close enough to the sideline that should he be tackled, the clock would stop. But that would at best only leave them time for one more play. That is if time hadn't already run out. They needed five points. A field goal would not be enough. They needed the touchdown, and their best bet was now, while the ball was securely in Alex's hands.

The free safety hit him with the force and impact of a Mack truck, and Alex, ready for the collision, turned his shoulders and drove straight into him.

"*Ummph!*"

The force of the impact carried Alex into the air, and he saw turf, sky, and bleachers all fold into one. When he did finally hit, the intensity of the landing almost jarred the ball loose, but he clung possessively to it.

A huge roar erupted from one side of the meagerly filled bleachers, but Alex was so turned around and so disoriented that he neither knew where he had landed nor where the Montgomery fans were located. A clump of grass clung tenaciously from his helmet, obscuring his vision. Not until he felt the thump of slapping hands on his helmet and the force of exuberant teammates pummeling the breath out of him, did he know that he had made it. That he had made the touchdown, and they had beaten the defending champions.

He no longer cared that he couldn't breathe. If he died right there on the field, he would die happy and a hero. Though his face was shoved into the turf at the moment, he felt on top of the world. Nothing could ruin this year. Nothing. It was going to be a great season.

Travis found an empty tree and lowered himself in its shade, leaning against its rough bark. For a guy usually cool and collected, he was feeling extremely uncomfortable. Had the tree been a dilapidated warehouse wall, or the rough brick of the tenements, or the splintering wood of a crack house, he would have rested comfortably. Even if he had been sitting here with a stash of crack on him, he would have felt easier—a man with a mission, a purpose. But this. This was a foreign concept, just relaxing on a college campus, and he felt weird.

He pulled out a cigarette and lit up, then drew in a long, slow draft so the warm, aromatic smoke could calm his jittery nerves. This was better. He released the billow of smoke that had collected in his lungs and relaxed. His knees were propped up casually in front of him, and he rested his arms on them, his cigarette hanging loosely from the tips of his right thumb and forefinger. From behind the safety of his Ray-Bans, Travis watched the collegiate world around him.

He reached for the paper bag that contained his new purchases and slid one of the books out and read the title: *Black Boy*. Securing the book against the ground, he flipped through the pages. *No pictures.* He smiled to himself. Travis really hadn't expected any, but that used to be his sole criteria for judging the worth of any book. The more pictures, the better the book.

He drew in another long breath of smoke and released it into the air and stared at the blue sky, still a little hazy from a summer of industrial pollution. Not until the fall rains came would the city finally be rid of it.

Turning back to the book, Travis wondered when his attitude toward books had changed. He couldn't remember any specific incident, any one particular book that might have influenced him. Plenty of teachers, he recalled, had told him that reading would be his ticket out of the ghetto, but even at ten, he had laughed to himself. Drugs were going to be his ticket out of the ghetto, not books. And he had already figured out that his thousand dollars a week as a mule was as much as what most teachers were making.

It was a cynical, worldly view for such a young man, but Travis could never really remember being innocent. Still, at some point he had needed something more than what the world was handing him, something deeper, and he had turned to books to look for the answers. He hadn't been disappointed. There had been plenty of answers—or theories really—and he had clung to each one hungrily until he realized the futility of it and discarded it like a used syringe.

But he didn't give up. Each book, each poem, each story for some reason seemed to make him more alive, seemed to bring his world into focus, and for that he was grateful. Travis set *Black Boy* aside. He really didn't want to start something so lengthy here. Why, he wasn't sure. He had no desire to go near his house. A quick glance at his watch confirmed this thought. *She* would be up and coping with a hangover. He felt a protective pang pierce through his middle as he thought of his younger brothers and sister. What were they doing to cope?

Since his own deliveries were over, Travis had nothing to do until he made a buy later that night. So, in all honesty, he had the rest of the day. He pulled the small book of poetry out of the bag and, with one hand, propped it up against his knee. He flicked the excess ash off his cigarette, took one more slow puff, and then tossed it away and settled himself deeper into the grass and the trunk of the tree. He flipped through the pages, searching out something short. His eyes caught the title "Dreams," and he felt an unexpected pang, followed by a sense of emptiness. He swallowed hard and read the poem.

Dreams

Hold fast to dreams
For if dreams die
Life is a broken-winged bird
That cannot fly.

Hold fast to dreams
For when dreams go
Life is a barren field
Frozen with snow.

—Langston Hughes

Travis just stared at the words. That pang he had felt had been fleeting, but it had been real, and it had a name: regret. He had dreams once, but he had learned very young that dreams didn't play out in the real world—at least not in *his* world. He stared once more at the page, set his jaw, steeled his heart, and read the last two lines again: "Life is a barren field/Frozen with snow." Then he willed an icy resolve over his heart and turned the page.

He pulled out another cigarette and lit it with one hand while he flipped the pages with his other, looking for something to take his mind off the last poem. He stopped when he saw "Feeding the Lions."

Feeding the Lions

They come into
our neighborhood
with the sun
an army of
social workers
carrying briefcases

filled with lies
and stupid grins
Passing out relief
checks
and food stamps
hustling from one
apartment to another
so they can fill
their quotas
and get back out
before dark.

Norman Jordan

Travis took another puff and and nodded, a cynical smile sliding easily across his face. This was more like it. This was the world *he* lived in. An ironic world where indeed an "army of social workers" converged on the ghetto, believing they were God's remedy to the poor by "passing out relief" through the "checks" they dispersed, as if money was the panacea for all the ghetto's ails. Yes, this guy Jordan knew what he was talking about. He wasn't living in a make-believe world, thinking dreams could actually come true like that first guy.

Travis turned his attention back to the poem. "Hustling," now there was a word with a true double meaning. He read the poem over again and puffed contentedly on his cigarette. He liked this poem. The images were straightforward and accurate. Travis was sure he could write a poem like this. He would have to give it a try. Letting the book rest against his leg, he took another puff, his eyes staring off into space as he contemplated the world he would create in *his* poem.

When the cigarette was finished, Travis crushed the butt in the grass next to him before flicking it away. He glanced at his watch: two thirty already. He slid the books back into the bag, stood up, brushed himself off, and turned to leave.

A young black man, neatly dressed and with close-cropped hair, stepped out to block his progress, startling Travis.

He cursed under his breath, upset with the young man for causing him to jerk and with himself for being caught off guard. Quickly, he checked the guy out. Face, eyes, mouth. He looked vaguely familiar. But where? His innate sense of caution kicked in, and he became wary.

"Excuse me," the young man said politely, and his voice was rich and deep and full. "I didn't mean to startle you, but I need to talk to you."

Though still wary, Travis stayed. Where had he seen him before? With his eyes still shielded by his Ray-Bans, he carefully scrutinized the young man, but he nodded slightly, giving him the okay to continue.

The guy was obviously nervous. He took a couple of deep breaths and glanced around the quad anxiously, his eyes flitting from object to person and back again. When they finally did come back to Travis, he forced himself to focus hard on Travis's lenses, and his jaw became firm.

"You sell drugs, don't you?" he said, and instantly, Travis's blood turned to ice.

Chapter 9

"You *do* sell drugs, don't you?" the young man asked.

Travis's face had become stony, and his jaw flexed viciously. "Whatever gave you that idea?" he asked.

"I saw you and the guard," he answered, and Travis silently cursed. Why hadn't he been more careful?

"I'm afraid you're mistaken," Travis said and started to turn away, hoping to put a quick end to the interview, but his abruptness bolstered the young man's courage.

"I know I'm not," he said forcefully and then lied, trying to secure any advantage he could. "Others saw the drop too. We've got it on video."

Travis stopped dead in his tracks, his icy blood now prickling his insides. If this guy was telling the truth, he could be in big trouble. He turned around and sized him up. Medium height, about five ten. Medium weight, say 175. He couldn't be more than nineteen. The only true way to shut the guy up would be to kill him or have him killed, but if he was telling the truth and there was incriminating video out there, then a dead body might lead directly to him. Best to play it cool and see what happened.

He gave the guy another once-over. He looked more desperate than anything. Too much sweat on the upper lip. Too nervous to be a narc. What was he after anyway?

"Let's say I do," he said. "What's it to you?" The kid released a quick breath but didn't seem any more at ease.

"I'd like to buy some," he said simply, and the struggle within seemed to wither away.

"Buy some what?" Travis asked.

"Drugs," he answered simply.

"What kind of drugs?" Travis asked condescendingly.

The guy now looked confused, and it was obvious to Travis that he had never toyed with drugs before. He had no idea what he was getting into. The young man licked his lips vigorously and looked around frantically, trying to maintain his knowledgeable facade, but finally he gave in.

"I don't know," he admitted, and his shoulders slumped forward. "I just need something to get rid of the pressure, to relax."

For some inexplicable reason, Travis felt sorry for the young man, who seemed completely distraught. He almost hated to get him started on the stuff. Perhaps just a little marijuana would do the trick. No harm, no foul. The kid looked like he had some money, and being a novice at the game, he probably didn't know the street value of anything. It was a sure bet that he hadn't been out comparison shopping. Travis shook his head.

"Sorry. Can't risk it. Not if there's video out there." He eyed the young man carefully, watching his mouth open then shut.

"There's—there's no video," he stammered hastily. "I just had to get you to stop and …" He paused and tried to grin. "And I saw it on TV once."

Travis nodded slowly. It was stupid enough to be true. He believed him and let out a wry smile of his own. "I think a little Mary Jane will do just the trick," he said. "It's a good—really good relaxer."

"How much?"

Travis seemed to contemplate the question for a minute before answering. "For you," he said, sounding like he was giving him a deal, "I'll sell you an ounce baggie for—say sixty dollars." The guy balked.

What did he expect? Travis wondered. *That the stuff was like aspirin?* The guy was licking his lips again, thinking.

"That will roll you about five good joints," he said, "and ten if you're frugal."

"Okay, but I don't have the money right now."

Travis shrugged. "No problem, 'cause I don't have the stash. When can you get the money?"

"By tomorrow."

Travis nodded. "I think I can arrange that. By the way, why didn't you just go through the security guard?" he asked.

The kid looked more dejected than ever by that question. "He knows my family."

Travis nodded again. No more needed to be said.

"So where should I meet you tomorrow?"

"Right here," Travis answered. "Bring a textbook, and we'll make like you're tutoring me. I think that cover will pass."

The young man genuinely smiled for the first time, and Travis felt a little sorry he had made the deal. The guy's life had taken a rotten turn today, and he still couldn't shake the feeling that he had seen him before.

"By the way," he said as the young man started to leave. "I always like to know who I'm working with. It's safer that way."

The kid didn't falter for a minute, having put his complete trust in Travis. "The name's Danny," he said. "Danny Richards."

Martha stood up, stretched her back, and then went over to check on the casserole in the oven. She glanced at the clock: four forty-five. Danny should be home any minute from the library, and dinner—she turned on the oven light—looked like it would be ready within the half hour.

She glanced over at the stack of papers she had corrected already. Saturdays were such fun, she thought sarcastically and smiled wryly. Yes, this was the teacher's life everyone soft-mouthed. "Oh, teachers have it so hard, don't they?" people would croon. "Have to work six hours a day, and only 184 days out of the year. Just have to take those three summer months off and those two weeks at Christmas."

It was true that you couldn't beat the vacation time, Martha admitted to herself, but you also couldn't call an evening or weekend your own until school was officially over. Papers continually hounded you, and lessons always had to be prepared or repaired. What had worked last year did not always work with this year's class, or, as was more often the case, you discovered something better.

She glanced at the clock and casserole again. She could probably get through a couple of the junior creative writing assignments. They were always a challenge. If she didn't have to struggle through all the technical problems, she might actually enjoy reading them, but years of teachers emphasizing fluency and feelings had left her with classes acutely deficient in any grammatical or communication skills. These kids certainly had a lot to say, but they had no ability to communicate those thoughts.

Martha shuffled through the papers until she saw a rather short poem in beautiful, flowing manuscript. She insisted that the kids put their names on the back so that she wouldn't be influenced at all, and she had to stifle an irresistible urge to see who possessed the beautiful penmanship. With everyone on a computer these days, you just didn't see kids taking that much pride in their handwriting.

The title read "Fire and Ice." She groaned. Plagiarism. When would kids realize that if they *were* going to copy, not to copy the classics like Frost. Go for the obscure poets whom she might not have read. Reluctantly, she read on just to see if the owner of the beautiful penmanship could also copy accurately.

Frost debates the end of the world
Whether by fire or ice,
But I know that both can kill you.
A couple of seconds suffice.

The fire sears a hole through your body.
The ice freezes the blood in your head.
But really—What does it matter?
The effect of both is—you're dead.

Martha's heart beat rapidly. She had had poems on drugs before, but never so cynical, so bitter. The beautiful, flowing handwriting belied a troubled and angry soul. She slowly turned the paper over and read the name, and her eyes froze to the page. Travis Johnson. Montgomery's own drug lord.

"More potatoes, Danny?" Martha asked.

Danny just stared at his plate and shook his head, pushing his food around with his fork. Martha looked across the table at Graydon. His eyebrows rose in the same question that was on her lips, and he too looked at his son with worry.

"Everything okay at school, son?" he asked. The question seemed to irritate Danny.

"Sure, why shouldn't it be?"

Graydon shrugged. "You just seem a little quiet, that's all."

"Can't a guy be quiet once in a while without getting the tenth degree?"

"You're not eating much," Martha said.

"Not hungry," came the reply.

"Are you feeling all right?" she asked.

Danny threw his fork on his plate. "I'm feeling fine, okay? Everything's going fine, all right?" He released a huge breath and leaned back in his chair and let his head fall backward. After a few seconds, he lifted his head back up and smiled wanly.

"Sorry," he said. "I shouldn't have lashed out." He straightened up in his chair. "It's just that I'm a little short on cash. My chemistry professor just said we need a supplemental workbook by Monday, and I don't have the money." His parents seemed puzzled by the statement.

"That's really odd," Martha said. "I've never heard of a professor requiring a new book once the semester has started, have you, Graydon?"

Graydon shook his head and looked steadily at his son. "What made him change his mind on the textbooks?" he asked.

Danny moved his fork through his food. "He didn't change anything; he just added the workbook," he explained, trying to keep his lie afloat. "He said this workbook had new applications that if we don't have, we'll be behind the power curve. Anyway, I don't get paid at the computer store till next Friday, and I have to have a chapter completed by Tuesday. Do you think you can lend me the money?"

"Why, sure we can," Martha answered quickly, but Graydon was still staring at his son, chewing very slowly.

"When did you find out about this?" he finally asked.

"Friday," Danny answered. "Yesterday."

"Why didn't you ask last night?"

"I was hoping I could pull enough together without bothering you and Mom. You know how I want to be independent and all."

Graydon nodded slowly, but his gaze remained on his son, and Danny felt warm all over. "He didn't give you much time to get the book and do the assignment," his father continued, and Danny shifted uncomfortably.

"If it's a problem, then just forget about it," he answered, avoiding his father's statement.

"How much do you need?" his father asked. Danny relaxed. The end was near.

"Only eighty dollars."

Graydon's eyes widened. "Only?"

"Hey, that's cheap for a textbook."

"It is, honey," Martha concurred. "Really."

Graydon finally leaned back. "All right, Mom, write him a check."

"I need cash." Graydon's head jerked up. "Where will I cash it before tomorrow, Dad?" he asked, and Graydon nodded.

"You have eighty?" he asked his wife. "Or do we need to get to an ATM?"

"I can take it out of the grocery money," she answered and went for her purse.

When Danny had the money in hand, he counted it carefully. An extra twenty for next time, he thought, and then shoveled a couple of forkfuls of potatoes into his mouth.

"Well, I'd better go study," he said and excused himself.

"Don't forget to get a receipt," Graydon reminded him. "We can write that off our taxes."

Danny stiffened just a bit. He had known his father was going to ask for some kind of proof, and he already had a workbook they hadn't seen, but he hadn't counted on needing a receipt. He would definitely have to go to the bookstore and buy something around eighty dollars and then return it. Something like that.

Graydon watched Danny go.

"My, but you were giving him a hard time," Martha accused, and Graydon pretended not to hear. He was staring at the doorway where his son had disappeared. "What was that all about?"

Graydon shook his head. "I don't know," he said slowly and turned back to his own plate. "But I don't like the feeling I'm getting down in my gut."

"What feeling's that?" Martha asked. He looked at her steadily before looking away and then sighed.

"That I don't trust my son."

"Are you ready, Mom?"

Alex had situated himself at the kitchen table, his legs propped up on one of the kitchen chairs while he leaned back in another, hands behind his head and waited.

"Put all four legs down on the floor," his mother commanded as she took her seat next to the computer. Alex plopped the two floating legs back to the floor. "One of these days you should learn to type and then *I* won't have to keep going to school."

Each time she sat down at the computer and made the suggestion, Alex's heart would skip a beat in worry. "I will as soon as there's room in my schedule," he promised, hoping to put an end to the topic. He also hoped there would never be room in his schedule, so his secret would remain safe. He waited patiently while his mother formatted the paper, typed his name, Mr. Jackson's name, the class, and date on the upper left-hand side of the paper.

"History?" she asked, and Alex nodded. "Okay, I'm ready. Number one." She waited.

Alex had purposefully sat at the far end of the table so that he couldn't see the sheet of questions he had placed next to the computer.

"I'm sorry," he said. "Could you read question number one for me? I forgot what it was."

His mother gave him one of her mock exasperated looks and then read the question: "How did the Iron Age help ordinary citizens gain power in Greece?"

Alex listened intently to the question, flipping back and forth through his mind all the discussion and lecture of the last week.

"The Iron Age," he began and then paused while his mother typed his words, "enabled the urban civilizations with the ability to make weapons and gave them a great advantage over the less settled people. It ..."

He continued his recount of the answer and settled back easily in his chair. His system was still intact. Yesterday, after Mr. Jackson had passed out the study guide of essay questions, Alex had listened carefully for any clues that might be given and then raised his hand, setting his system into operation.

"Could you explain what you mean in number four?" he had asked. Mr. Jackson had then read the question aloud and explained exactly what he was looking for. Alex nodded, satisfied that he now had enough information to answer the question. Gary was the next to raise his hand, about question number two. Then Mark, and finally Stuart. For their part in the minireview, they knew Alex would pay them each three bucks.

Mr. Jackson never caught on; in fact, he relished the questions because it showed an interest. And in a class of delinquents and rejects, interest was a rare commodity. Alex's buddies never asked why he had them play the game. Why bother if you get three bucks just to ask a question? But he had given them some lame excuse anyway about making Jackson work for his paycheck, and they had seemed satisfied.

Alex finished reciting his answer and waited for his mother to type it out. With a flourish, she hit the key for the period and then looked at her son with pride.

"That is a wonderful answer," she said proudly. "You are *so* smart."

An uncomfortable rush of heat flooded his face. "Number two," he said and waited for his mother to read it.

"Blessed assurance, Jesus is mine! Oh what a foretaste of glory divine! Heir of salvation, purchase of God, Born of His Spirit, washed in His blood."

"This is my story, this is my song, praising my Saviour all the day long; This is my story, this is my song, Praising my Saviour all the day long."

The entire congregation of First Neighborhood Church bellowed out the chorus and then slowed down for the second verse. Reba sang lustily along.

She loved Sunday mornings. First Neighborhood wasn't a

wealthy church, but it did have stained-glass windows, and now in the early fall, the sun started coming in from a southern slant, and the pulpit was bathed in a prism of light.

"This is my story, this is my song ..."

A warm sensation coursed through Reba's veins. She looked down the pew. Her mother and father, sharing a hymnal, sang along, harmonizing with each other. They had beautiful voices. Willie, resting his hymnal on the back of the pew in front of him and then leaning all his weight on it while he rocked back and forth, was hopelessly singing along. Reba smiled. Willie hated to sing and could never stand still, yet as she mouthed the words she could hear the painful off-key notes emanating from his throat.

Jake, on the other hand, loved to sing, and at seven he had a beautiful soprano voice. Mr. Washington said if he followed in the footsteps of the other Washington men—those who could sing, he added, smiling and throwing a look at Willie—it should deepen into a rich baritone by the time he was an adult.

Jocelyn, standing on the pew under her father's arm, watched and listened in awe, her thumb unconsciously raising to her mouth, until Mr. Washington would reach up while still singing and pull it back out. At four, she was too old to be still sucking her thumb. Little Chris stood under his mother's arm, and though he knew only a few of the words, he knew all of the notes, and he sang impressively.

Reba didn't think she could be any happier or content. Life was wonderful. For her, the world consisted only of her family, her church, and her school. She was totally oblivious to the world of drugs and crime that made its home in her neighborhood. It didn't affect her; therefore, it didn't exist.

The song ended.

"Let us pray," resonated Pastor Rayburn, his deep voice reverberating off the old brick walls of the church.

Reba bowed her head, and as she thanked God for her wonderful life, she added as she always did, "And bring Travis into your fold as well, dear Lord. Amen."

Chapter 10

Travis studied the few lines he had drawn on his paper and then looked back at the photograph next to him. A field of clouds stared back at him, and he contemplated what his next move should be.

He had never paid attention to clouds before. In fact, if the truth be known, he really hadn't looked above street level for a long time. Too dangerous for one thing. An eye in the sky meant one less watching the ground, and that could be lethal. But now he was going to have to draw lots of clouds, using charcoal, brushes and paint, and pencil.

These firsts were in oil. They had just finished their color wheels, and clouds were their first assignment. Though they weren't supposed to use any pencil, Travis had cheated. He needed to get a feel for the cloud.

"No more pencil, Travis," said Mrs. Rameriz sternly, but there was a twinkle in her eye because she knew that such concern on Travis's part at least showed that he cared. "Just the outlines. You have plenty there. Trust me. It will be much easier if you use the oils. They are more malleable. You can soften the edges easier, and the wet paint is more pliable."

Begrudgingly Travis put his pencil away. He had no intention of getting on Mrs. Rameriz's bad side—if there was one. She never seemed upset. She was one of the few teachers who didn't treat him like some gang member to be feared. Granted, he was a gang member, and he was to be feared, but that didn't mean they had to watch his every move. He wasn't out to kill anybody.

Instead, Mrs. Rameriz treated him like an artist. Like he actually had talent. Maybe he did—he really didn't know. Travis had only signed up for the class because he liked to draw and didn't think it would be too tough. He had never realized there would be so much to learn.

He picked up his palette where his paint lay waiting. He had white and black and then a little mixture of the two to make gray. He painted the sky area with the gray first, leaving spaces big enough for the clouds. Already he could see their form taking shape.

I'll have to take some time and look at the clouds today, he told himself and then studied his canvas. *They're kinda peaceful looking.*

He mixed a lighter shade of gray as he was instructed and started on the edges of the clouds. They started to come to life right below his number six brush, and he grew more excited. He brought in the white for the main part of the clouds and then mixed three more shades of gray for their underbellies.

"Now, what did I tell you?" whispered Mrs. Rameriz over his shoulder as she placed a warm and friendly hand on his back. "You have created beautiful clouds, Travis. You must have stored them in your soul because we don't see such beautiful clouds here in Detroit, do we?"

Travis shuddered involuntarily at the touch of her hand, but she didn't move it. It had been so long, too long to remember, since he had felt a loving, gentle hand on his back. The girls that fed his physical hungers didn't have that feel. They were too busy trying to satisfy themselves. No, this was the hand of a mother, a warm, tender, caressing hand, coupled with the words that fed his soul. He looked up at her gratefully, and despite his resolve to keep a cool exterior, he let a small smile pass his lips.

Though she seemed to be looking only at his painting, she must have sensed it, for she patted him gently on the back and whispered, "Keep up the good work, Travis. You have much to show and tell us through your painting."

He didn't know if she told all the kids that; all he knew was that she told *him* that, and by God, he for sure didn't want to let her down.

"Alex, will you please read?"

Martha saw the panic that flashed briefly across Alex's face and then disappear behind a stony exterior.

"I'm afraid I don't know where we are," he said. "Why don't you come back to me once I've found my place."

Martha looked at him carefully. He had been turning his pages along with the rest of the class, albeit a second behind as though he were using the others as a clue.

"We'll wait," she said pleasantly. "We're on page fifty-six, top of the page. Garrison, will you please show Mr. Kowalski where we are."

Alex's already ruddy cheeks burned a bright crimson as the small black boy next to him leaned over and pointed to the top of the page. Alex mumbled his thanks, shifted to get more comfortable, and then peered intently at the book. Martha watched. Suddenly, the book shot from his fingers onto the floor.

"Man, I'm sorry," he apologized. "Why don't you just go ahead. I'm putting a cramp in the story."

"We'll wait," Martha repeated softly, patiently, and Alex's shoulders began to rise and fall. *He looks like a cornered animal,* she thought, *trying to find an escape. Desperate.* Alex leaned over to pick up his book. He licked his lips over and over, and his eyes looked wild.

"I really would rather not read, Mrs. Richards," he said. "My throat and all."

"I would like you to read," she said evenly, and looked him straight in the eye. He stared back at her. This was their showdown.

All week she had carefully kept an eye on him to see if he would read, and if not, how he got out of it. One day he didn't bring his book. Another, he would drop it, or lose his place, or claim a sore throat. She had accepted each excuse readily, not pushing, just waiting, and he had seemed confident in his ability. Today she forced him to show his hand.

"We're waiting, Mr. Kowalski," she said.

Alex glanced around the room at the other students who were staring at him in bewilderment. They had never seen him refuse a teacher's request. He had always been polite, obedient, even helpful. Martha knew all this, too. She had forced Alex to find a new modus operandi.

"I won't," he finally said belligerently, and his eyes flashed both anger and worry at her.

Martha tilted her head questioningly. "Am I to understand then that you are defying my request?"

She saw Alex's Adam's apple rapidly bob up and down a couple of times as he swallowed to gain confidence, but his eyes never wavered.

"That's right," he said.

She nodded in understanding. "Then I expect to see you after school today," she said evenly, without anger or malice.

"But I can't," he objected. "I have football practice."

She looked at him with raised eyebrows. "I will speak with Coach Bauer," she replied, and with that she asked another student to read. Alex folded into his seat and fretted over not only his fate in this class but also his fate on the football field when he didn't show up for practice on time.

He was not aware that while the rest of the class settled back into the plot of *The Chocolate War*, Mrs. Richards was watching him out of the corner of her eye. From her perspective, she saw a miserable, unhappy young man, and for a moment she wished she hadn't pushed. She hated to see him hurt, but if her instincts and perceptions were right, he had probably been hurting a lot more for a long time.

"Lennis? This is Martha. I need to keep one of your players after school today."

She heard the heavy sigh on the other end of the phone. The two had had their differences over the years. During her first years of teaching, Martha would hold football practice over the head of the football players who threatened to cause trouble, and she was firm to her word. For any infraction, no matter how small, she would detain them, which would then disrupt Lennis Bauer's practice and hurt his starting line up since he required perfect attendance to start.

It wasn't that he was trying to undermine Martha—she had the right to her discipline. It was just that she was undermining herself. The players grew to resent her so that even though they were now behaving—in a manner of speaking—they were refusing to participate and consequently learn.

Finally, in his own frustration, he had brought it to her attention and was surprised to find that she was extremely receptive to his ideas. That confrontation had begun a unique but wonderful professional relationship between the two. Therefore, if Martha was now, some eighteen years later, calling to tell him a player was being detained, something was drastically wrong.

"Who is it and what did he do?" he asked, the irritation noticeable over the line.

"Alex Kowalski."

"Kowalski?" came the astonished reply. "I know the kid's a little slow, but I never thought he was a discipline problem."

"He's very bright," Martha corrected, "and he isn't a discipline problem. He just refused to read for me today." There as a sudden silence on the other end of the line, and Martha knew what Lennis was thinking.

"That's not why I'm keeping him after." She heard a rush of air come through the receiver.

"Glad to hear it, Martha," he said. "I thought you were reverting to your old ways."

She chuckled. "Sorry to disappoint you," she replied and then added, "I think the reason Alex refused to read is because he can't."

"Kowalski can't read?" Bauer asked incredulously. "Come on, Martha. The kid's never failed a class in his life, and he gets A's and B's in most of them."

"I know, I know," Martha agreed. "But I still believe he can't, and I want to check it out. If I'm right, we need to do something right away. You know how devastating it could be for him to graduate and be illiterate." Another silence on the other end.

"Yeah, I know," came the reply. "Keep him as long as you want, and if you need me to, I'll talk to him, too." Martha smiled.

"Yeah, I hear you smiling, but I'm no softy. Work something out but don't take football away from him. It's his life's blood, and it might be his ticket to college."

"I know, but *you* know he'll have to know how to read to make it *through* college."

"Yeah, I agree." More silence.

"Thanks, Lennis. And someday I think Alex will thank us both."

Chapter 11

The knots in Reba's stomach were growing tighter as the hour wore on. In only a matter of moments, she would have to go in front of the room and perform her two-minute sketch. It was something she looked forward to with mixed emotions.

Every day in Mrs. Richard's drama class was an exciting yet nerve-racking adventure. She learned some new technique or insight, but it was always accompanied with on-the-spot practice. Reba couldn't understand why her desire to be an actress could be so strong when her aversion to getting up before the class was just as formidable. Nevertheless, both were true.

Today's assignment was an impromptu one. At the front of the class sat a table and a chair, nothing more. Each student selected a card on which was written the situation he or she was to perform. Then all members had five minutes to mentally formulate what their dialogue and scenario would be.

Jarvis, a friend of hers since second grade, had selected a job interview and had taken the role of a nervous recruit in search of his first job. Reba thought he had done wonderfully and had told him so, to which he confessed that half of it wasn't acting. He was really that nervous.

The next two students were both juniors whom Reba hardly knew, but both thought they were pretty hot stuff. The first played a principal reading the riot act to some imaginary culprit, and Jarvis whispered that he was sure this scene was biographical. Reba stifled a laugh. It would be rude.

The second was a tired sales clerk waiting on a finicky customer who wasn't really in the market to buy anything. Reba had to admit, she did a good job with her scene as well, and unless someone really fouled up, Reba knew she would be going into her scenario with no way to go but down.

"Reba, please select your card," Mrs. Richards directed. Nervously, she pulled one off the chair in the front row, took a deep breath, and glanced down at it: "Actress out at lunch."

It was pretty ambiguous, and Reba wondered how she should play it. Should she be a struggling artist with only a few coins to her name? Or a famous one hounded by a slew of adoring fans? Should she be incognito or flaunting her fame?

She glanced around the class. Of all the students, she looked least likely to play the role of a successful actress, but then, wasn't acting putting on a convincing facade? She hadn't really done anything yet to establish herself as an actress. Of course, most of the assignments and exercises were not for show, but for the working of mechanics. Voice, carriage, and so forth.

Reba had no idea what the next two students performed. She was too busy mentally preparing and praying. Then her heart quieted and her confidence grew. She knew what she could do. She would push herself and the others to go with her. She would take a chance.

"I specifically asked for two slices of lemon in my tea, not one," Reba said haughtily, and her eyes closed slightly, her chin lifted, and her nose rose to the air. No one answered her, for no one was there, but she carried out her end of the conversation as though she were surrounded by people.

Her face, with her large eyes, nose, and cheeks, all of which seemed too big for such a small girl, were well suited for the stage. Each expression was visible to even the back seat, and Reba, realizing this in the first ten seconds, worked to exaggerate her expressions even more.

One eye flew open in astonishment at the silent rebuttal of the waiter.

"What do you mean *I* must pay for it?" she asked, and the class laughed at both her comical expression and her nasal intonation. "You, my dear boy, will be the one to pay if I don't have that second slice of lemon."

Again the room burst into laughter, and Reba warmed to her task. A rush of adrenaline pumped through her. It was what she had always dreamed of. To be onstage making people laugh and cry. Of becoming someone new. The class quickly grew silent as they noticed Reba ready to speak again. She could feel their anticipation. She had made them laugh for two minutes with her character's humorous quips. Now it was time to pull the rug out from under them and reveal the truly pathetic character she really was. She waited till the silence was complete and then spoke.

Martha sat stunned as she watched Reba Washington perform. She had been so wrapped up thinking about Alex that she had really tuned out the drama improvisations. But when Reba began her performance, she was drawn back in. The homely little girl had a power over her audience, pulling them into the life she was creating. The big, bulging eyes, the buck teeth, the wimpy almost anemic body were all forgotten as she played out the scene that was obviously already running through her mind.

She's wonderful, Martha thought. *So poised, so in control. She is definitely the comedienne, and she has the whole class right in her hand. Laughing as though on cue.*

She sat back to enjoy the performance, laughing with the others when she noticed, ever so slightly, a transformation in the character before her.

"Surely you know who I am." Reba's voice carried through the room. Her silent counterpart denied knowing.

"Why, I am famous," she retorted. "I have played opposite Cary Grant and Gregory Peck, and …"

The character continued recounting her glorious career that was lost on the exasperated waiter, and right before the class's eyes, she became a pathetic creature. A person who leeches off the past, laying claim to privileges she is no longer entitled to.

"Surely, you don't expect *me* to have to pay the bill?" she asked incredulously, and again the tacit consent that she was indeed to pay her own way.

The class had grown hushed; not a heartbeat could be heard. Not a shuffle. When Reba was finally ushered from the restaurant by invisible security men, still claiming that she was a star and the studio would cover her meal, not a breath escaped. Reba had them.

"Please sit down," Martha directed Alex as he stood before her desk. He still wasn't happy, but he had lost some of his aggressiveness of the morning. She smiled slightly, but he didn't return it. She was still the enemy.

"Before we begin," she said standing and moving to the front of her desk, "I want you to know that your being here in no way jeopardizes your position on the football team."

Alex glanced up at her skeptically.

"What I mean," she continued, "is that your missing practice today won't hurt you from playing on Saturday. Whether or not you keep your starting position, of course, is up to your ability. True?" She smiled at him, and her eyes twinkled. Despite himself, Alex felt himself smile slightly. Martha walked to the windows and looked out at the practice field below, which was just now beginning to fill with players.

"You should also know that you are not here for disciplinary reasons," she said, and she could feel his head jerk up and stare at her back. She turned slowly around and looked him straight in the eye. "Though your behavior in class today, your refusal to obey my instructions, would pass as defiance of authority and is punishable in a number of ways—suspension being one."

She saw the blood rush to his cheeks, partly from fear, partly from anger.

"But I pushed you to that point, didn't I, Alex?" she asked, not expecting an answer. "You're a nice guy. Polite, cooperative. You do your work. You use your class time well. You participate. All your teachers like you as a student, and so when you drop your book, or lose your place, or claim to have a sore throat, they all buy into your excuse, and you're off the hook. Right?"

Martha paused, and when Alex's mouth dropped open slightly, she knew she was on the right track. She walked back over to her desk and sat on the front edge.

"Well, I think you are all those things I just said and more, Alex," she said, leaning forward. "You are one of the brightest, most insightful young men I have ever met, and I like you too. But I'm not going to let you off the hook, because I think you have a problem. I think you can't read."

She stopped and watched his reaction. His eyes had widened at her abrupt assessment of him, and then his Adam's apple started working overtime with the accusation.

"What do you think?" she asked.

"I think I can read," he answered bluntly.

Her head tilted slightly, questioning him. "All right," she said, pulling a book off her desk and handing it to him. "Read."

He took the book and gazed at the front cover. He recognized it as one they had read last year.

"*Of Mice and Men*," he said triumphantly as he pretended to read the title.

Martha nodded. "Continue," she said, and Alex felt his flesh grow warm.

He opened to the first chapter and wet his lips. "A few mills … south of …" He had no clue what the next word was and so mumbled something under his breath, " … the …" Stuck again. He recognized "river" and just skipped the word ahead of it, "… river prods in … closet … to the …"

He was concentrating so hard on the mishmash of letters in front of him, trying to recognize the shapes of words he had seen before, that he had no idea that what he was reading was making no sense at all.

"That's fine," Martha said softly and took the book gently from his hands. Alex looked up at her, his eyes full of worry, of hope.

"See, I read it," he said.

She nodded. "Do you know what you read?"

"It's about these two guys. One's mentally retarded—" She shook her head and raised her hand to stop him.

"Not what the book's about, but what you read today. The sentence you just read?"

Alex just stared up at her. Lost. His mind searched desperately for something that might click, but nothing fell into place. Finally, he let his eyes and head drop, and he shook his head sadly.

"Not a word," he confessed. Martha slid into the seat next to him.

"I want you to tell me what these words are," she said and opened the book to the first page again. "How about this one?" she said and pointed to "close." Alex looked the word over carefully.

"Clothes?" he asked, not remembering that he had said "closet" before.

"And this one?" she asked, her finger under "pool."

The letters looked familiar. "Loop," he said and then looked again. "Or pool," he added, suddenly confused.

"Alex, how do you tell what a word is?" she asked.

He shook his head. "I don't really. I mean, if I've seen it before—a lot—I kind of remember, but then some of the words look alike."

"Do you sound them out at all?"

He looked at her quizzically. "Letter by letter?"

Alex licked his dry lips again. He hated to confess that he really didn't know what letter made what sound. He just tried to memorize words. It worked for some. He shook his head again, and with it came out his years of frustration.

"I'm just stupid," he said. "I don't even know what letter makes which sound." He was so close to tears that Martha felt very uncomfortable. Alex was a proud boy and would probably never forgive himself if he broke down in front of her. Not to say what it might do to his already floundering self-esteem. She needed to salvage the situation.

She jerked her head back in amazement and stared at him as though he had just made the most ridiculous statement she had ever heard, which he actually had.

"That is the last thing you are, Mr. Kowalski," Martha snapped. "If anything, you are the most intelligent and hardworking person on this campus. Without being able to read—that is, fluently," she added, "because you *can* read some, you have never failed a class. In fact, you have excelled in math, which means that that mind of yours is a steel trap. What you hear, you never forget."

She paused. "Your problem is not your intelligence at all. I believe you suffer from dyslexia." Alex looked at her puzzled.

"For lack of a better way of explaining it," she continued, "it means you get letters mixed up. Something in your brain—"

"Doesn't function," Alex finished for her.

"Doesn't function the same as some other people," she corrected him. "You would be surprised how many people suffer from it."

He looked at her steadily. "So can they ever learn to read?" he asked, and she could see the desperate hope in his eyes as well as hear it in his voice.

"As well as anyone else," she said with a smile. "See, the problem with education, Alex, is that teachers teach the way *most* kids learn, or sometimes just the way they themselves learned. That doesn't mean other ways of learning are wrong or bad—they are just other ways of learning. And that's what we need to figure out for you. How you can learn to read. Just by our time today, I've discovered how you've tried to learn, but I think we can both agree that it hasn't been very successful for you."

He nodded his head in agreement.

"I'm afraid I don't have any answers right now either," she confessed, "but I'll start reading up on the research, and I promise, by the end of the year, you'll be a reader."

The light in Alex's eyes flashed brightly and then suddenly flickered away as the memory of other promises that had been made but broken came to mind. It could be another disappointment, and there was no reason to raise his hopes. Still, at least *this* teacher had a name for his problem—and it wasn't "dummy."

Chapter 12

Danny stared at his chemistry test: 72 percent. Most people would be happy with that, but in this class, where the professor's main thrust was to weed out half of them, a 72 percent equated to an F. He looked through the test at the questions he had missed. Some had just been stupid mistakes or careless errors. He knew this stuff. He had studied for hours and hours.

Inside he felt empty, totally deflated. He had been a straight-A student at St. Christopher's, and even though he had studied there and liked to study, it had still come easy for him. Now he felt pressured. He knew he should be doing better, and so he pushed himself harder and harder and then choked on the day of the test—afraid he might fail it—and then what happened?

He crumpled the paper slowly with one fist. Those closest to him watched silently, but he didn't notice. The professor didn't notice either because he was about two hundred students down and most likely didn't care, except for the fact that he was succeeding in weeding out yet another wanna-be doctor who really didn't have the stuff to make it.

The lecture started, but Danny didn't hear a word, insuring that he would now most likely fail his next test. His mind drifted. He wondered what he was doing here, why he wanted to be a doctor at all. Who was *he* to think he had what it took?

When he had mentioned majoring in premed, his mother smiled triumphantly, and his father had nodded with approval. "A noble profession," he had said and then his mother had warned, "It will take a lot of studying, but I know you have what it takes."

Danny looked at the crumbled paper now lying on his desk. No he didn't. But how could he ever let them know it?

"Now remember," his father had said. "You may find you don't like that major once you start studying it. Don't be afraid to change. A man should be happy in what he's doing."

Changing because of not liking something was one thing. Changing because you didn't measure up, because you were a failure, was another.

He stared off into space, contemplating his possible options. Nothing came to mind, and as the professor droned on about various catalysts, he sank deeper and deeper into his own despair.

"Alex."

Coach's voice was uncommonly soft. It was unnerving, and Alex wasn't quite sure what direction this conversation, or rather lecture, might be taking.

"Alex, I understand Mrs. Richards wants you to come in for tutoring twice a week."

Alex was cautious. How much did teachers talk? Mrs. Richards and Coach Bauer did not seem the type to be friends, so maybe he didn't know much.

"She's mentioned it," he answered.

"Are you going?"

"I told her I couldn't make it until after football was over," he said, still nervously wondering what was up.

Coach Bauer, who had been pacing his normal figure eight, turned to look him over carefully. "Why did you tell her that?"

"Because I can't miss practice," he said, somewhat amazed that the coach would even have to ask.

"Why can't you?"

Alex looked shocked. "Because if I miss practice, I can't play in the game."

"You can't *start* in the game," Coach Bauer corrected.

Same difference, Alex thought. "And for each day you miss," Alex added, "you sit out a quarter and run extra steps in practice."

The kid know the rules, Bauer mused. "So football's pretty important to you, huh?" came the question.

"Yes, sir," Alex replied, and Coach Bauer winced. The kid was so polite, such a good kid and a great player with huge potential. He hated to have to be the tough guy. He also hated to have to sacrifice a possible championship season.

"Is it your number one priority?"

Alex knew a trick question when he heard one. He also knew the expected answer for most teachers—"No, school is"—but he wasn't sure what Coach was looking for.

"Well?" Coach Bauer's eyes bored tiny holes into him, and he shifted uncomfortably.

"I don't know," he answered truthfully, and strangely enough, Coach Bauer smiled.

"A very honest answer," he said softly again, almost to himself. He paused for a moment, his hands clasped behind his back, and recommenced his pacing. "Why does Mrs. Richards think you need tutoring?"

Alex felt his throat tighten again. How much did he know? "I just need some help in English."

"Thought you were getting a C minus in English?"

Alex swallowed again. "I am."

"Then why the tutoring? Are you a discipline problem?"

Alex's eyes shot open. "No, sir," he said with conviction.

Coach Bauer watched him from the corner of his eye. He hated to take the kid through this insidious interrogation, but he knew that the boy had to admit what his problem was, face it head on, and accept the challenge before he could ever tackle it.

"Then why?" he asked slowly and deliberately as he sat down two feet from Alex and looked at him hard.

Alex had never felt so distraught in all his life. His lifelong secret, a secret not even his parents suspected, was on the line. At the present, only Mrs. Richards knew, and she was an English teacher. She seemed to understand. But Coach Bauer was his coach. Coach Bauer was the guy who yelled in his face, who flushed with rage when he turned left instead of right, who thought he was an idiot already. Coach Bauer wouldn't understand.

Alex felt his strength ebbing away. Coach Bauer would also recognize a lie and not take too kindly to it. He was stuck in a corner. A dog caged. There were no options; there was no way out. He bit his lip till he thought it would bleed, swallowed three more times in quick succession, wiped his sweaty hands on his pants legs, and looked up weakly.

"Because I can't read," he finally said, and his voice seemed small and echoed in the quietness of the room.

The stench of heavy beer accosted Travis as he pushed open the apartment door. He tried not to breathe too deeply.

Ten minutes max, and you're out of here, he reminded himself as he crossed the small living room and set the two bags on the counter.

"That you, Travis?" The question came from the dark of the nearest bedroom.

"Yeah. It's me," he answered unenthusiastically.

No one answered, and Travis set to emptying the bags of groceries. With his back to the living room, he didn't see his mother stumble out of the bedroom.

She was a tall woman, with long, shapely legs that she showed off with a tight, form-fitting knit skirt and matching top. She had light chocolate-brown skin, thin aristocratic hands and fingers, and a soft, shapely mouth filled with mostly white teeth and one gold cap. From anybody's standpoint, she was a very striking woman—with her mouth closed. She made her way toward Travis with a slight weave in her walk. He heard her, felt her, without turning around, and the hair on his neck involuntarily stood on end.

She had a lit cigarette in her hand and drew on it heavily, then held the cigarette out away from her at arm's length and with her other hand began tentatively pawing through the contents of the unattended bag. Travis continued emptying the other and silently waited. She pulled out a box and looked it over.

"What did you buy these for?" she asked in a whiny voice and held up a box of Captain Crunch. "This is pure junk. Those kids don't need none of this. You're jes wastin' our money."

Travis held his tongue while his mother ranted. She spoke of his brothers and sister as if they didn't belong to her.

"The kids like it," he said mildly, ignoring the comment about whose money was being spent. He had specifically purchased the sugary cereal because it really was the only treat the kids had. He bought it for them weekly, and they knew the secret hiding place. Now the secret was out. What was she doing here anyway? Usually she was out drumming up business right about now.

"Well, they don't need it, and I don't want you buying any more of it. Kids these days need to be eating healthier than that!"

And what do you know or care about how they eat? Travis silently seethed but said nothing. His mother took another long puff before throwing the box back into the bag and rummaging through the rest of the contents, grunting disapprovingly at occasional purchases, but throwing nothing away. Nothing positive came from her mouth. There was another long pause.

"Give me some money," she said suddenly. Travis grew wary and tense.

"What for?" he asked.

She shrugged in irritation. "What difference is that to you?" she said. "I said give me some."

"I don't have any," Travis answered. "Just spent it all on groceries."

"You're lying," she hissed, and her eyes flashed, and Travis could see the red around the pupils. She was high. "You've got all kinds of money. Now hand some over."

"No," he said firmly.

She slapped him hard on the side of the face. He just stood there and took it.

"*Give it!*" she screamed.

"*No!*" he yelled back, and she ripped her fingernails down his cheek. He stood there and took her assault, a guy who had killed two others in cold blood would not touch his mother, and he himself didn't know why.

"I'll have to sell myself if you won't," she threatened. "Do you really wanna see your mama walking the streets?"

No, he thought, *but you'd do it anyway. Money or no money.* "I don't have any money," he said quietly. He knew she had probably already searched his room, which is why he never kept it there. It was all safe.

"You're worthless," she spit between clenched teeth and then turned and strutted and stumbled out of the apartment.

A cynical smile played on his lips as he realized the irony of her statement. *If you only knew,* he thought.

"Now, Willie, you need to make noise like you're shooting birds, but you need to be offstage, so go in the closet and come out on cue," Reba directed. "Jake—you, Jocelyn, and Chris sit on the bed. You're the audience."

"You want me to go get Mom?" Jake asked.

"Not yet. I want to make sure I know my part first," Reba answered.

"Why are you trying out for such a weird part anyway?" Willie complained. "Weezer's a geezer," and then he laughed at his own joke.

Reba didn't answer while she situated the two younger children on the bed. What should she say? The truth? That she already knew that her looks would stand in the way of many of the premier high school drama roles? That she was already settling on second best because she knew she couldn't get first?

It wasn't like her at all, yet she was doing it, wasn't she? But she had read through all the parts, and this one did appeal to her. She looked too young for Malyn, the mother. She had thought about Anelle's part, but that character was too wimpy for her taste; and then there was Shelby. She thought it through again. Just exactly why was she going for Weezer's part?

"I think you should try out for the girl who dies," Jake said, sitting down next to Chris and pulling the big three-year-old into his lap. "You've always died really great." Reba accepted the compliment and then smiled at the two brothers. Jake loved to hold his little brother, and if he were allowed to hold him as much as he wanted, Chris would have never learned to walk. There wouldn't have been a need for it.

"I wanted to try a comedic role," Reba answered. "They're the more difficult parts to play anyway."

This seemed to satisfy them, and the three on the bed quieted down, while Willie stepped into the closet to commence his shooting noises, and Reba stepped outside.

"Bang! Bang! … Bang! … Bang!"

From outside the door, Reba yelled, "Stop it! Stop pulling, Rip. Come on!"

The shooting continued, and Reba appeared in the doorway, half bent over, legs spread for footing as though pulling on an imaginary dog that wouldn't budge. The kids giggled.

"Come on, Rip," she said, struggling with the imaginary dog and then knocking on the wall next to her. "Drummond, I'll kill you if you don't answer."

Willie stuck his head out.

"Good morning, Weeza," he said pleasantly, in a nice Southern drawl. "My, but you look like—" Willie stopped abruptly and a frown covered his face. "Reba, I can't say that word. Mom will wash my mouth out with soap."

Reba never stopped her imaginary struggle. "Just substitute then," she said.

The smile returned. "Good morning, Weeza," he repeated. "My, but you look like a dog turd today."

Jake howled with laughter, and little Chris followed suit because Jake was laughing, but Jocelyn gasped and covered her mouth with her hand in embarrassment. Reba just threw her younger brother a withering glare, but he fielded it with a smile. He had broken no rules.

"I have such a bone to pick with you," Reba said, staying in character *and* looking straight at her brother and then almost had her herself pulled back out the door much to the delight of the youngsters.

"Stop it!" she yelled at the dog and then struggling, turned her attention back to Willie. "I've just come from the vet. He said all this noise that you've been making the last few days has been causing a nervous condition in my dog. His hair's falling out, and I've got to get him on tranquilizers."

Willie just grinned at her, the kids laughed and clapped in delight, and Reba continued to do battle with the dog and Drummond.

Chapter 13

Lennis Bauer looked carefully at his young charge, who was squirming uncomfortably before him. It had taken a lot of guts for Alex to admit what he did, but he was unsure if Alex was willing to go the distance he needed. The kid needed to be tutored after school. The kid wanted to play football. At present, the two were conflicting.

He mused over his own options. True, Alex could wait until after the season, but that wouldn't straighten out his priorities, and Bauer was one who knew how wrong they were, or if not wrong, at least how fragile they were. He could allow Alex to go to the tutorial and still start the game. It would make both of them happy. Alex wanted to play, and he wanted Alex to play, both for the good of the team and for the good of the kid.

The coach had never had a son—three girls—and Alex was everything he would ever want in a son. Ironically, he even had a few of his own traits. But he knew before he ever let the idea bloom that it wouldn't work. You didn't play favorites. You didn't make allowances and still keep a good team concept and good team morale. It just didn't work. There was only one answer.

"You will be going to tutorial twice a week beginning tomorrow," Coach Bauer said with a finality that surprised even himself.

Alex looked up in shock. This was not the answer he had been expecting from Coach Bauer. "But then I can't play football," he argued, and the hurt and disbelief was evident in his eyes.

"No, that's not true," Bauer stated. "That means you won't be able to play two quarters a week, but you can still play."

Alex breathed in rapidly, trying to calm himself and catch his breath. This wasn't fair. This wasn't right. Coach Bauer had no right to tell him he had to go to the stupid tutorial. Sure he wanted to read, but he wanted to play football too, and according to his plan, he could do both. But the way Coach Bauer had it figured, he had to give up one for the other, at least most of it. His disappointment and disbelief dissipated while his anger grew. Maybe this was Coach's way of just weeding him off the team. Well, it would take a lot more than that.

"You can't make me," Alex said stonily.

Bauer paused. "No, I can't," he finally replied, "but I can keep you from playing football." He set his jaw. "And if you refuse to go, I'll cut you from the team."

Alex's mouth dropped open involuntarily, and he quickly shut it again. This was blackmail! Now he couldn't play either way. Now just confused and mad, Alex wasn't thinking straight.

"I'll save you the trouble," he spit out. "I'll quit and then *no one* can make me go to the stupid tutorial."

He rose from his seat and strode to the door in two steps, whipped it open, and then slammed it behind him. Coach Bauer winced at the noise and then stared at the closed door and questioned what he had just done. Had he in his effort to help actually shut two more doors for Alex Kowalski?

Travis found Byron and Jasmine out on the street where most of the neighborhood spent the good part of the day. Jasmine was skipping rope with some of her friends while Byron was keeping a wary eye out on the street scene. He had no idea where Tyrone was. Travis watched his younger brother. He truly wished Byron and Tyrone didn't have to be a part of all this … this … he smiled ruefully. What was all this? A game? A living? A death trap? He let out a sharp, shrill whistle, and his brother turned instinctively.

Travis never moved his head, and even though the autumn sun was not as menacing as the summer one, he still wore his Ray-Bans. His brother recognized him immediately and came running.

"Hey, Travis," he said.

Travis seemed not to hear at first, looking first one way down the street and then the other. When he was satisfied with what he saw, he looked down at Byron solemnly.

"Who you workin' for?" he asked.

"Marcus," Byron answered.

Travis scanned the street again. "What's he paying you?"

"A tenth of his take."

Travis nodded as if in approval. "He makin' you go on the east half?"

Byron shook his head, and Travis nodded in approval again. "You make sure he doesn't, you hear?" He started walking down the street, and Byron followed him.

"Travis? Why don't you let me work for you?" he asked. "Marcus says you don't let anyone work for you. That you want to keep all the money for yourself. I wouldn't take much," he said. "I—" Travis turned on his little brother and sparks flew, even through the heavy coating of his sunglasses.

"Don't you believe a word Marcus Wilcox tells you," Travis spit. "You think for a moment why he has *you* working for him. Do you think he wants to share his money? Do you think that's why you're working for him? No way, kid. Wake up! You're working for him because he doesn't want to take the fall if something comes down. He doesn't want to get his hands dirty should the cops come around." He paused. "He's not working you out of the kindness of his heart, Byron, and you learn that fast. He's working you for his own protection."

The speech released a lot of pent-up emotion in Travis, and he was physically relaxed when he was through.

"Then why don't you work someone, Travis? I don't want you gettin' in no trouble."

Travis let out a weak smile. "Any trouble," he corrected, "and I don't want to be responsible for anyone getting hurt but me," he said. He paused and let out a slow breath. "Just me."

"How come you let me work for Marcus then, huh? How come?"

It was easy to see the question pained Travis, and his eyes fell on his little brother before looking over and seeing ten-year-old Jasmine taking her turn jumping.

It really didn't make much sense. Here he was protecting Willie Washington, and yet he let his own brother get sucked up into the mess. He tried to sort out his own hypocrisy. There really wasn't much to sort out. His family was already mired in it, while the Washingtons seemed untouched. He wanted to protect and preserve that purity somehow. Byron, like himself, would have to work his own way out.

"Because believe it or not, Byron," he said simply but with more than a little truth, "you're safer if these guys are on your side than against you, and though there's no sure way, helping them out is a plus. Just don't go on the east side, you hear? And don't do any dirty jobs. Just run stuff, that's it. You understand?"

Byron nodded, his eyes glued on Travis's face. Byron adored his brother, and that just kicked the living crap out of Travis. He looked again at Jasmine. Byron was safe for a while as long as he played the game. But Jasmine? Even at ten, she was beginning to show signs of growing up. How long would she be safe? What could he do? How could he protect her?

The weight of his burden hung heavy on his shoulders, but he couldn't think of it now. He rested his hand on Byron's shoulder, and the young boy moved closer to him.

"I need to get some work done now, okay?" Byron looked up and nodded. Travis smiled wanly.

"You'd better get back to your post or you won't earn your 10 percent, and I know you've already got it spent."

Byron grinned. "A pair of Air Jordans," he said and scooped up an imaginary basketball and went up for a jump shot.

Travis let out a rare laugh, rubbed Byron's head affectionately, and walked off.

"How were classes today, Danny?" Martha asked pleasantly.

Danny toyed with his food and didn't look up. "Fine," he said. Martha wasn't too disturbed by his lack of answer. After all, he had been quieter ever since he started college, and she just attributed it to maturing.

"You were getting a test back today in chemistry, weren't you?" she asked, passing him the mashed potatoes.

He took the potatoes from her and placed them on the table in front of him. "Yeah," he answered.

"How did you do?"

"Got a 72 percent."

Martha picked up on his disgusted tone and tried to console her only child. "Well, a seventy-two isn't bad, a C, and I know you'll do better next time."

Danny never looked up and kept swirling food with his fork. "Yeah. Whatever."

Graydon Richards had just been sitting back, taking in the whole scene, and he was not liking what he saw.

"I think your mother deserves to have you at least look at her when she's speaking," he said sharply, and his son's eyes shot up to look into his father's. No words were spoken, but Martha could see the battle being waged, and she wanted to avoid it.

"Oh, it's okay," she said, hoping to mollify the situation, but her two men continued to lock eyes.

"If you'll excuse me, I think I'll go get some studying done," Danny said and pushed his chair back and left the table before anything else could be said. Graydon followed him with his eyes.

"Now why did you go and do that?" Martha wanted to know. "He's having trouble in school, and you're just adding pressure."

Graydon Richards didn't answer her, but instead looked at the empty doorway that had just swallowed up his son. How much of what he suspected should he tell his wife? And how long should he wait until he took action?

Danny closed the door to his room and quietly locked it behind him. His father was already suspicious and should he hear the click of his lock, well, it was a scene he really didn't want to relive. Without turning on the light, he walked over to his window and opened it, letting in the crisp October air. He breathed in deeply, and the freshness helped alleviate a little of the stress he was feeling.

He sunk into his desk chair and looked out at the stars gathering in the sky. He remembered when it had been enough just to breathe in the fresh air and look at the stars. His world had been so uncomplicated, even just last year. Now it was a mess: a maze of choices and decisions, a mine field of competition, and he wasn't surviving well at all.

Danny slid open his left desk drawer and dug beneath the piles of papers until he felt the tiny baggie at the bottom. In the gathering dark, he pulled out a rolling paper, then the baggie of marijuana, dropped the last of it into the paper, and rolled it skillfully. This was his third purchase. He thought the stuff would last longer, but he had underestimated the calming effect and his own desire to feel free and easy. What he had expected to be a once-a-week relaxer had turned into an every-other-night habit.

He licked his fingers and sealed down the edges and then pulled out a match and lit it. He still felt qualms of guilt knowing that he was indulging in something his parents strictly prohibited—and in their own home no less—but he could think of no safer place. His parents respected his privacy. Anywhere else and someone might see him.

He drew in a deep puff, and the warm sweetness of the marijuana oozed through him, giving him a light-headedness. He closed his eyes and released his breath slowly, subconsciously aiming the smoke out the open window where it would dissipate into the evening stillness.

He took another long draw and felt his muscles relax, and many of his worries seemed to float to the back of his mind. He stayed in this repose, eyes closed, feet propped up on his desk as his joint burned slowly down. A full forty-five minutes slipped away and with it, all the troubles that had been bombarding him.

But when he opened his eyes to crush the small stub, the euphoria was already beginning to vanish, and reality was flooding through the window with the increasing chill. He felt more depressed than ever. He reached deep into his desk drawer and felt one baggie left. He could smoke it now, but what good would that do? He would feel the same letdown after it and then what would he use on Monday?

Staring out the window, Danny pondered the state of his affairs. He would just have to get something stronger—but not cocaine or crack. He didn't need to get high; he needed to get mellow. Someone had mentioned that heroin was making a comeback and could make you feel great. He would ask Travis if he could get some. Monday. That was their next deal. He would ask then.

The cold was starting to chill him, so he waved any excess fumes out and shut the window. He pulled his books out. *Might as well try and make a comeback,* he thought as he opened his chemistry book and started to study, but his mind was still so weak and fragmented from his joint that he found it hard to concentrate, and he never heard the quiet creak of his doorknob being twisted as his father checked to see if it was locked.

Alex lay in the dark of his room and stared up toward the ceiling. This had been an all-around rotten day, and it was all Mrs. Richards and Coach Bauer's fault. Who were they to tell him what to do?

He let out a long sigh and contemplated his future. He had asked for it; he knew that. He had prayed every year for God to help him learn to read. He had pleaded for the chance to learn, and well, here it was. Only it was at the expense of his football. That was the part he *hadn't* counted on.

Alex rolled over and stared at the little red light on his stereo that indicated it was on. The CD had been over an hour ago and yet he hadn't realized it, so wrapped up was he in his own thoughts. He rolled over on his back and rested his head in his hands. The dark was strangely comforting, probably because it matched his mood so well: forlorn, depressed, heavy. He reworked his meeting with Coach Bauer. Why had he threatened to quit? He didn't have to. He could still play, just not start. Was that really so bad?

But how long would he have to be tutored? Even though Mrs. Richards had said he would be reading by the end of the year, she didn't say how *well* he would be reading. This could go on for years. Would he have to give up football for good? Man, that was something he hadn't bargained on. Why did God make a person sacrifice one thing to get another? It just wasn't fair. Why did he have to make a choice?

Alex turned his head and glanced at the clock on his nightstand. Eleven thirty. He should be asleep, but he wasn't even tired. Still, he should at least make the attempt. He had a football game tomorrow—what could be his last game of the year. He had better make it count.

Chapter 14

"All right, guys," Coach Bauer said as he paced back and forth across the front of the locker room. "We've got three wins under our belt. That's good." He pursed his lips and continued pacing. "That's real good, in fact. I like that." He stopped and turned to face them, looking at each player, all forty-five, directly in the eye.

Alex wanted to look away when Coach Bauer caught his eye, but he knew it would show weakness. Though he was quaking inside, he returned the coach's gaze with a steady one of his own. "But it's not enough," added the coach. He held Alex's eye, and Alex felt himself weakening.

"The last two teams we've played haven't been too strong. Maxwell is young, lots of juniors, yet they played us close enough; and Jefferson, as always, had tons of talent and no discipline. They self-destructed.

"We, on the other hand, have a pretty mature group here. Twenty-five of you are varsity veterans. You know the ropes. You know what to expect, what the opposition might throw at you, and that counts for something." He had stopped his pacing again and turned his gaze back toward Alex.

"And we all played pretty fair. But today you are going to be tested." He paused as he passed his eyes over every player in the room. No one breathed. No one moved. "Today, all your skills, talents, and desire will be on the line. And let me tell you, boys, you'll need all three.

"Heart alone won't win this one for you. Skills we've practiced and drilled into you for the past two months alone won't win this one for you. That raw talent and instinct some of you possess won't win this one for you today. Today, men, you have to possess and display all three." He paused once more and then added softly but forcefully, "But I know you have all three."

The energy rose visibly in the room. Faces were glued intently on their coach, adrenaline was pumping, hands were opening and closing in anticipation.

"Are you ready?" Coach Bauer asked softly.

"Yeah," came the sporadic reply.

"*Are you ready?*" he asked more forcefully.

"*Yeah!*" came the shout.

"*ARE YOU READY?*" he yelled, shooting his right arm into the air.

"*YEAH!*" came the pumped reply as the players rose to their feet.

"*Then let's go show Madison what you've got!*"

"*Yeah! Yeah! Yeah!*" they yelled, and shoved and pushed each other out of the locker room.

"Umph!" Alex hit the ground hard and felt the full weight of the 220-pound linebacker who fell squarely on him. Every bone and muscle in his body ached, and usually that didn't happen till the next morning. But today's game was so punishing, the pain was coming early.

The whistle blew and the back judge cleared the linebacker off, and Alex struggled up. Madison's linebacker was bent over, catching his breath. Alex glanced at the clock. Less than a minute left, and they were more than a touchdown behind. There was no chance to win, but there was no way they would give up after the grueling battle they'd been through. Coach had been right. Today had required skill and talent, and now when it came down to the wire, pride and heart were really all they had to keep going.

Alex jogged back to the huddle and bent over, his hands resting on his knees. He glanced around at the faces of his teammates. They were tired and dirty but still determined.

"Give me the ball," Alex said. "That middle linebacker is dead tired. Pass it right down the middle, and I'll beat him."

"But if you don't, we're out of time, Piston," Greg protested. "And we want one more touchdown. We need a sideline pattern. I'm passing long to Richard, Red 94, which means you get down there and pick off the free safety and then block anyone open."

Alex nodded. It wasn't the way he wanted to end his season, but he was a team player, and he knew Greg was right. In *his* mind he saw himself breaking tackles and powering into the end zone with two or three would-be tacklers hanging on. Now he was relegated to a supporting role, but he wouldn't let Richard down. He looked toward his buddy and nodded. Richard grinned.

The huddle broke and Alex lined up, quickly checking over Madison's zone defense. They were playing right into Montgomery's hands. The ball was snapped and despite his fatigue and pain, Alex pushed off the line, drove right, and then cut toward the goal posts. His pattern crossed right in front of the free safety, who instinctively moved to cover him. Richard's defender dropped off to pick up Alex too, which left Richard free to cut across the open field and head down the sideline.

The ball landed gently in Richard's hands. There was no need for Alex to cut back to block. Richard literally danced into the end zone with no time remaining.

Alex let out an exhausted breath. They may have been beaten today, but they did not lose. He could hold his head up to Coach Bauer when he dropped off his pads—he was leaving a winner.

"You're a quitter, Kowalski," Coach Bauer said softly, and Alex stopped in his tracks, the hair on his neck standing on end. This was not what he had expected to hear. Though normally controlled, he felt his anger slowly building. Man, this guy never gave anyone a break, anyone credit. Here he had been pushed into a corner, and all Coach Bauer could do was criticize. He turned around slowly, squared his shoulders, and faced his coach.

"I am not," he said evenly, already feeling the heat flush in his normally red cheeks. "I'm just setting priorities." The bitterness seeped through the words.

Coach Bauer pursed his lips, looked down at the floor, and shook his head slowly. "No, you're not," he almost whispered. "You're getting even."

He looked up. "You're saying 'so there.' You're saying you can't handle or don't want to try and handle what's come your way, and so you're quitting. No one said setting priorities meant quitting football. That was *your* idea. All yours. Own it."

Alex stood and listened to Coach Bauer but had no idea how to retaliate. *Man, why am I so stupid?* he wondered. *Why can't I think of clever things to say that would make this man feel as small and worthless as he's making me feel?* He floundered within his own mind while Coach Bauer paced casually back and forth.

"Sit down, Alex," Coach Bauer said gently, and Alex, caught completely off guard by the use of his first name, could think of nothing else to do, so he sat. The coach ended his pacing and sat on the edge of his desk facing Alex. For a few moments, the room was deathly quiet while Bauer tried to sort out his thoughts, tried to decide where to start.

"Alex," he began, and again Alex jerked involuntarily at the mention of his first name. *What had happened to "Kowalski"?*

"First of all, I want to apologize if I ever made you feel like you were dumb. I never, *ever*, thought you were dumb. In fact, the reason

I rode you so hard was because I couldn't understand why such a smart kid like you could make such stupid mistakes."

He smiled ruefully, and Alex blushed but said nothing. *Was that supposed to be a compliment? What was Coach driving at?*

Coach Bauer eyed Alex evenly before looking away. "I know you're dropping football to spite me, and perhaps Mrs. Richards for telling me, and to make me feel sorry or guilty or who knows what else," he said and cast a casual eye at Alex, who was watching him hard. "But it won't work. Because the only guy who's going to be spited, or feel sorry or guilty … is you."

Alex's lips tightened. He was in no mood for a lecture. Life was bad enough already. He had quit. He didn't have to sit here and take this, but he couldn't make himself move. Coach stood up and started pacing again, back and forth across his office.

"I know you want to play college football, Alex." Alex's head popped up ever so slightly. "I can see it in your eyes." He turned toward him. "And I'll be honest with you. You could make it. In three years, barring no injuries, you could make any college team you wanted."

Despite his mood, Alex's face lit up. This was more like it. This was what he wanted to hear.

"But could you make college, Alex?" Coach asked, and the bombshell fell. Coach had hit his greatest fear and deepest secret. "I'm not asking you this to put you down," he said gently. "I'm asking you this to make you think."

He stopped at his desk and sat down in his chair as though exhausted and leaned back, his hands behind his head, and swiveled back and forth as though debating about continuing. Finally, he swung back to face Alex, and he looked tired.

"You see, Alex, I *didn't* think."

Alex looked up at him, slightly confused, puzzled. *What was that supposed to mean—Bauer "didn't think"?*

"Like you, Alex, I couldn't read in high school, but I made it all the way through and stood on the platform with my diploma, which to me was my ticket to the pros." He smiled ruefully. "Do you know that except for my name, I couldn't recognize another word on that piece of paper?" He shook his head sadly.

"But," he said optimistically and sat up in his chair, "it got me to college. At least through the door. I had a full ride to Michigan State—a full ride, mind you. My life was set. All I had to do was play football and pass some classes." He stopped and his eyes rested on Alex, which made the boy squirm uncomfortably.

"Well, what do you think happened? Oh, I could play football all right, but I couldn't pass a one of my classes, and I'll tell you, it wasn't from trying either. Oh, yeah, at first I goofed around, figuring I could just slide through like I had in high school. You know, those classes were so crowded that a professor would almost rejoice if a kid missed an assignment or two, just to have a little break. But then I saw it wasn't working, and I saw my whole career, my whole life slipping through my fingers like running water, and there was nothing I could do.

"To my credit, I wasn't a cheater. I had morals, so my options were few. I hired tutors and started going to every class and every study session I could find, but it was too late. I was out by semester break. I played one game that year. When the coaches found out I was having trouble in school, they didn't waste their time on me. Why develop a kid who was going to flunk out? Football players were plentiful."

Alex sat silently, listening in rapt attention. This was tough for Coach Bauer. How many other people knew he had flunked out of college and ruined his chance at a pro football career?

"But you're teaching now," Alex said. Coach Bauer nodded.

"Now, yes. But I was hired at first only to coach football, and I was lucky. Usually, they want someone with a credential who can teach as well as a coach, but the school was desperate. Let me tell you, coaching high school football does not make a living. I had to pick up some pretty bush jobs just to eat."

Alex felt himself smile in spite of himself. It felt kind of good to have the coach confide in him. "Then when did you get your ..." He paused, trying to recall the word.

"Credential?" Coach Bauer filled in. Alex nodded and the coach stood up, stuffed his hands in his pockets, and stared out the window as though looking into the past. "That didn't happen until almost ten years later," he said softly and then turned slowly around and gazed at Alex levelly. "When a new, young, black, energetic English teacher came to me for help with how to handle one of her students—one of my football players."

"Mrs. Richards?" Alex asked in astonishment. Coach Bauer grinned.

"But how did she learn you couldn't read?"

Coach Bauer's eyes rose in surprise. "*You're* asking *me* that? How did she find out you couldn't read? That's one smart lady."

"Well, what did she do?" Alex asked, his interest piqued.

"To make a long story short, she baited me. Sent me little memos about my players, asked me what I thought of certain articles about football, anything until I finally had to confess to her that I couldn't read. I mean, I didn't want her to go and start asking questions that might let everyone know."

"What did she do then?"

Coach Bauer shrugged his shoulders nonchalantly. "She taught me." He sat down again. "Every night after practice, I would stop by her house, have dinner with her and her husband, and she would teach me to read."

Alex's eyes widened. "Why did she do that?"

Coach Bauer leaned forward. "Because that's the kind of woman she is," he answered simply. "And that's all the explanation you need." He relaxed again. "Of course, once she had me up to speed, she had me enroll at the JC to start working on my degree and then introduced me to a friend of hers so that she and her husband could have some time alone again."

Alex grinned. "Was this friend a good cook?" he asked, feeling both strange and good about talking to the coach on such a personal level.

"Good enough to marry," he answered and winked. Alex laughed. "The point is, Alex, Martha Richards saw a need in me and a hope for me. Through all of that, she still treated me as a professional equal. Don't throw away what she's about to offer you. She knows football's important to you. But she also knows that you won't succeed unless you can read. And Alex, no one will ever know unless you tell them. And only you will know when that will be important."

It almost sounded like a plea, and Alex felt ashamed for having been so dense for thinking they were out to get him. He swallowed hard twice to regain control of his voice, and a third time to swallow his pride. He looked at his pads lying on the floor where he had dropped them.

"Do you mind if I reclaim my pads and give it another try?" he asked tentatively.

Coach Bauer feigned surprise as he looked down at the gear lying on the floor. "Gee, I thought you just dropped them off to have them cleaned," he said with a grin.

"All right now, who wants more spaghetti?" Travis held out the skillet while he brooded over the table, checking out everyone's plate. "Jasmine, you look like your plate is just about empty."

Jasmine shook her head vehemently. "I'm too pull," she mumbled.

"Don't talk with your mouth full," Travis scolded while trying to suppress a smile. "Tyrone, Byron, how about you two?"

Both boys nodded fiercely.

"You make the best spaghetti, Travis," Byron said as he held up his plate for more. "I think it's 'cause of all that catsup you pour in."

Travis dished up some noodles and then poured a healthy spoonful of meat sauce over the top. It was nice to receive a compliment, but he knew with Byron's hollow legs, probably anything tasted good. He did wish, however, that he knew how to make more than spaghetti, macaroni and cheese, and hamburgers, which provided the staple of their diet. But the kids never complained.

His mother wasn't home, and Travis was glad. He enjoyed this time with his brothers and sister. He glanced at his watch. Six thirty-eight. He had a drop at seven and then he planned on doing a little relaxing himself. He needed the release.

"All right, whose turn is it to wash tonight?"

"Tyrone's," Byron yelled before anyone else had a chance to answer. "Jasmine dries, and I clear."

"No way," complained Tyrone. "I washed last night. It's your turn."

"Then it's Jasmine's," countered Byron, but Jasmine shook her head furiously.

"It is not," she denied and puffed out her lower lip.

"By the way you're passing it around," Travis observed, "I'd say it's your turn." Byron opened his mouth to protest, but Travis held up his hand and narrowed his eyes. "You wash," he said, "Tyrone dries, and Jasmine clears."

"Jasmine always gets to clear," complained Byron sulkily. Travis gave him another hard stare.

"Now I've got to go out for a little while, but I'll be back by eleven. I want you all to do at least one hour of homework, understood? And then you can watch TV till nine and then to bed."

The three nodded their heads, although Byron was still holding a grudge. Travis kissed Jasmine lightly on the head and then ran his hand over the head of each boy. Neither pulled away. His heart pulled into a painful knot. They deserved better—a better mother, a better home, a better life. They all did. But how? He grabbed his coat and headed out the door.

Travis pulled the collar of his jacket up around his neck and then stuffed his hands into the pockets and felt the wad of money in his left hand. The drop had gone without a hitch. He fingered the money without feeling and skillfully peeled off two bills. He would use those tonight.

Ten o'clock on a Saturday night, and the streets were alive. Though he appeared nonchalant, both his ears and eyes were alert to the sights and sounds of the street. The sudden rev of a motor and the squeal of tires caused his heart to stop momentarily, and he stepped into the shadows of one of the doorways until the car passed. Turf, drugs, girls, boredom. Any were good enough reasons to shoot.

He waited until the car was out of earshot and then stepped back out on the sidewalk and headed toward the warehouse, occasionally sidestepping a staggering drunk or stepping over someone who had given up on finding any shelter for the night. Travis felt nothing for these people, having anesthetized himself long ago to their plight. In fact, he felt nothing whatsoever. He needed company, companionship. It was weird that in a city of thousands, he could feel so isolated, so alone.

It took only a couple more minutes to reach the warehouse, which from the outside looked dark and deserted. A dark figure lingered in the doorway.

"Whas up, Blueboy?" Travis asked somberly.

Blueboy shook his head and chewed his gum with exaggerated slowness. "Not a thing, man."

Travis's face remained expressionless. Blueboy spit and then the whites of his teeth showed in the darkness.

"Cecile's fixed up fine and waiting for you in the back room."

Travis said nothing but nodded. He took the stairs two at a time, passing other guards along the way who all nodded him through without greeting. These were his "friends." When he finally entered the main room, it reeked of smoke and booze and vomit. He stifled the urge to gag, swallowing everything boiling up from his stomach, and walked placidly through the room, scanning the scene.

Cecile saw him, rose from out of the smoke, and shimmied toward him, and he felt his body involuntarily heat up. She smiled coyly, and he stared back. She swayed toward the back room. Travis followed, but as much as he tried, he could not engage either his feelings or his heart. They were dead.

When Travis left Cecile and the party, he headed for the streets. The crispness of the air did wake up some of his senses, and he glanced up at the wide expanse of sky. The brightness of the streetlights produced a solid blackness above him. Travis stopped his progress and took stock of where he was.

Two blocks away was a vacant field with no lights. He slid down the alley and then jumped a fence at the far end, holding his breath as he passed the stench of an open doorway. In the distance he heard sirens wailing, growing louder as they worked their way toward his neighborhood. He stopped only momentarily to locate where they were going. Perhaps he had left the warehouse at a good time.

In the darkness behind him he heard shuffling, and he instinctively ducked behind a trash bin that had more garbage lying around it than in it. A stooped figure—old or young, hard to tell—shuffled across the alley and then slumped against the back of the building. Travis released his breath before he realized that he had been holding it. Was he scared? The thought made him laugh. He had never been scared. Just cautious—smart. But then, why was his heart pounding?

Travis pushed the idea out of his mind and continued toward the vacant lot. He hopped one more fence and dropped into the relative darkness. Lights still seeped around the corner, but they were muted enough that if he looked hard, he could see some stars. He cupped his hands around his eyes to try and block out more, and it helped, but the city lights still washed out most of the stars. Still, as he stood there in the darkness and concentrated, more and more sprinkles of tiny white began appearing.

The sirens were still crying, gunshots would split the air on occasion, and traffic droned on monotonously on the streets around him, but they all drifted to the background of his mind, and the stars and their stillness took over. The peace Travis had hoped to find here was absent. Instead, he felt a growing void of emptiness and insignificance as he stared at the great vastness above him. And though he may have flinched earlier at the sounds in the alley, this time he knew for sure that for some inexplicable reason, he was truly scared.

Chapter 15

"Have a seat, Alex, and I'll be right with you," Mrs. Richards instructed. Alex found a desk at the front of the room and sat down self-consciously. He had never been with a teacher one-on-one before for any length of time. It was the one situation he strove to avoid at all costs, and he found it very unnerving.

Mrs. Richards gathered a few materials together—flash cards, Dr. Suess books, papers—and then sat down in the desk next to Alex and turned toward him smiling.

"Are you ready to get started?" she asked enthusiastically, and he tried to return her smile with assurance.

"Sure," he said.

"Good," she answered, ignoring his nervousness. She had Alex's whole program worked out. She would begin her diagnosis today and Wednesday and then recruit a peer tutor to practice with him. She had learned early in her career that she did not have the time nor the energy to tutor all the students who needed help and that they usually responded better with their peers. She had even coerced the school into giving her a small fund (the operable word here was *small*) to pay the tutors.

Alex, however, might be dyslexic, and she had never had a tutor work with a dyslexic student before. She would need to make sure she knew what she was doing before she turned him over.

"Okay, Alex," she said, "let's see what we can find out. Today and Wednesday I just need to make sure I know where your strengths and weaknesses are before we start you on a program. It's a lot like your coach does in football. He sees what you do well already, and what you're weak in."

She had meant for the football analogy to set him at ease, to make him more comfortable, but she could see by his sudden wince that it had a more disturbing effect.

"I'm sorry you're missing practice," she said softly, sincerely. "You are a wonderful player. The fastest receiver with the surest hands I've ever seen, and I'm a diehard football fan thanks to Coach Bauer. But I think in the long run, you'll be glad you made the decision you did. It shows an incredible amount of maturity on your part, which just adds up to what I've already noticed in class. You seem to be here to learn, Alex, and we're going to help you do that."

Alex grinned weakly, trying to make her feel better. Martha continued.

"I already have an assignment for you tonight," she said, and Alex looked up in surprise. "I want you to come up with a couple of goals for this year that would relate to your learning how to read. Be ready to share them with me on Wednesday. Understood?"

Alex nodded. If there was one thing he knew how to do, it was to make goals, and this should be an easy assignment. He had been dreaming for years what he would like to do if he could read, but he knew he had to be realistic. She had said for this year. That was a little tougher considering he didn't know how difficult it might be to accomplish. But he was used to working hard, so he resolved to aim for the highest.

"So, let's get down to work," Martha said, breaking into his thoughts by placing a sheet of paper on his desk. "Please read this for me," she instructed, and Alex stared at the mess of letters on the sheet in front of him and tried to create some sort of order out of the chaos.

Travis crumpled up the piece of paper and heaved it at the wall. His entire insides were wrapped up in knots. Inside of him, whirling around at breakneck speed were all these ideas and feelings and fears and hopes, and yet he couldn't get even one of them down on paper so that he could cope with it without it sounding like six-year-old gibberish.

He opened the huge Bible and began thumbing through it, looking for another unfinished poem. Writing, he had learned long ago, offered him a sense of control over this out-of-control world. And if there was one thing Travis Johnson wanted and needed, it was to be "in control." He passed a loose sheet and turned back to recover it, but he couldn't take it out before his eyes caught one of the verses on the page: "He counts the number of the stars; He gives names to all of them."

There were those stars again! Since Saturday night, he had been plagued by that feeling of insignificance and smallness, a feeling that he really wasn't as important and in control as he thought he was. He felt a sense of unfamiliar panic rise, and he pulled out his poem and shut the Bible on his disturbing thoughts.

Where had they gotten this stupid book anyway? It was a joke to be in this house. All it did was collect dust—and hide his poems and his money. He smiled in spite of himself. The one sure place in the entire house his mother would never search was this Bible. He shook his head and turned the paper over to read what he had written some days or weeks before.

> In the valley of tainted darkness
> I'm a panther on the prey
> Stalking innocent victims
> Who have

He looked at the writing in disbelief. It was childish, stupid, contrived. And what was "tainted darkness" anyway? It had sounded clever at the time, but now it seemed completely idiotic.

He crumbled it up and slammed it into the corner with the others and then ran his hand over his hair. Maybe he should just give all this up, this writing, this art bit, and just get back to what he was good at: selling drugs.

Travis stood up and grabbed his coat. Sitting in this room just gave him too much time to think, and right now, thinking was not pleasant. He needed to get back out on the street, with the hard concrete under his feet, the cold wind in his face, the feel of money in his pocket, and power in his fist. He checked to make sure his .357 Magnum was secure in the back of his waistband and then slid his leather jacket on.

Today was initiation day anyway, and he had a few recruits that he needed to give instructions to. He went to his room and pulled out his flip camera. No phones—they linked a person to a crime. Flip cameras were anonymous. Travis would film this initiation himself. He needed to feel in control again, to feel that power and purpose in life, and this was one way to get it back.

"I need a student who is good at teaching phonics. Do any of you know of such a beast?"

Martha laid her question out on the table for the lunch group to ponder. In such a large school, there were many students she was unfamiliar with, but perhaps some other teachers might be able to help out.

"Reba Washington."

The reply came so quickly and with such assurance that Martha glanced at the provider with surprise. Bill Moxley, the chemistry teacher, who had supplied the information, never missed a beat in tackling his cheese enchiladas.

"Reba Washington?" Martha asked skeptically. "How do you know her? She's only a freshman. And how do you know she has knowledge of phonics?"

Bill laid down his fork and took a much deserved breath. "Her reputation precedes her," he answered simply, but Martha was not satisfied and Bill continued. "My wife teaches at the elementary school the Washington children attend," he said, "and she tells me that each of them knows how to read before he or she ever enters kindergarten, and the kids claim it's Reba teaching them. Rumor has it that she taught her parents to read as well."

Satisfied that he had supplied as much information as was necessary, he resumed his attack on his enchiladas. "So you see," he said as an afterthought and around a mouthful of cheese, "Reba Washington is your girl."

Martha looked around at the others for verification, but they only shrugged their shoulders.

"Do you think she could use the money from tutoring?" she asked.

Bob nodded vehemently. "Based on what my wife says about the average income of the families in her school, the girl probably would beg for the job."

Martha mulled the idea over in her head. She had Reba—twice—so contact wouldn't be hard, but there was another problem, a bigger one: the play. Tryouts started tomorrow, and she knew Reba was aiming for a major part. If she landed the role, then she wouldn't have the time to tutor. Would Reba be as willing to sacrifice the play as Alex had football? Besides the money, there was little for her to gain. The question plagued her as the lunch hour rolled by and her food grew cold.

"Hey, Piston! Where were you yesterday anyway?"

"Yeah, man. That's not like you to miss a practice."

"It's going to cost you a quarter you know."

"You feeling okay?"

"I think you might be able to slide by. Coach never even asked about you yesterday. Maybe he didn't even know you were missing."

"Bet you're going to have some stairs to pay if he did."

Alex listened to all the questions and prophecies and just shook his head. "I'm okay. No big deal. Just had to get a little extra help for a class."

The other guys stopped in their tracks and just stared at him.

"Are you crazy?" asked Brandon. "You're going to give up a quarter of football and run stairs just for a class? Come on, Piston. I knew you weren't bright, but I thought you had *some* smarts up there."

The accusation stung. So the guys really *did* think he was stupid. That he was only a jock with a jock mentality and a jock brain. He spoke before he thought.

"Well, you were wrong, Masters, weren't you? I don't have a *single* brain cell in my entire head." He could feel his cheeks reddening, and he silently cursed his white skin and Polish background. *Man,* he thought, *why do I let these guys get under my skin?*

The outburst caused the small congregation to do a double take. Alex rarely lost his cool, so a raw nerve had been struck somewhere.

"Hey, man, I didn't mean anything by it," Brandon backpedaled. "Just thought you had your priorities a little screwed up is all. A guy can go to school forever, but football …" He shrugged. "One bad accident, and the season's over."

Alex was fighting for control as he gazed steadily at Brandon Masters. Had the guy listened to what he had actually just said? He contemplated calling him on the fallacy of his thinking but thought better of it and turned on his heel and headed out to the field. The others trailed skeptically behind him.

Coach Bauer saw Alex step onto the track and noticed his distance from the others and frowned. What was happening? Had the pressure already started?

The guys fell into warm-up formation, and an assistant ran them through their stretches. Once over, Bauer blew his whistle.

"Kowalski! Front and center!" he yelled.

"Guess the guy *did* notice you weren't here," one of his teammates whispered, and Alex ignored it.

He jogged over to where Coach Bauer was standing with his back turned slightly toward him as he gazed over the empty bleachers. He wasn't smiling, and Alex felt his skin crawl uncomfortably.

"Yes, sir," he said, and he could feel the eyes of his teammates staring at his back.

Coach turned toward him, his face never changing expression.

"The guys giving you a hard time?" he asked.

Alex shrugged slightly. "They're curious."

"How do you want to play this?" Bauer asked.

Alex looked confused. "What do you mean?"

"You already know you'll miss a quarter Friday, but if I don't assign you the traditional discipline of stairs, then they'll be suspicious and think I'm playing favorites."

Alex stood silently, waiting.

"Alex, I have no intention of disciplining you further for what I consider a wise decision, but that's only if you're willing to be candid with your teammates and tell them why you're missing practice. A lot of them go in before school for additional help, so just saying 'extra help' isn't going to cut it with them. If you want to keep it to yourself, then you'll need to run the stairs. Which way do you want to work this thing?"

Alex's lips tightened into a thin line. One decision seemed to precipitate others, and none of them were easy. The burden and punishment seemed to be growing. It just didn't seem fair, yet … He glanced back at his teammates who, although lined up into formations, were still keeping a close eye on the proceedings, and he felt a small knot grow in his stomach. They already thought him stupid, dumb. He had no desire to confirm their suspicions by telling them he was learning how to read.

"I'll run," he said with resolve, and Coach Bauer nodded.

"Ten stairs now, and another ten after practice. *Go!*"

Travis grabbed his coat and stormed out of the apartment right as Jasmine was coming in.

"Where ya going, Travis?" she asked.

"None of your business," he growled and brushed past her. She stopped in surprise. What had gotten into him? He was rarely rude to her. That was their mother's area of expertise.

Travis took the steps two at a time and felt a pang of remorse for lashing out at his sister that way, but not enough to apologize. In fact, in his life, he could never remember apologizing to anyone. To apologize meant you were wrong, which meant you had some weakness somewhere, and if there was one thing Travis did not want to imply it was that he was at all weak. If Jasmine had been hurt by his remark, she would get over it. It was good for her anyway. The world wasn't a nice place, and she needed to be reminded of that.

He glanced at his Rolex and swore under his breath. Why didn't he buy more? He was worth it. A car would be nice, some new clothes, DVD player, and a big, flat-screen TV. But the thoughts vanished as quickly as they came. To flaunt all that would be inviting trouble. Though his gang and opposing gangs knew he was dealing, his low profile kept him out of the public eye and the police limelight, which was just fine with him. And it kept his mother off his back. The minute he were to bring home something lavish, it would be all over.

Travis rarely waited for a bus, usually planning his arrival at the bus stop with the arrival of the bus. Should he be early, he kept going; late, he walked. This time he just needed the walk. Danny Richards had wanted to meet him early in back of the library, and he had agreed, which worked out perfect since he needed to meet the recruits later at the warehouse.

He knew what Danny wanted. He knew what this meeting was

all about—it was always the same. The guy wanted to move up. Marijuana just wasn't cutting it anymore. It took too long for the buzz and then the buzz wasn't as satisfying. What should he offer? Coke? PCP? Bennies? No … heroin for this kid. He liked to mellow out. Of course, that meant needles, and they were going for about three dollars a pop, which was why so many users shared needles. Should Danny head in that direction, he could be a prime candidate for HIV.

Again he was plagued with a pang of guilt, but he shook it off. So what? It was Danny's life. If he wanted to ruin it, he could. All Travis was doing was helping him feel good—if only for the moment.

Danny was waiting for him, his hands jammed into his pockets nervously, his shoulders tensed, and he was pacing. Travis tried to look even more casual than usual to tighten Danny up even more. He lit a cigarette, and even though it was almost dark, he refused to remove his sunglasses. He inhaled long and slow, released it, and then flicked away the ash. It worked. Danny was edgier than ever.

"So, what do you want?" Travis asked.

Danny licked his lips nervously. "I—I don't know really," he answered. "Something more. Something with a little better buzz."

Travis pursed his lips, pretending to be deep in thought. "Heroin okay?"

Danny shrugged. "I guess so. How does it work?"

"Injection," he answered.

Danny balked, and Travis felt his advantage waning. Danny was an intelligent boy, and all the hazards of injection were running through his mind.

"Hey, I'll include clean needles if you want," he said, hoping to push the sale. It was a first for him, and he wondered why he did it. Control? Over whom? Danny? His mother? "Injection works a heck of a lot faster than anything else. So what do you say?"

He could tell he had swayed Danny with his pitch about clean needles, and the young man nodded. "How much?"

Travis shrugged. "You could probably get a teaspoon from

someone for say … twenty bucks, but it won't be as pure as mine. I charge forty dollars, and that's with the needle."

"Is one teaspoon only good for one shot?" he asked hesitantly.

"That's up to you," Travis said and smiled slightly.

Danny seemed deep in thought as he stared blindly at the trees before him. "All right then. Give me three teaspoons."

Travis nodded, another small smile playing on the corners of his lips.

"When will you have the stuff?" Danny asked.

"Friday."

"Meet you here again?"

Travis shook his head. "Never meet in the same place twice in a row. Looks suspicious." Danny nodded, and Travis continued. "Meet you in the bookstore, four thirty on the nose. Got it?"

Danny nodded. "Anywhere in particular?"

Travis's grin broadened now. "Yeah, chemistry section. That should be appropriate, don't ya think?"

Chapter 16

Martha rubbed her eyes tiredly. It had been a long afternoon. When she had posted the change in the fall play from *Steel Magnolias* to *To Be Young, Gifted, and Black*, she had done it to throw a wrench in the preaudition rehearsals, hoping that Reba perhaps wouldn't fare as well.

What it had done, however, because of the numerous small parts, was convince tons of kids to try out this year. She still had another twenty to look at before she called the first day of auditions to an end. The two on stage were muddling through, or rather, unmercifully massacring the small prologue scene between Ruth and Walter.

She rubbed her neck again, trying to relax. Even with the short scene, the afternoon was dragging. Too many things on her mind, she guessed. The two finally ended their annihilation, and the other hopefuls clapped politely. Martha looked down at her clipboard and checked the "no" column and then looked at the next two names.

"Reba Washington and Carlos Mendez," she called out and felt herself perk up a bit. Reba was turning out to be a rare talent, one that any teacher might cherish the chance to nurture and lay claim to, but today, ironically, Martha was caught with mixed emotions. She really wanted to see what Reba could do with the minimal role of Ruth. She knew she couldn't cast her in a major role if she wanted to have her work with Alex, so maybe something small like this. It really wasn't fair of her to make Reba's decision for her, but she still felt compelled to push the young girl in a certain direction.

Reba and Carlos took the stage. They had had no idea that they would be auditioning together, but both instinctively moved to the right side of the stage and waited for Martha to give them the okay. She lifted her hand, and Reba morphed from the awkward ninth grader into a young black woman, shuffling toward center stage, tired and dreading the day. She pantomimed breaking eggs into a bowl, beating them, and then stirring them in a skillet. Carlos waited a few seconds more and then entered, yawning and stretching and looking at her appreciatively.

"You look young this morning, baby," he said and moved to put his arms around her, but she stiffened at his touch.

"Yeah," she answered caustically.

Carlos dropped his hands. "Just for a second—stirring them eggs. You looked real young again." He paused when she showed no signs of emotion and then dryly added, "It's gone now—you look like yourself again."

Reba turned to glare at him as if he were crazy. "Man, if you don't shut up and leave me alone."

Martha watched critically and appreciatively as the two finished out the scene. They were good, both of them. Of course, Carlos wasn't black, but he was dark enough that she could cast him in a major role, but Reba … she felt her heart sink again. Reba deserved more than just this one-page scene. She was one of the best so far this day, but … Martha wrote some notes in the margin and then next to Reba's name wrote "Ruth." It was only a bit part, but maybe as a freshman she would be happy with that.

The two finished their audition and then went to sit with the others in the audience.

"Marcus and Gladys," Martha called and tried to hide the weariness in her voice. She still had eighteen to go before she could call it a night.

Alex toweled off his wet hair and then combed it smoothly into place. The locker room was empty except for him. It had taken him an extra half hour to run the additional ten flights of stairs after practice, and everyone else had already showered and taken off. He sat down on the cool bench and reached for his socks. His legs ached. Geez, here he had thought he was already in great shape, but these stairs were going to be the death of him.

He stood up, pulled a fresh T-shirt over his head, and then pulled out his forest green Pendleton his grandparents had purchased for his birthday. He loved the shirt with its soft, warm fabric and the tan, suede elbow patches. A lot of the guys laughed at him for wearing it, joking that his family was so poor he had to wear patches on his clothes, but Alex didn't mind. He knew they were only jealous. He pulled on his tan pants and then carefully tucked his shirt into his pants, zipped them up, and buckled his belt. He sat back down and slid on his Rockports and then went back to the mirror to recomb his hair.

It mattered little to him that no one would be around the school to see him. He didn't look nice for anyone else anyway. There was just something within him that said, "look good; be your best." Maybe his mother had drilled it into him when he was little when she taught him how to keep his drawers neat, or maybe his father by his constant reminders to work hard, like those army commercials that challenged you to "be all that you can be."

It could have been all or one, but he did know this: that part of it was Mrs. Rojewski telling her young charges during Sunday school that they should "do their work as unto the Lord, and not men," and that their "body was a living sacrifice" for the Lord. Those two verses he had taken to heart.

He closed his locker and pulled on his jacket as he walked out of the locker room. He wondered if he should ever tell Mrs. Rojewski that he still remembered those verses. That whenever he felt pressured by school or friends, he always found comfort in those two verses. He could because she still went to St. Andrews and still taught the boys' third grade class. He smiled sadly to himself as he pushed open the locker room door. He wondered if any of the guys ever told Mrs. Rojewski thank you for anything she did.

He sighed. Maybe that was true for all teachers. Maybe none of them ever knew how much they affected their pupils. But then again, if most of their students didn't realize what they had learned until—what was it now?—seven years later, like he had, then the probability was that teachers never heard anything.

Alex pursed his lips and decided that this Sunday he would tell her. He would root Mrs. Rojewski out of the rest of the congregation and tell her what a great teacher she had been and what he remembered.

With that off his chest, his mind returned to the present and the teachers at Montgomery. Three days ago he had thought his life had been falling apart between Mrs. Richards cornering him and Coach Bauer nailing him. At that point, he had felt that even though God seemed to be answering his prayers, it was as if he had completely abandoned him.

He smiled ruefully in the dark. What a difference two days could make. Even though Mrs. Richards had only tested him, she had nodded a lot and smiled and said all kinds of encouraging things. The hope of actually learning to read seemed almost within reach.

And then to have Coach Bauer not only face off against him and force him to be a man, but to actually admit to a seventeen-year-old that he too hadn't known how to read. That must have been pretty humiliating. Alex felt warm inside. It was funny how that humbling experience had actually raised Coach Bauer to the level of hero in his eyes. The two shared something: a disability and a secret. Coach Bauer was going out of his way to keep Alex's problem a secret, and Alex would return the favor. Coach Bauer's past was secure with him.

True, the tutoring would require a lot of work, and he would have to give up a little football, but now football and life didn't seem to end with high school. Instead, the tunnel was beginning to widen, and he was excited. Even the stairs might turn out to be a good thing. After all, after only one day, he was feeling stronger.

"Better watch where you're going there, stud."

Alex's head popped up just before he ran into a hip-high cement post designed to keep traffic out of the campus. His mind had been so far away that he hadn't even seen it. His face burned profusely, and he hoped the darkness hid his embarrassment. He turned to see who had saved him from what could have been a very emasculating disaster.

He looked up to confront his savior and found himself staring into the quietly laughing face of Amanda Donahoe. Even in the dim light of the streetlamp, her strawberry blonde hair shone and her green eyes sparkled. It was impossible for Alex to know her eyes were green in the dark of the evening, but he had stared at her enough in the hallway, in the cafeteria, in assembly, to know that they were the color of a Bermuda bay.

He felt his entire chest cavity tighten. Of all the people to stop him from castrating himself, it would have to be Amanda Donahoe, the girl he was in love with in his dreams and felt sure he could be in real life too if only she knew he existed. Well, he had gotten his wish. After this mishap, she would know him for sure, but as a bumbling idiot, so his chances of getting anywhere with her now were slim.

Alex averted his eyes in embarrassment and then looked back, not wanting to take his eyes off that face … that face that was still smiling in amusement. He wasn't sure how much time had elapsed, but he knew he should probably say something or she would think he was truly a dummy and extremely rude.

"Thanks for the warning," he said sheepishly. "It could have been rather, uh, awkward."

Her perfectly formed eyebrows lifted in surprise. "To say the least," she said and chuckled softly. "What were you so engrossed in anyway?"

Alex was so enamored and embarrassed and confused that whatever had been on his mind was completely gone now. He shrugged sheepishly.

"You know, I can't even remember now," he answered truthfully, and the conversation stopped rather abruptly. Alex racked his brain for something to say, feeling extremely awkward with the ten-second lull that followed, but Amanda seemed at ease.

"Well, just make sure that I get credit for saving the honor of Montgomery High's star receiver."

Now it was Alex's turn to look surprised. How did Amanda Donahoe know who he was, and why would she give him such a compliment? She was a junior, in all the top classes, with a body of cheerleader material but too sane to enter that arena. He found it hard to even think she followed football.

"You watch football?" he asked in disbelief.

She returned his Neanderthal look with a withering stare. "Yeah, I watch football," she said in a deep moronic tone and then laughed and spoke normally. "I love football," she said. "And I love watching you catch passes. You're really a talent."

It was not a come-on, or a pass, or anything like that. Her statement was one of genuine admiration. Alex was so caught off guard that he didn't even think to downplay her praise.

"Well, thanks," he said, glad the night was hiding his crimson face. Then came another ten seconds of awkward silence, and he racked his brain for something else to say. *Come on,* he prompted. *Think!*

"Why—why are you here so late?" he asked, realizing that they had been talking about him the entire time.

"Play auditions," she answered simply. "Just got out."

Alex's eyebrows rose. "Are you going out for the play?" he asked and wished that perhaps last year he had gone to one of the productions. Perhaps then he could say something complimentary to her about a performance she had been in—or something. Amanda threw her head back and laughed—a full, resonant laugh—and Alex found it musical.

"Not this year, I'm afraid," she said, and Alex looked puzzled and worried that he had said something wrong. She caught his reaction and reached out to touch his arm reassuringly. Alex felt a jolt of electricity course up his arm.

"No, no, it's all right," she said. "It's just that the play is *To Be Young, Gifted, and Black*. I know I can pass for young, and with a little acting, gifted—but black?" She spread her arms out to let him take a look at her. "I'm afraid that's one category I don't fit."

Amanda started walking, and Alex followed. "I thought the play was going to be that *Steel Magnolias* one," he said, glad to have remembered something he had heard.

"It was supposed to be," she said, "but Mrs. Richards suddenly moved that to spring. Wants to fill the entire auditorium with fresh flowers, she said. You need spring for that."

Alex grinned, but he was still confused then as to why she was here. Was he that dumb? "Then why were you at the auditions?" he asked, numbly praying that he wasn't making a fool of himself.

"Oh, that," she said and nodded her head in understanding at Alex's perplexity. "I'm the student director."

Alex's eyes widened. Now that sounded important—something he could take advantage of. "Wow! That's impressive. What do you do as the student director?"

Amanda laughed. "It is demanding," she agreed and then paused to figure out some way to put five pages of job description into a manageable sentence. "I guess the best way to describe it is to say that I do everything Mrs. Richards doesn't have time to do and help her out with the things she does do: practices, blocking, lighting, casting."

Alex was impressed. "Sounds like it takes a lot of time."

She nodded emphatically. "Oh, it does. Once the cast is selected, which will be this Friday, it will be every day from three to six o'clock, just like football practice."

Alex nodded in understanding, but something was puzzling him. "Is Mrs. Richards there every day?" he asked.

"Just about," Amanda answered. "I think in the past she's only missed about two practices for each production, and those were for extreme circumstances."

Alex's mind was racing. If she had this commitment, then how was she going to teach him to read? And who was she to make him give up football if she had no intention of giving up the play? He knew already he was being unfair, but he couldn't help it. He began to feel a bitterness building within him.

"Is something wrong?" Amanda asked, and Alex realized that his mind had drifted. He smiled apologetically.

"Sorry," he said. "Just thinking … Does this mean that you'll be leaving this late every night?" he asked and then realized that she might take the question the wrong way and think he was being too forward, but she merely nodded.

"Yes, most likely."

Alex looked around. "Where are the others?"

"They left earlier. Only Mrs. Richards and I stayed after to discuss the prospects."

"I would have thought she might have given you a ride home or something," he said. "It really isn't too safe for you to be walking home alone, you know."

"Are you being sexist?"

Alex flinched in surprise. "What do you mean?"

"Well, it looks like *you* are walking home by *yourself*," she said.

Alex grinned ruefully. "True."

"Are *you* afraid?" she asked.

Alex pondered the question briefly. His faith in God seemed to be his preventative from fear, but he was occasionally a bit nervous.

"Just cautious," he answered, and Amanda smiled that overflowing smile of warmth and acceptance.

"Good answer," she said. "Anyway, I didn't mean to attack you. I'm really not a feminist, though I do flare up on occasion. If you want to know the truth, Mrs. Richards did offer me a ride home, but I saw you coming out of the gym and told her you lived nearby and that I'd just catch up to you. She seemed satisfied."

Once again Alex was pleasantly shocked. Not only did Amanda Donahoe know who he was, but where he lived as well. Of course, he knew where she lived, but what guy with two functioning eyes didn't?

"Sounds good to me," he responded.

"Now for the same question you asked me," she pressed. "Where's the rest of the football team? Don't tell me only the stars stay late."

Alex felt a seeping depression fill him, and he mentally fumbled over a couple of lies before settling on the truth.

"If the truth be known," he admitted, "I had to run extra stairs because I missed practice yesterday."

"Oh," Amanda said, and to Alex's surprise she seemed more disappointed than curious or judgmental. However, her tone turned lighthearted again. "Then I guess I shouldn't count on this personal escort every night."

Alex looked off into the distant darkness and released a long, slow breath.

"Actually," he answered, "I think you can count on it more often than you think."

Chapter 17

Reba walked nervously down the hall, her heart pounding ferociously in her chest as though at any minute it would burst through her rib cage. She was oblivious to the warm hustle of students around her, some grabbing books and slamming lockers, others blatantly closing a drug deal, a few groping each other without shame in the middle of the hallway, and a remaining few throwing snide remarks at her.

"Your face really that ugly or did a truck hit it this morning?"

A peal of coarse laughter followed, coupled with a series of high and low fives. Reba could feel her face grow warm, her body tingle with embarrassment, and her already overworked heart twist in hurt. But she tried to ignore them and focus only on the door at the end of the hall. She pushed her way through the masses toward that door on which her future was hinged. The door that held the cast list for *To Be Young, Gifted, and Black.*

The nearer she got, the louder her heart beat. Now her head throbbed, and she felt she might be sick. Even though she had little chance to rehearse because of the last-minute play change, she felt she had done well, perhaps even the best. Carlos had said so, and as a junior, he was a veteran. He had grinned when they had finished their first audition.

"Man, I'll work with you anytime," he said, his pearly white teeth sparkling beneath the glare of the theater lights. "You made me really mad at you. You were such a … a …" He stopped, his politeness preventing him from telling Reba exactly what she had been, and instead said, "Exactly what you were supposed to be," and Reba blushed beneath his compliment.

"You know, tomorrow we can choose our own scene and partner," he added. "Would you mind working with me? I really want to get a part, and I think I have a good shot with you."

There was no way Reba would say no, and she felt lightheaded as she accepted. Here was Carlos Mendez actually asking her, a freshman, to be his audition partner. She readily agreed, and the two of them had selected a scene and then Reba had gone home and memorized it and rehearsed it until her parents insisted the lights go out and she get in bed so everyone could get to sleep. She had obeyed, but in the darkness of her room, her mind had refused to quit. For hours after, she had reviewed the scene over and over in her head.

Reba awoke the next morning tired and worried that she would not perform well and that she would let Carlos down. Her mother caught sight of her drawn face, and after setting the oatmeal in front of each of the kids, sat down and took the hand of each child next to her. The others followed suit until the circle was closed. Then all heads bowed and waited.

"Our dear Lord," she began, and her rich, mellifluous voice filled the tiny room, sending a soothing calmness around the table. Mrs. Washington had a powerful voice, one that could excite you one minute, calm you the next, and put you in your place a second later. It was the same voice Reba had inherited.

"You know how hard we work and the desires of our hearts, and you have told us not to worry about what the day might bring, for worrying accomplishes nothing." She squeezed the hands next to her and waited until she thought the squeeze had worked its way around to Reba.

"I pray that your peace, which surpasses all understanding, might fill us now as we give you authority over the events of our day. We know you are in complete control of not only the world, but of our lives as well, and that you want only what is best for us. This we pray in your precious Son's name, amen."

"Amen," chorused the table.

"Amen," Reba echoed softly and looked up into the loving face of her mother. Her mother winked, and Reba felt the flood of anxiety bottled within her rush out. God would take care of her.

The audition had gone superbly except for a line Carlos had forgotten, but Reba had ad-libbed so adeptly, they were sure no one was the wiser. Then it was just a matter of waiting and wading through another hour and a half of auditions, then an evening and night of uncertainty until this morning.

Now the door was in sight, and even though she still knew that God was in control, she couldn't control the racing of her heart as she drew near the white slip of paper before her.

Reba's eyes scanned the list of names, her heart beating in syncopation as she moved down the list. With each name, a sense of dread began to fill her. Finally she saw it: "Reba Washington." She slid her eyes across the page to the part she had been assigned: Ruth. She blinked once and ran her eyes back to her name and then, more carefully, back across to the role.

But there was no mistake. She had only been given the part of Ruth. Though one of the first on stage, it was a minor, insignificant role to say the least. Her disappointment overwhelmed her. She had thought she had done so much better. Carlos had assured her that she would be one of the leads. But no. All she was was Ruth.

She stared at her name. Her heart had stopped beating completely, leaving her entire body in an ear-piercing silence. Reba struggled with herself. *I am being so ungrateful,* she scolded herself.

After all, I'm only a freshman. Maybe I was too confident. Maybe I really don't know what they look for.

Reba tried to cheer herself up, but nagging her in the back of her mind were all those other doubts that she had hoped to avoid. *You're too homely and skinny for acting. You'll never be an actress. This is a wild fantasy of yours. Why don't you just give it up?*

The bell rang and startled her. First period was about to begin. How would she ever make it through an entire period with Mrs. Richards? How could she face the woman? She was filled with a mixture of anger and shame. She was upset with Mrs. Richards for not recognizing her true talent, and she was completely embarrassed for having strutted out on stage so confidently.

There was no place to run, no place to hide, no one to find shelter behind. She turned and ran toward the stairs. There was also no way she would be late for class and give Mrs. Richards a chance to focus on her.

Reba sat in her chair and half listened to the discussion about the short story of the day: "The Most Dangerous Game." Normally, she would have joined in. She had picked up the meaning of the work. How the external was never a true indication of what the internal was like. General Zarroff appeared to be the most civilized and courteous man around, yet he hunted people. Reba mentally jumped to Jesus and the Pharisees. What had he called them? Whitewashed sepulchers?

She glanced at Mrs. Richards and felt a twinge of bitterness. Had she had Mrs. Richards pegged all wrong too? Was this friendly, caring nature only an external facade, and she really didn't care about anyone?

Danny stood nervously in line for the teller, shifting his weight from one foot to the other, carefully watching the progress of the line and windows. The first or second window would be better. Those tellers didn't know him. But he *definitely* didn't want the third window. Beatrice Carmichael was behind that one, and she was a close friend of the family. Should *she* help him, it would be only a matter of minutes before his parents caught wind of it.

Danny silently swore. *Why hadn't he remembered his debit card? Then he could have avoided this whole scene and used the ATM.* But it was too late to go home and get it. He needed money *now.*

With each movement of the line, Danny recalculated where he might end up. *Don't move too fast.* Wouldn't you know it, the two lines he needed were bottled up while Beatrice was just pumping 'em through. Finally, he was at the front of the line, and his heart was pounding ferociously as he waited. He watched the lady in Beatrice's line collecting her stubs, and he ducked his head and looked through his paperwork and then mumbled for the guy behind to go ahead. He hoped Beatrice hadn't recognized him.

"Can I help you?"

The question came from his left, and he jerked his head up to see teller number two smiling at him. He nervously smiled back and walked over. Sure, Beatrice wasn't waiting on him, but it would only be a matter of looking over and seeing him.

"I'd like to make a withdrawal," he mumbled, trying to keep his voice low. The teller leaned over to hear.

"A withdrawal?" she asked loudly, and he almost withered but managed to nod. "How much would you like to take out, sir?"

"Two hundred," he said quietly, praying Beatrice Carmichael wouldn't look his way.

"Would you like that in twenties or fifties?" she asked, and he felt himself dying a slow death.

"Twenties would be fine," he said as she began processing the transaction. It took only a matter of minutes, but Danny felt like he was standing naked in front of everyone for hours. Finally, she turned back to him with a smile and began counting out the bills.

"Twenty, forty, sixty, eighty, one hundred," she said, and Danny prayed that she would quiet down. What was she trying to do? Tell the whole bank he was taking out $200? He'd probably get mugged right outside the door.

"Twenty, forty, sixty, eighty, two hundred," she completed. "Have a nice day."

Without replying, he stuffed the bills in his wallet and nodded and then headed to his left away from Beatrice Carmichael right as she looked up to call over her next customer. She caught sight of him as he turned to leave.

"Dan—" she called but cut herself short as he hurried away, obviously not wanting to talk. She watched him hustle out the door, puzzled by his odd behavior, and then filed the event in the section of her brain reserved for neighborly trivia for when she next saw Martha.

"I just don't understand," Amanda said, shaking her head as she and Alex walked in the crisp October air off campus and toward Hamtramck. "I could have sworn Reba Washington was going to get the lead."

"Who's Reba Washington?" Alex asked. It felt good to have Amanda talk about drama rather than focusing on football.

"Reba Washington is this skinny, little, freshman black girl who's not very pretty, and if you were to pass her in the hallway, you wouldn't think twice about her, but when she steps onstage, she just carries you away. I'm telling you, for such a young kid, this girl is going to be something."

"Then why didn't she get the lead?" Alex asked. He liked it when Amanda got all wound up. She could sling out five sentences without taking a breath.

Amanda shook her head. "That's what I can't figure out. Last night, Mrs. Richards and I were mulling over the potential leads, and I was pushing for Reba, and she was balking and questioning me on some of these others. At the time, I thought she was just playing the devil's advocate, making sure I had taken everything into consideration, but now," she stopped and stared at the cement in contemplation. Alex stopped and waited until she resumed her walk. "Now I am beginning to think she never wanted Reba to get the lead in the first place."

"Why wouldn't she?" Alex asked, and he began to get these disquieting qualms in his stomach. Was Mrs. Richards toying with someone else's life too? Maybe she just didn't want certain kids to succeed in what they were good at. But then why would Coach Bauer tout her so highly. It just didn't make sense—but then a lot of things weren't making too much sense right now.

"What did Reba say?" he asked. "I mean did she seem to mind?"

Amanda shook her head. "No—not really. She showed up today for the initial run-through and practice schedule and seemed eager enough to be there. She was hanging on every word Mrs. Richards said, and sometimes she even took notes in the margins. She didn't seem to mind her meager part, and I mean meager. The kid will only be on stage a total of two minutes max!"

Alex thought about the young girl and felt a certain affinity for her. He knew how she must feel. Putting in a remarkable performance and then being relegated to the back. He admired her for her attitude.

"Well, enough about the play," Amanda said, grandly switching the subject. "Tell me about tomorrow's game. Will you be the star as usual?"

Alex felt himself reddening in the darkness. Now what was he supposed to say? What reasonable explanation could he give for his not starting?

"It should be an okay game," he said, downplaying the whole thing and hoping that she would drop it.

"An okay game?" she said incredulously. "You're playing Commerce. Aren't they supposed to be the up-and-coming team?"

He silently cursed her for being so well versed in football. Why couldn't she be like most girls, or at least the way most girls were supposed to be, and be completely ignorant and apathetic toward football? He cleared his throat, trying to buy time.

"Well, yeah, that's true," he said. "I didn't realize you kept up with football so much."

"It's in my blood," she answered. "My dad played in college and so," she spread her arms, "the rest of us learned to love it." She grinned. "Though for me it wasn't much of a fight. I truly do love the game, Alex."

He caught a glimpse of hope for an escape in her short speech, and he brightened. "Where did your dad play college football?" he asked.

"Michigan State," she answered. "Class of '78. Middle linebacker, all-American. Team captain two years in a row. Never beat Michigan."

Alex grinned broadly as she spouted off her father's accomplishments as though well practiced.

"Don't tell me you've never heard of him?" she asked in mock surprise.

"Actually, now that you mention it," he said, grinning slyly, "I have. John Donohoe. Played in both the North-South game—for the North, of course—and in the Senior Bowl. You also failed to mention that he still holds the Michigan State record for lone, open-field tackles."

Now it was Amanda's turn to be surprised. "My, you do take your football seriously if you know all that about a guy who played in 1978."

Alex held his pleasure to himself. Not only was she impressed with his knowledge, but they had also arrived at Amanda's street, and he had successfully evaded the question of tomorrow's game and his part in it.

Chapter 18

"Reba, would you like to call your parents?" Martha offered. "They might be worried if you come home a little late."

Reba shook her head. "I usually call right before I leave so they know when to expect me, unless this will take a long time?" she queried. She didn't tell her that Travis Johnson would also be waiting outside to walk her home. She had no idea why Mrs. Richards had singled her out to stay after practice. She had been paying attention, and she already knew her part, and Mrs. Richards knew that. What could be the problem then?

"No, it won't," Mrs. Richards said and pulled up a chair near Reba's and smiled. Reba waited.

"Reba," she began. "First of all, you have the potential to be a wonderful actress. You already have that ability to know your character and then just pull the audience into her with you. That's something that really can't be taught. Blocking, poise, voice control—those are some of the things a drama teacher can instruct a student in, but not …" She paused as she thought of the simplest way of explaining it, "not how to bring a character to life. Not how to make the audience care. That's something only a few people ever learn, and personally, I don't think they learn it. I think they're born with it."

Reba listened politely. *Where was this conversation going?* she wondered. This didn't sound like a reprimand, but why would Mrs. Richards be praising someone so highly who only managed to land a minor part? Not much of this was making sense. Mrs. Richards seemed to be reading her mind.

"You're probably wondering why I am showering you with such glowing praise after I only cast you in a minor role."

The thought had just *crossed my mind,* Reba said silently in a rare moment of sarcasm, but she was much too polite to ever voice such an opinion.

"My student director, Amanda Donahoe, wondered the same thing. She had you cast for the lead."

Reba's heart quickened. Maybe this little meeting was to tell her that the list had been a mistake, that Mrs. Richards had reconsidered her decision and meant to give her the lead role, or maybe at least the understudy spot. She felt her heart beating rapidly and warned herself to calm down.

Mrs. Richards pursed her lips in thought as she mulled over the best way to continue. "I hope you won't hold my decision against me forever," she said, smiling weakly, "but I didn't give you the lead, and I gave you only a minor role because I needed you somewhere else."

"You need me to do something else for the play?" Reba asked.

Martha shook her head. "No, something that doesn't deal with the play at all. I wanted you as the lead, too. You would have been the best, but there's a young man who needs your assistance now more than the play needs you."

Reba was growing terribly confused. "I'm afraid I don't understand."

"There's a sophomore boy on campus who does not know how to read, and it's beginning to catch up with him. He longs for a football career, but if he can't read, he can kiss any chance of college out the window. I was told that you are very adept at teaching people to read.

That you have taught your sister and brothers to read. I want you to tutor him so that he has a chance at his dreams."

An unaccustomed rebellion grew in Reba's throat. *What about my dreams?* she wanted to scream. *What about my desire to be an actress? Doesn't that count for anything? And who gave you the right to decide what I would and wouldn't do?*

She wanted to hurl these thoughts at the woman in front of her. Here she had been chiding herself for thinking she was better than she was, for being overconfident and proud of her performance when, in fact, she had every right to be proud. She, in all rights, had won the lead role, but this woman—*this woman*—took it upon herself to use her somewhere else. She felt herself shaking both in anger and disappointment.

"You will be paid, of course," Mrs. Richards answered when Reba didn't say anything. "And there will be more plays."

Unless you have something else for me to do, Reba countered silently and then bit her tongue. This was not a Christian attitude at all. This was a selfish, childish response, and she was ashamed, but that didn't help the resentment or anger go away.

Her feelings battled within her. Sure the money would be nice. She could buy Christmas presents for her family without having to do odd jobs for her mom to get the money. And she had no doubt that she could teach this guy to read.

"I'll help you get started," Martha prompted, a little worried when Reba was taking so long to answer.

Reba looked back at her, her disappointment riding in her eyes, but then she let out a resigned sigh. "When do you want me to start?"

"So are you in trouble?" Travis asked as he fell into step with her.

"No," Reba answered simply.

"Didn't think so," he replied and then grinned. "That would be the day."

Reba said nothing, not feeling like talking to a suddenly talkative Travis. Travis noticed her reticence and the lack of bounce in her step.

"Anything wrong?" he asked, and he couldn't keep the worry out of his voice.

"No," she said simply.

Travis felt the wall springing up between them. Usually it was he who would build the wall, keeping everyone else out. It seemed very odd and disquieting to be on the opposite side.

"She didn't put you down or anything did she?" he probed, growing angry. He would love to have a reason to be mad.

"*No!*" Reba shouted.

Travis was completely taken aback by her hostility. This was not the Reba he knew. Something was wrong, and that something was caused by that teacher. And when Reba's world was out of sync, the one safe spot in his own life was too. He cursed silently and vowed that he would find out what it was and make it right.

Travis walked the street aimlessly, watching, listening, always on the alert. He had made three deals already that morning and was heading to Wayne State to cash in on a little more. Danny would be there waiting for his first delivery of heroin. Travis grinned. Not only was he striking back at Mrs. Richards for whatever she had done to Reba by doping up her son, but he was also going to make a bundle off of the guy and eventually blow this whole town.

The frustration with his writing and those weird feelings of insignificance he would get whenever he was alone were beginning to wear on him, and he didn't like it. He stayed out later and later, opting for large crowds. Never before a real partier, he found some satisfaction, albeit hollow, with having others around. His mind was beginning to plague him, and for the first time in his life, he felt tempted to try the very stuff he was selling. *Maybe this is why they take it,* he thought one night, *to get rid of these oppressive thoughts and feelings.*

He checked his jacket pocket to make sure the "quarter teaspoons" were there along with the syringes. He shook his head. He couldn't believe he let himself get talked into providing needles for this guy, but he made up the money elsewhere. Danny had no clue what the strength of true heroin was, so Travis could cut it down with sugar or starch, save himself a bundle, and the guy would never know.

The qualms he had had earlier about selling stuff to the son of one of his teachers had vanished. She had hurt Reba, so he would hurt her. It was his way of staying in control. But these feelings, these thoughts … he felt his mind going again to those doubts, and he silently cursed and clapped his hands to his head, trying to squeeze them out.

"Ahhhhh!" Travis screamed and became more resolute in his vow. "I *won't* waver. I *won't* feel. I *will* be in control."

The October afternoon was sharp with the first real feel of fall. Alex breathed in the crisp air and felt nostalgic for a boy of sixteen. All during grammar school, he could remember watching Saturday afternoon TV, which showed ancient college football films like *The Knute Rockne Story*, and a host of other no-name movies that sometimes showed throngs of people dressed in the raccoon coats of the twenties or cashmere sweaters and lettermen's jackets of the fifties, all coming to enjoy an afternoon of college football. The whole town would turn out with their pennants waving and the band playing.

Alex took another deep breath while waiting for the whistle to blow to start the game. Those old movies were probably the reason he was the only one on the team who did not mind the Saturday afternoon games. Sure they were moved from Friday night to Saturday for security reasons, but for Alex, it had only heightened his enjoyment of the game.

Most college as well as professional teams played their games in the afternoon. Only high school had played in the evening. And in Detroit, once the weather turned cold, evening games were very uncomfortable for both player and spectator alike.

His eyes swept over the stands, and he felt a small wave of disappointment. Only a few hundred huddled together in the chilling air. There were no pennants flying, no white section of student rooters, the cheerleaders were huddled together in a circle, and only a remnant of the band had shown up for this game, and they sat talking to each other.

Alex swallowed his disappointment and turned his attention back to the field. Regardless of what was going on up in the bleachers, on the field, football was football, and he loved it.

The whistle blew, and a sharp pain seared Alex's diaphragm as Brian Watkins moved in to kick the ball. This was the first game he had not started this year. He had earned his starting spot and then had given it up for a chance to read. It had seemed tough to deal with during the week, but nothing compared to what he was feeling now. Standing here on the side watching was tough. How did some of the guys do it?

As the Commerce receiver caught the ball and began his run back upfield, Alex's eyes drifted once again up into the stands. Somewhere in that small, pathetic group sat his mother and father, watching and probably wondering by now why he wasn't starting. He hadn't told them and really had no intention of doing so, yet he had better figure out a story by four this afternoon that might wash with them.

His eyes drifted down the seats, and for a moment he thought he caught a flash of strawberry blonde hair and thought of Amanda. What might she be thinking? His heart sank a little more, and he averted his eyes from the crowd and returned to the field. After all, football was football. It never changed.

Chapter 19

First period. Alex slid into his seat next to the window and slouched down so as to remain inconspicuous. Monday mornings usually were a thrill for him. The game on Saturday, the write-up in the paper on Sunday, and then the applause and accolades from his friends on Monday. But today he wanted to avoid attention.

Sure Montgomery had beaten Commerce, but it had been an ugly and sloppy fight. The first half wasn't an offensive show or a defensive battle. It was a mess of turnovers, and by the time the gun sounded putting an end to twenty-four elongated minutes of misery, the score was a pathetic and paltry twelve to eight after the first half in Commerce's favor—and not a legitimate offensive touchdown in the lot.

Commerce had fallen on a fumble in the end zone and then picked up another loose ball to account for their second touchdown, but couldn't hit either point after. Montgomery had sacked Commerce's quarterback for a safety and then settled for two puny twenty-yard field goals.

In the locker room, the Montgomery team sat in sullen silence over their sloppy play, and Alex was more than aware of a few sulky stares turned his way, so he knew a few of them were blaming him and his absence for the present state of affairs. Coach Bauer had not been easy on them.

"What in God's name do you call this game you're playing?" he bellowed. "It's certainly not football. Oh no. Football is a game of precision, a game of sureness and intelligence. Football is a game of aggressiveness and quickness, agility, brute force, and finesse. What you're doing out there isn't even close. You look like a bunch of farm rejects trying to slop hogs in a quagmire, and there hasn't been a drop of rain in weeks!"

He let his words settle in and watched the eyes cast furtive glances about the room, trying to lay blame on someone else.

"Commerce is a good team, that's true," Coach Bauer continued, "but there is no way on God's green earth that they should beat *you*! Now let's get a little intensity and focus and a boatload of brains out there this second half and play *football*, not this sissy foot game you've been piddling with this first half.

"Kowalski!" he shouted. "You start the second half and see if you can get some life back into this team. Now let's go!"

The second half had gone better, but Alex felt that a couple of the guys blamed him for their getting chewed out, and he was sure a few blocks were missed or assignments screwed up on purpose so that he might get a little physical reminder that they didn't appreciate his absence. Montgomery had won, but it was neither impressive nor pretty.

Now from his window seat, he waited grimly for someone to make a comment on the game, to ask why he hadn't played the entire time. But no one said anything. He looked around the class, most of them bantering with each other, making crude comments, and comparing weekend conquests. How many had even gone to the game? How many even cared? He let out a long breath and opened his book. Football may be important to him, but that certainly didn't make it important to everyone else.

"Please turn to Act III, Scene 1," Mrs. Richards directed, and the xeroxed pages began shuffling. Alex followed suit, looking for the familiar Roman numerals that would indicate the right spot.

"Who was assigned the part of Cassius?" A hand raised in the back of the room.

"How about Brutus?" Another fluttered.

"Caesar? … And Calpurnia? Good. Then shall we get started? Greg, please begin."

Greg cleared his throat and began reading, and Alex looked at the strange figures on the page and tried to make sense of what he was seeing with what Greg was trying to read. The "doths" and "ayes" and "want'sts" were a bit too much for Greg, but he doggedly kept going.

Alex shook his head. Even if he knew how to read, this stuff would be the death of him. Shakespeare could confuse a nuclear physicist he was sure. Yet, to his surprise, he was enjoying the story about Julius Caesar. Despite the language, Shakespeare had a way of getting to the heart of men. Take Cassius for example. If he could read, that would be the part he would take. The guy was a devious conniver and really knew what made men tick. He also had an acute chip on his shoulder.

Alex listened and thought. Was he like Cassius? or Brutus? Brutus was too trusting, so noble minded that he didn't realize the rest of the world was busy getting what they could any way they could. Had *he*, Alex, been too trusting? He looked up at Mrs. Richards, who was following along, nodding, prompting, encouraging. Today was his first official tutorial, and yet she had scheduled play practice, and Amanda swore she never missed. So what was the story?

He had done his homework and set his goals—well, only one really—and that was to be able to enroll in a regular class next year rather than a remedial one. Now he felt the anger rise in his stomach, leaving the bitter taste of betrayal in his mouth. He had laid himself out there, but for what purpose?

Perhaps he should be more like Cassius: suspicious of people's motives, wary of what they do and say and want. Yet Cassius did not seem like a happy man, and for Alex, that didn't seem to be the best route either.

"Hands, speak for me!" yelled Sam, really getting into his part, and Alex's attention was drawn back to the play. Caesar was being stabbed to death, and he had almost missed it. He glanced at the page number of the girl next to him and then flipped his pages until he was on the right page. True, Mrs. Richards didn't call on him to read anymore, but he still didn't think she would take too kindly to it if she caught him daydreaming, and right now she controlled more of his life than he wanted.

"Alex, this is Reba. Reba, this is Alex. Reba is going to be your official tutor."

Alex's eyes shot up at Mrs. Richards and burned with accusations. He had thought *she* would be his tutor. She had given both Coach Bauer and him that impression. She had lied to them both. And what right did she have to go and spread it around school that he couldn't read?

No one was supposed to know about this except her. His eyes burned fire as he stared accusingly at Mrs. Richards. Though Reba's name sounded vaguely familiar, at this point he could care less. Who she was was less important than why she was here.

Reba, meanwhile, was taking in her own fill of her new pupil and didn't like what she saw. He seemed indignant and angry and intent on not having her for a tutor, though she really couldn't blame him. It must be quite humiliating to have a freshman teaching you how to read your second year in high school. Alex felt her staring at him and turned his angry gaze on her, only to be met by one of equal disdain.

Oh, this is just great! he thought. *Neither of us wants to be here, and yet here we are.*

Martha picked up on the hostility. "I'm sorry I didn't explain it to you earlier, Alex, that I would not be doing all of your tutoring, but I thought if I did, you wouldn't agree to come."

Well, you got that part right! he thought angrily.

"Reba comes highly recommended."

His eyes looked her over carefully and then shifted back to Mrs. Richards. *You mean you don't know personally if she is any good or not?* His eyes accused her, and she read his thoughts.

Keeping her voice calm, Martha continued. "She's a freshman and new, but she has taught her brothers and sister to read as well as her mother and father."

The two teenagers stared at each other again, each taking a careful measure of the other one.

She's pretty ugly, Alex thought.

He's pretty stuck up, Reba mused.

"Well, if you'll excuse me," Martha interrupted, "I will leave you two to it while I get to play practice."

The mention of play practice caused Reba's head to jerk involuntarily, and Alex caught the response. Her full lips pulled tight with controlled anger, and he thought he saw her chest move in and out more rapidly as she tried to control her feelings.

My, but that caused a response, he thought.

"I hope you two get along," Martha said and smiled reassuringly. "But I know you will because you are both fine people."

Alex resented the patronizing attitude and the attempt to reconcile each to his or her fate when it was obvious that neither of them really wanted to be there. Martha exited the room, and the uncomfortable silence hurt Alex's ears. Neither Alex nor Reba moved for a few moments, and the clock could be heard making its rhythmic *click-click* on the wall.

Alex just stared ahead, in no hurry to get started. He was still too mad about being shoved off to some freshman. He wouldn't admit to himself that her being black had anything to do with it. Heck! Over 80 percent of the entire school population was black. But deep inside, he knew her superiority over him was only heightened by the fact that she was black. He took another deep breath.

Father, he prayed, *I'm having a tough time with this.* He sighed in resignation and looked up at Reba with remote expectation, but she was still staring at the door, dealing with her own feelings.

Lord, help me, she prayed silently. *I know I should be thankful for the opportunity to help someone and earn money at the same time. I know I should be confident that you know what you're doing. I know I should not be resentful of Mrs. Richards's decision and be taking it out on this boy here—but I am.* She too, took a deep breath and then looked over at Alex, who was staring at her, only this time he did not appear so hostile or angry, just disappointed. She smiled despite herself.

"I guess I really don't look too impressive," she said, "but I do know that I can teach you to read."

Alex nodded his acknowledgment, and Reba moved over to sit down in the desk across from him. She began pulling out a series of cards from her book bag. Alex watched with suspicious curiosity. Suddenly Reba stopped with her hand in the bag and turned to him.

"You *do* want to learn to read, don't you?" she asked. Alex was taken by surprise.

"Sure," he said indignantly. "Why do you think I'm here?"

Despite her anxiety, Reba smiled again, this time more warmly. "There could be a number of reasons you're here," she said slyly, "but it's important that you *want* to read. Otherwise, you won't learn."

Alex relaxed a little, but she had opened the door for him to pursue his question.

"Now the next question is do *you* want to be here?" he said, and Reba looked up at him. "I saw the way your eyes narrowed when Mrs. Richards said she was going to play practice. What was that all about?"

It was rather bold on Alex's part, and Reba wondered how much she should tell this stranger. She bit the inside of her lower lip and decided to be honest. After all, he was unknowingly sharing his secret.

"Mrs. Richards has told me that you want no one to know that you are being tutored in reading, is that right?" she asked. Alex nodded. "Then will you promise not to tell anyone what I tell you?"

Alex thought about it and nodded his head slowly. That was a fair trade. Reba took a deep breath. She was not used to sharing her problems. She didn't like to complain or hold grudges, and she was afraid that's what this would sound like. But for some unknown reason, she felt compelled to be honest with this boy.

"I tried out for the play and thought I had done well," she confessed. "In fact, a lot of people told me they thought I had one of the lead roles." She stopped. "I've learned since that you shouldn't take too high of stock in what other people think. Anyway, when the cast list was posted, I was given only a minor part and was disappointed because I had set my sights so high."

The pieces of where he had heard her name before and who she was were naggingly close, but he couldn't make them all fit, so he just nodded. "I know how you feel. Happened to me in baseball once."

Reba smiled. "Anyway, once I had reprimanded myself for being ungrateful for the part I did get, which for a freshman was still pretty good, and reconciled myself to a supporting role, Mrs. Richards called me in and told me that she wanted to give me the lead, but that she had another job she needed me to do."

Alex looked at her in confusion. "Another job? What job?"

"This one. Tutoring you," she said without wavering, and Alex felt his ears shatter from the full repercussion of what she had just said.

"You mean you didn't get the lead for the play because Mrs. Richards arbitrarily decided that you were going to be my tutor?"

"That's one way of putting it."

"Hey, man," Alex said, throwing his hands up in defense. "I don't want to have that guilt trip hanging around my neck. Let's just call it quits right here, and you can go back to the play, and I'll go back to football practice."

"You gave up football to learn to read?" Reba asked.

Alex nodded. "Yeah, sort of. My starting spot anyway. But it was with the idea that Mrs. Richards would be teaching me. I didn't ask anybody to give up something. You just go back to the play." He stood to gather his books, but Reba stopped him with her hand.

"Too late for that," she said simply. "The cast is chosen, and I've already said okay. Plus, I am getting paid for it, and as hard as it was for me at first to accept it, I have this philosophy that there's a purpose for everything."

Alex had stopped midway in his ascent. Reba's last comment had caught his interest, and he slowly sat back down. Should he pursue it?

"Kind of like there's a plan?" he stated tentatively, feeling his way. "Like an ultimate power?" He could hear his heart start to pound in his chest. He always had a hard time sharing his faith.

"Like God is in control," Reba stated flatly. "And that he is presiding over this," she said and stretched out her hand to imply their session.

Alex felt the pressure escape from his lungs. "Are you a Christian?" he asked.

"Uh-huh. Are you?"

He nodded and then smiled ruefully. "Yeah. Guess I haven't acted like it though, have I?"

Reba laughed and then Alex's eyes lit up, the pieces having fallen into place.

"Say, Amanda Donahoe was talking about you. She's the student director of the play. She said you were great and that you *should* have had the lead."

Reba warmed to the compliment. So Mrs. Richards hadn't just been feeding her a line. She *had* been good.

"I have to confess," she said. "I've been pretty resentful toward Mrs. Richards the past two days."

Alex's face clouded over. "I guess that makes two of us," he admitted. "But I kind of think she understood."

Reba smiled warmly and decided abruptly that she liked Alex. He wasn't as cocky as she had thought. Alex grinned back and decided that Reba was not bad looking at all. Her eyes and that warm smile just pulled you into her confidence.

"Then what do you say. Let's do some things here that will really surprise her," Reba stated and returned to pulling out the remaining cards from her backpack.

The lights were just coming on as Alex left the main entrance of Montgomery High. He glanced at his watch. Five ten. He stood on the steps and contemplated what he should do. Amanda wouldn't be through with play practice for almost half an hour. Out of courtesy, he should wait. After all, he was pretty sure she would be expecting him. But somehow he really didn't want to see her tonight. Football may not be important to 90 percent of the students around here, but it was to her, and she would be sure to ask questions.

He glanced at his watch again and then zipped up his jacket and headed down the steps. He would just have to think up something to tell her.

"How was practice?" Mr. Kowalski asked.

Alex felt himself choke on his mashed potatoes. "Fine," he mumbled.

"Coach didn't keep you guys as long today," his father continued. "Thought after Saturday's game he'd have worked your tails off."

Alex managed a grin. "Yeah, me too," he said, his eyes never leaving his plate.

"Are you feeling all right?" his mother asked with genuine concern. "You're not eating half as much as you usually do." Alex felt his neck redden.

"Yeah, I'm fine," he said, feeling uncomfortably warm all over. "Coach just didn't work us as hard today."

Out of the corner of his eye, Alex could see his father shake his head. "Bauer must be going soft in his old age," he said. "There was a day, and not that long ago mind you, that a game like Saturday would have meant practices till seven o'clock. Hope he hasn't lost his edge."

Alex gritted down another forkful of mashed potatoes. "He hasn't lost it," he said reassuringly. "Just think he was trying a different approach today. I have a feeling tomorrow will be a long day."

His father nodded approvingly. "I guess I shouldn't second-guess Coach Bauer yet. He's always fielded winners. By the way, did he give you any reason for not playing you the first half?"

Alex shook his head. "Just said he wanted to give a few of the backups a try," he lied.

His father looked at him carefully. "Well, you were the only starter who was backed up," he stated.

Alex shrugged, praying his father would just drop the subject. "He's the coach," he said. "I just do what he tells me."

"Well, that's a good attitude to have," Mr. Kowalski agreed. "I just hope he doesn't decide to do it again this Saturday. Central is a must-win game, and you guys can't afford another half like you had this last time."

For the second time, the mashed potatoes lodged in Alex's throat. What was he supposed to do now?

Chapter 20

Alex pulled the flash cards from his backpack and spread them out neatly on his bed. A picture of a cat, book, dog, fire, and about thirty others stared up at him. Even in the privacy of his own room, he blushed from embarrassment. He felt like a kid—looking at pictures and then saying the word out loud.

He heard footsteps outside his door and held his breath until they passed, then quickly walked over and quietly locked it. His parents were already concerned about his behavior. They had questioned him about his shortened playing time but had seemed to accept the excuse that Coach was letting some of the second string play against the weaker Commerce team. He had been a little worried when his dad noticed that no other first stringer ever came out of the game, but the crisis had passed without further incident.

Amanda would be more difficult to convince. Just last week she had been singing their praises, so he could almost hear her response to his fabrication.

"Commerce, *easy*? Who are you kidding? Why, they run a phenomenal wishbone, have two great nickel backs, and …" No, he would have to think up something better to tell her. And what might she say about this week's game against Central? They're always a powerhouse, so letting backups have a little playing time would certainly not ring true. He wasn't sure which lies were going to be harder to maintain: the ones to his parents or to Amanda.

A gentle knock on the door brought him quickly back to the present, and he shoved all the cards into a pile and stuffed them into his backpack. "Yeah?" he called.

"It's Mother," he heard through the door. "You need anything before your father and I sit down to do a little reading?"

"No—nothing," he called back and felt his heart pounding. *Please don't try the door,* he prayed. *Please, don't try.* He never locked his door, and for her to find it locked would only raise more concern—not suspicion, but motherly concern.

"All right then," she answered. "We won't bother you. Get a lot of studying done."

She respected his privacy and walked away, and he felt a flood of bad air explode from his lungs. He hated secrets and lies. *Sorry, Lord,* he prayed quickly, but he felt his conscience nagging him, which he silenced by spreading the cards out again in order. Then he pulled out his notebook and opened to a blank page.

"All right," he said with determination. "Let's see how much I remember from my first lesson. Bat, cat, dog, fire, gate …" He continued through the cards, identifying each picture and saying the word clearly, listening for that first sound. When he was finished, he went back to the beginning and started again.

"Bat," he said firmly and then wrote a capital *B* on his paper for that first sound. Reba had shown him only capitals this first day because the lower case *B* and *D* caused problems for some people, she had explained.

"Cat," he repeated and then thought a moment, sorting through the symbols he had seen today, trying to associate the right one with the sound. For a full hour, he methodically went through the cards, and after completing all he could, he turned them over and compared answers.

"Ten out of twenty-one," he said flatly, not really knowing if that was good or not. He looked down at the cards and picked up the ones he had missed, turning them over in his hand, looking first at the picture and then at the symbol of the sound on the opposite side.

"Teepee," he said with frustration. "I should have known that one."

Then he gathered them all into a pile again, shuffled them, and laid them out in a random order, turned to a fresh page in his notebook and started again.

"I'm going to learn these tonight," he said with a fierce determination.

Martha sat curled up on her sofa in her midweek pose and stared at her grade book and the row of blank boxes following Travis Johnson's name.

"What happened to this kid?" she asked herself softly. "He was doing his work and wasn't a bad writer and then—this? Lord," she prayed quietly, "help me reach this young man. I thought I had a line to him through his writing, but he's severed it. Help me be a part of that healing process."

She chided herself for not recognizing the problem sooner. School policy said she should have notified the parents two weeks ago about his failing grade. She had been so busy with the play, Alex, and Reba, that she had let Travis slip right through the cracks. It was easy to do. Alex and Reba were likable; the play was fun. Travis fell into the "problem" category. Well, not in class, but he was harder to reach, and since she didn't have a lot of time to make that effort, she had slid him to the side.

"Well, I know how to fix that!" she announced and untangled herself from her papers, walked to the phone, and pulled out the phone book. Martha opened to the *P*'s and slid her finger down the list of names until she stopped at Patton. She dialed the number at her fingertips and waited.

"Hello?"

"Hello, Greg? This is Martha Richards from church."

"Why hello, Martha Richards from church. How can I help you?"

Martha paused for a moment, pursing her lips, debating about the best approach to take. "Remember when you said to call if there was anything you could do to help me with my classes?"

"Sure do. What do you need? A lecture? A field trip? What?"

Martha paused for a second time and took a deep breath. "A mentor," she replied.

Martha checked the student reminders she had written on the board, looked over her lesson plans for first period, set out all the handouts on a front desk, and then checked her Post-it note to see the order of events for the first class of the day. Then she checked the clock. Fifteen minutes before class started. She still had time to get a few more things done.

Walking back to her desk, she looked over two more Post-its on her desk that laid out the plan of attack for the day: get all tutors set up on the payroll, call Mrs. Johnson, run off the next essay assignment, print up the play practice schedule, talk to Travis after third period, pick up the laundry on the way home.

Despite the long list of items, Martha smiled. She definitely was one to have all her little ducks in a row and then just check them off as the day wore on. When all the items were checked off, the day was a success.

She double-checked her lesson plans for the day. The class hour was jam-packed with activities and discussions. One of her strengths was her preparation and organization. As a student, Martha had loved assemblies and rallies—actually anything that broke up the monotony of the day. As a teacher, she hated them. They broke up her perfect day, her perfect quarter schedule, which in turn just messed up her semester, which in turn destroyed her year.

No, she liked things to go according to plan—her plan—and right now things were. Play practice was scheduled right down to the dress rehearsal; Reba and Alex, despite their initial standoff, seemed to be working well together. She had sneaked a peek through the window during a break in practice, and the two were more than just going at it. Her classes were working. Only Travis seemed to be a kink in her otherwise perfect world, and after third period, she would have that fixed as well. She smiled and let out a contented sigh. She had time for one call to the office to check on that payroll status and then she could scratch that item off her list as well.

"Travis, may I see you for just a moment after class, please?" Martha asked as the bell rang.

Travis's head popped up at Mrs. Richards's request.

"Guess so," he said with a shrug, and he lowered himself back into his chair. Once all the other students had vacated the room, Martha walked over to him, sat down in the seat next to him, and smiled. Travis squirmed uneasily. He didn't care for her being so close, or smiling so sweetly, like she was his mother or something.

"I'm worried about you, Travis," she began, and Travis rolled his eyes. Now she was beginning to *sound* like a mother. Not *his* mother, but a mother. He didn't answer. She pulled out her grade book and opened it to his class and laid it before her, running her finger under his name and the row following it.

"You were doing all of your work when school started," she said, "and good work, too. And then, all of a sudden, you just seemed to stop. Is there any reason?"

Yeah, he thought sarcastically. *The reason is I couldn't see the point. Where was it going to get me?* But he said nothing and stared stonily at the whiteboard in front of him like he wasn't listening. If he had had his sunglasses on, he would have stared at her, but she wouldn't allow them in her classroom, and he didn't feel all that secure in front of this assertive lady without some protection, so he just stared straight ahead and said nothing.

"You showed a lot of promise, Travis," she continued, apparently not caring if he responded or not. "And I'd like to help."

Then why was it so frustrating and hard? he thought. *And maybe you should think about helping your own kid instead of me. Do you know what he's into, lady? No, I don't think you have a clue. You're living in some fairy-tale world where everybody can be exactly what they want to be if they just work hard enough. Well, let me tell you, lady, that ain't the way it is.*

He ran the angry conversation through his head and tightened his lips, but remained silent.

"Of course, your writing wasn't very disciplined, and you have a lot to learn, but you do have a lot of potential."

You already said that.

"I think I know what could help if you're willing to give it a try," she offered, and for the first time Travis's head turned, and he looked at her with a distant curiosity.

"I have a friend down at the *Michigan Press* who is a very good writer. I know you lean toward poetry, but learning the journalistic approach would certainly give you a handle on the language. It would really make you grow. Greg Patton, the man at the *Press*, does all kinds of writing himself and swears that journalism is what groomed him. He said he would be willing to take you on as an apprentice if you want to give it a try."

Travis's eyes looked at her skeptically. "What does that mean?" he asked. "To be an apprentice?"

"It means that you will work for him at a reduced wage, and in return he will be your writing mentor. He'll teach you everything he knows and help you groom your own style."

"Yeah, I guess I know what a mentor is," Travis said as a slow, sinister grin spread across his face. Martha felt a chill pass through her. "I'll get paid, huh?"

Martha pushed the sense of foreboding to the back of her mind and nodded. "Minimum wage."

Travis couldn't help but smile wryly. *If only you knew, lady, that right now I am making megabucks doing something that takes no effort whatsoever, and you're offering me a job at slave labor rates for something that takes all my energy. How's that for irony?*

"Well?" Martha asked, back under control. "Would you like a little time to think about it? Say a week?"

Travis shook his head and rose to leave. "No," he answered, the grin still plastered on his face. "I don't need any more time." He turned to face her. "Tell your friend that I'll take it."

Martha breathed a sigh of relief after Travis left the room, and she mouthed a quick prayer of thanks for the Lord's protection. Though she had always prided herself for her calm and control, her lack of fear in fearful situations, she could not deny the foreboding feeling she felt whenever Travis walked into the room. It was as if there were a darkness around him, a blanket of evil.

Of course, at times it seemed to have holes in it, and she thought she could catch a glimpse of the young man inside. A young man who yearned to be loved and wanted to learn. A young man with exceptional perception and incredible suspicion. All those things she had perceived as he sat in her third period class. There was even a time, brief as it may have been, that she could have sworn she thought he was a little frightened, but of what she couldn't imagine. Other gangs? That was about the only logical explanation that she could think of.

But in the last couple of weeks, his whole demeanor had changed. He withdrew from class discussions completely. He had repeatedly left his sunglasses on so as to add another barrier between him and the rest of the class. At first she hadn't hesitated to remind him to remove them, and he would and then he would stare blankly at the whiteboard.

But when he continued to leave them on, she became angry, threatening to keep them the next time she had to tell him. He had removed them, but the blank stare had turned into a defiant, smirking one, daring her to try it, and she had felt another cold chill course through her body.

The next day, he came in, slouched into his seat, and stared at her through the opaque lenses of his glasses. Martha had felt her heart pound both in her chest and her ears, but she refused to let herself be intimidated by this youth. She had just opened her mouth to speak when he slowly removed them with a faint cynical smile and then meticulously folded them and slid one of the arms down the neck of his T-shirt.

This same procedure occurred day after day. Martha thought about insisting he take them off when he entered the room, but why? She had never demanded that before. Was it just to assert her authority? Instead, she said a quick prayer prior to third period every day and then the two reenacted the same scenario. But even though he never tested her resolve past this point, he had also refused to take part in anything. No more work was turned in. No comments were made and no direct questions were answered. He had removed himself from this world, and there was nothing she could do.

Which led to her puzzlement over his answer today. Why on earth would he, without hesitation, accept the job when he seemed so set on alienating himself from the rest of the human race? She really hadn't expected him to say yes at all, and had really only pursued the opportunity to let Travis know she cared. Martha wanted to believe that she had hit a sympathetic chord with him, but the realist in her knew that there was some other, more plausible reason for his reaction, and that unknown reason was sending slivers of fear up her spine.

Chapter 21

"*Faster!*"

Alex pumped his arms harder and pushed his legs faster as he propelled himself up the stadium steps for what seemed like the hundredth time. Despite the crispness in the air, he was already sweating profusely. Running stairs was bad enough, but running with full pads on was torture.

He reached the top and slowed to a jog to catch his breath as he crossed to the next aisle and then started his descent. Going down wasn't much easier.

"*Ten more!*" yelled Coach Matson, Bauer's assistant.

Alex felt his legs rebel as he started back up. Even though every muscle in his body screamed in pain, it was still better than being on the field right now. Not that practice was that difficult today. All they were doing was reviewing blocking responsibilities. No, the tough practice was yesterday. It was the kind of practice his father had spoken about last Saturday night at dinner, and from what he had heard, it left *everyone* lying on the ground at the end. That was the problem. He only heard about it because he had been with Reba for tutoring, and the minute he walked into the locker room, he was the target of icy stares and frosty comments.

"Nice of you to show up, Kowalski."

"What are you, Coach's pet? He doesn't make you come to the tough practices?"

"Almost cost us the game last week. Thought you might have learned your lesson and decided to come to practice this week."

"Too good for us these days?"

Even Richard was a little miffed. "What gives, man?" he asked softly once the other guys had started to file out of the locker room. "Why are you so gung ho on all of this help all of a sudden? You've never been much of a student. Why try now? Why don't you just let it go, give it up? Football's your ticket, man, and you're blowin' it big time. With the guys, Coach, even yourself. Colleges aren't gonna offer scholarships to a guy who sits on the bench all of the time. Come on now. Get your head screwed on straight."

Alex watched Richard grab his helmet and follow the others out to the field and then he grabbed his own and quietly shut his locker. Richard's words had hurt. Did Richard really think he didn't have a chance at making the grades? Maybe he *was* fooling himself. He shook that last thought from his mind. Now was not the time to be second-guessing himself. He ran out to catch up with the others.

The grumbling hadn't ceased once they had reached the field. Coach Bauer started where he had left off yesterday, running them up and down the field. At each rest, Alex could hear the grumbling and feel the accusing stares. When they were matched up for hitting drills, the guys took extra pleasure in releasing their pent-up anger on him. Only when things calmed down and they began walking through their blocking assignments had Coach sent him off to run his stairs for missing practice yesterday.

"Thirty!" he had yelled. "Ten for every hour you missed."

"*Five more!*" Matson bellowed, and Alex sensed some relief that the end was near. But then he would return to the field, and what would he encounter there?

He gritted his teeth and steeled his body against the agonizing flight of stairs that rose before him and his mind against the slings of arrows that awaited him below.

The darkness and the walls of his room seemed to close in on him, pressuring him, confining him. His curtains were closed, obscuring the one streetlight that usually provided a ray of light into his room. When he was younger, that light had made him feel safe. Now it only served as a means of exposing him, of shedding light on the things he was doing behind closed, locked doors.

The window was shut tight against the bite of the late October cold. Danny sat in the darkness, staring straight ahead, fingering the strip of rubber tubing while he sat looking at nothing and thinking of nothing. Finally, he pulled himself out of his daze and wrapped it around his left arm. He opened the curtains just slightly until the streetlight illuminated the veins popping out. He picked up the syringe and skillfully inserted it into the biggest one and slowly pushed the liquid into his body.

It had bothered him immensely the first time he tried it, and his hand had been shaking so much that it took him three tries to catch a vein. But the aftermath had been so relaxing that he had no trouble inserting the needle the second time.

When the syringe was empty, he pulled it out and then released the rubber tubing from his arm, thought enough to remember to dump the syringe into the trash can, and then crashed on his bed to wait for the effect. He was surprised by how long it seemed to take and how short the downer lasted. Danny had expected more, but he couldn't complain. Heroin left no telling after-smell and took him to a deeper sense of peace.

He felt his mind and body begin to numb and tingle at the same time. He felt alive yet muted, sensitive yet anesthetized. Colors became more vivid while the world seemed less clear. This was his escape and he laid back to enjoy it, for it would only last a couple of hours at the most and then he would start to come back out. That thought made him start, and he shook it from his mind. Danny hated to return. If only he never had to return.

Reba sat at the table surrounded by her younger brothers and sister. All were working diligently, scratching out math answers, biting lower lips over a geography book, or silently mouthing the words to the story being read. Reba checked over her own rough draft and let her mind wander. She felt all warm inside. How could she have been so upset yesterday or last Friday over missing out on the play?

Actually, she wasn't missing out; she was still a part of it, and that was more than evident today at practice. Mrs. Richards had her run through her part and then work with some of the other actors to help them learn their lines and then with Amanda Donahoe to run through some blocking ideas. If anything, she was getting more of a theatrical experience by *not* playing the lead than if she had.

She shook her head and let out a small sigh. When would she learn, or rather, *not forget* that God really did provide—that he really *did* take care of her. All during her short fourteen years, she had come up against disappointments or complications, like the year they couldn't go visit Aunt Lucille in Baltimore because Dad had lost his job.

That had been a major disappointment because they had planned on driving up to Washington DC and seeing the Capitol and the White House and the Smithsonian. But hadn't that turned out all right? Because her dad had learned to read and then had found another job, and the next year they were able to go anyway. Wasn't that proof of God's timing and providence?

And then what about when Willie got sick and all their money had to go to pay for his doctor bills, and so they had to do without a Christmas tree and presents. That wasn't much fun. But God had been watching over them then, too, for hadn't the church sent gifts and a tree and a complete Christmas meal? Yes, God had provided. God had watched over them.

And now the play. Reba didn't get the lead and was railroaded (at least it had felt like it) into tutoring a football player. She grinned. But look at the results. Alex had smiled at her in the hallway this morning, she was earning her own spending money, and she was learning more about the theater than she had ever dreamed. She felt her spirits rise even more. Yes, God had helped her weather disappointments and failures in the past, and he was still beside her now, so nothing could go wrong.

Chapter 22

Danny sat in his regular cubicle in the back of the third floor behind the stacks and stared at the pages before him. He had been here for hours pretending to study, going through the motions, looking every bit like the student. He had to keep up the facade. There were too many people who knew his parents. They were everywhere, and in places he would least expect to see them. They might even be people he didn't recognize.

In his mind, his mother's influence had fingers that reached into unseen portions of the city. He had to fool everybody because he wasn't really sure who would get back to his parents, who might tell them that he hadn't been at the library, that he hadn't been studying. Then what might happen? His throat tightened at the thought, and his mouth ran dry. He licked his lips, but his heart raced. Man, he couldn't let them find out.

He turned another page in his chemistry book and stared at the headings, but they blurred before his eyes, and he couldn't concentrate. As worried as he was about his parents, it took a back burner to his primary concern, which wasn't school.

He glanced up at the clock: ten fifteen. He swallowed again, but his throat was dry. He was supposed to meet Travis for another buy this afternoon at three. The first teaspoons hadn't lasted half as long as he had expected. Somehow the high hadn't been as high or as long as he had anticipated, and so he had shot more.

Now he needed more, and he needed it fast. His pulse raced when he wasn't drugged. Sounds were too clear, too loud. Life was too raw. Yeah, he needed the stuff. The problem was he didn't have the money, and he couldn't think of a way to get it. He had depleted his savings, and he couldn't hit up his parents again.

Maybe Travis will give me credit, he thought hopefully. *After all, he has done me some favors in the past like the needles and all.* Danny let out a short breath of relief. It was the first ray of hope he had had in a long time.

Martha sat down to an early lunch of tuna and carrot sticks and looked over her list. She had gone walking, cleaned the bathrooms, changed the sheets, dusted and vacuumed the bedroom and living room, and started the laundry. She ran a line through each of the items as she named them off, then took a bite of her sandwich and stared out the kitchen window where leaves of gold and red were floating softly to the ground.

It was a beautiful fall day, she thought blissfully and chewed her sandwich slowly. She took a deep breath, letting her mind drift with the leaves. Martha thought about absolutely nothing for almost ten seconds; then, she let out a deep sigh and turned back to her list. She had a few papers to grade still and some reading to do in preparation for Monday.

She felt her conscience gnaw at her. She should also probably go in and clean up Danny's room a little too. He had been working so hard, and he looked so tired and worn out. It would only be to help him but not enough to be too noticeable because she didn't want him to get the idea that she was going to be his maid. Just enough to make it livable by her standards. She hated clutter and mess, but the last thing she wanted to do was to be constantly cleaning up after men who were old enough to pick up after themselves.

How long had it taken her to get Graydon to throw his clothes in the hamper instead of on the floor? The first year they were married, she had followed him around like a dutiful servant, picking up socks and shirts. Then the thrill of *serving* kind of paled, and she began to grow resentful because he just expected her to pick up after him. She had fumed for weeks, but really had no one to blame but herself.

Finally, she had voiced her frustration and said she would not wash anything that wasn't in the hamper. To her surprise, he readily agreed. Of course, the first two weeks he forgot, and Martha battled with herself not to pick up the clothes littering the floor throughout the house. Graydon hadn't seemed to notice having to sidestep socks and move dirty shirts off of chairs to sit down, but when he wound up wearing dirty underwear to work because there weren't any clean ones in his drawer, he learned fast. From then on, the dirty clothing was found in the hamper.

Danny had been much more difficult; he hadn't cared how dirty the clothes were that he wore … until high school and then suddenly both clean clothes and his privacy were necessities. So Martha had won again, and she carried that winning technique of "grittin' it out till the troops fall in line" with her to school with more than adequate success.

She wistfully looked back out the window to where the sun was now shining brightly. The sky was a brilliant blue, and the leaves continued to float. All three called to her.

"I deserve a treat," she said abruptly. "I'm going to the game." She laid down her list and stood up in a moment of decision and freedom. Then she picked it back up and scribbled out a revised list, keeping all the same items but placing new deadlines on them. She stood up and went to get her coat, then wrote a note for Graydon and Danny so they wouldn't worry.

It had been a couple of years since she had been to a football game, and yet she really enjoyed football. Just too many other priorities had gotten in the way. Anyway, Alex was on the team, and right now she felt she had a personal investment in him. Plus, she deserved a little reward herself.

Travis stared at the slip of paper in his hand and then up at the numbers above the door. There must be some mistake. This couldn't be the *Press* office. In a gesture not common to him, he pressed his face against the window to get a look inside. The ever present sunglasses inhibited his vision, so, in a second uncustomary act, he shed them and then shielded his eyes from the sun and took another look inside. *This is just a hole in the wall,* he thought cynically, and backed away for a moment and reconsidered his decision.

His visions of working in a huge cavern of activity, surrounded by copy boys running up and down the aisles, keyboards clicking away, coffee being spilled on clean copy (followed by a stream of expletives) vanished. He had believed there would be editors leaning over desks, demanding a story while the writer shrugged and lit up another cigarette. That was what he had dreamed, but that was *not* what was behind this plate glass window: three desks, of which only two were occupied, and three computers.

He slowly backed away from the window and the office as if it carried some insidious disease he was afraid of catching and stared first at the numbers and then the bold script on the window: MICHIGAN PRESS. This must be some sort of satellite office. He shook his head slowly.

No, this was not what he was looking for, though up until this moment, he really hadn't been sure what he was looking for, but now part of it dawned on him. He was looking to get lost, to be surrounded by people and activity so that those nagging, disturbing thoughts couldn't get to him. Those thoughts that he was nothing, insignificant, a nobody, a grain of sand in the realm of the universe.

Travis didn't want to be alone with time to think. He needed to be busy, to be active, to be in control, and he had thought working for the *Press*, no matter how petty the pay, would be that ticket.

He took one last look at the window before he turned to leave. This place would not allow any of those options. Here he would stick out, be noticeable and accountable. He didn't work that way—naked. He worked undercover.

As Travis put his sunglasses back on and turned away, out of habit he looked at his watch. It was ten thirty. He would have been prompt. He would have made a good impression. He would have been hired. Instead, he shoved his hands in his jacket and left.

"I want you to put last week's game out of your mind. I want you to put aside your petty differences and squabbles of the past week. I want you to put aside *everything* except this game before you today. *This* is the time. Seize *this* moment. Be a *team*, not a bunch of individuals. Be *men*, putting aside all else for the war, not a pack of backbiting old ladies. Have *character*, *pride*, *fortitude.* Go out there and do the job you came here to do!"

Alex sat on the end of the bench and listened intently to Coach Bauer's pregame speech. Usually his speeches were filled with gut-moving, adrenaline-pumping, hormone-producing invectives, designed to get the blood driving through every limb in every player. But today's speech wasn't like that, and it was for his benefit. The week had been horrendous, and it wasn't all from the miles of extra stairs he had had to run. His punishment from the coaching staff was mild compared to what the players dished out.

Tuesday had been bad enough with unwarranted below-the-belt hits and uncalled-for roughness, but after he missed again on Wednesday, Thursday was torture. First, he had been met by stony silence. Then came the hits again. Then, while Greg was calling the shots from the huddle, he was intentionally shunned. Backs were turned toward him, and his number was never called.

Finally, Coach stepped in and demanded his plays be called, but that didn't stop the ostracism. Every pass was just out of reach or just high enough or just behind him enough to leave him vulnerable to the defensive hit. And when that ruse was looking a bit too obvious, the play was telegraphed to the defense so that even if he did make the catch, the defender was there and crashed into him without any mercy. Coach Bauer finally blew the whistle to end the scrimmage before someone was seriously hurt.

"We've got a job to do, men," Bauer continued and let his eyes settle on each player for a few seconds, "if that is truly what you are. … Central is a good team … a very good team. If you have so little confidence in yourselves to believe that your only chance of winning hinges on one player" … the heads shot up … "then you aren't a team; you're parasites.

"No team should rest on the performance of one person. It should rest on the shoulders of the eleven men out on the field. Prove to me and yourselves that you are a good football *team* today. Go out and kick a little Central butt!"

"*Yeah!*" came the battle cry as helmets were raised toward the exposed water pipes above them.

"*Are you ready?*" he asked.

"*Yeeaaahhh!*"

"*Then get out there!*"

The command was followed by the clattering and sliding of metal cleats on concrete as players jockeyed for position to be one of the first out the door. All except Alex, who really didn't mind bringing up the rear today.

Alex stood on the sideline, hopping from foot to foot and pulling the warming jacket tighter around his shoulders. The gentle autumn breeze had picked up some velocity since the start of the game, and the temperature had dropped suddenly. He never realized how cold a guy could get standing on the sidelines. He was used to playing, and when you played, even if the weather was ten below, you could manage to break a sweat. Now, his toes almost felt numb, and the game was only a little over a quarter old.

He alternated lifting his knees high to get the blood flowing as he watched the action out on the field. The game was close, and the teams were pretty evenly matched, but he could just feel Central starting to pull away. They had been gaining an extra yard or two on each offensive down, while taking a couple away from the Panthers. With only three minutes left in the first half, Central held a slim three-point advantage.

"Come on, guys," he whispered to himself. "Hang in there till halftime and then we'll get things rolling." It wasn't that the offense wasn't any good without him; it was just that their threats were limited. Without Alex, Richard was really the only pass receiver to worry about, so once he was double-teamed, the passing game was eliminated.

Central had always been known as a run stopper, and they were proving it again today. His eyes darted from the clock to the action on the field. The Montgomery defense was already showing signs of wear, and small wonder. They had been on the field twice as long.

"Just hold 'em one more time," Alex encouraged under his breath, "and then we'll get one more shot to put a few points up there on the board ourselves. … C'mon."

The defense must have heard him, for on fourth and two, they dug in and pulled the running back down, inches from the first down marker. The little crowd in the stands let out a cheer that blew down toward the defense with a gust of wind as they raised their tired arms in victory and jogged off the field, helmets in their hands, pants streaked with dirt and grass. Alex ran over and slapped a couple on the back.

"Way to go, Jimmy!" he said forcefully. "Way to stick it to 'em!"

Jimmy looked at him blankly, let out a contemptuous breath, and then turned away. Alex felt the cold of the day rush through his veins, and he swallowed hard. *So Coach's little speech had little effect,* he thought. *These guys hate me. They really do.*

Alex felt his breath come in short little bursts, and his body tensed up with energy. He watched the rest of the team gather around the heroic defense, intentionally and unintentionally ignoring him. He pulled his lips tight in determination. The second half would be different, he vowed. Just watch.

"What is Bauer thinking? Why doesn't he play that white kid? Kowalski? The kid's a natural. If he were out there, we wouldn't be scrapping for points; we'd be ten points ahead!"

Other murmurs of discontent followed the initial complaint.

"Heard he's not playing for disciplinary reasons," offered a second voice.

"Discipline?" countered the first. "Whad the kid do?"

"Skips practice … a couple of times a week from what my boy says," said a third.

"You're kidding," said the first. "Then why's he even still on the team?"

"Good question," said the third. "My boy Eric says it's causing a lot of hard feelings out there and that it's really affecting team morale."

"Bet it's 'cause the kid's white," piped in a fourth. "If it was any of our boys, I bet they'd be out on their butt. That's what I think." Some more grumbles of assent.

"I always thought Bauer's head was on pretty straight, but he's sure screwing up this team and their chances for a championship by playing favorites to one white boy. If that kid doesn't want to be out there, then cut him. It's as simple as that."

The discussion died down a little.

"Bauer's been coaching for over twenty years now, hasn't he?"

brought up the first. A series of nods and verbal assents. “That’s a long time to be coaching,” he continued. More assents. “Maybe too long,” he concluded.

The crowd came to a slow, uneasy silence and looked back out on the field where the weary Montgomery players were trudging toward the locker room for a well-needed halftime breather.

Martha pulled her coat up around her ears and hugged herself. What happened to that beautiful weather that had enticed her out? This weather change was making her football revival much less enjoyable than desired. That and the discontented talk floating about the stands, and the struggling players on the field. A gust of cold air shot through the stadium and chilled her ears. She pulled her collar up even higher.

Maybe she had been wrong to make or encourage (or whatever it was she had done) Alex to start his tutoring now. She looked down at the field as the players jogged off, noticing the obvious gap between the team and Alex. Not only had he lost some of his football, but his friends as well. And now Coach Bauer could be under fire by some of the disgruntled parents. Maybe, and she hated to think it, but just maybe it hadn’t been the right decision.

Amanda sat sullenly in her seat in the bleachers and watched the team leave the field. Most of the players were caked with mud and grass stains; it had been that kind of a game. But not Alex. Alex was jogging off the field in a pristine uniform. Not a speck of dirt. Not a smidgeon of grass stain.

She pursed her lips and stared after the last, vanishing player. Though she had bought Alex’s thin excuse for not playing last week, she wouldn’t this week. Something was definitely not right here, and she was going to get to the bottom of it.

Chapter 23

After caving in on his journalism job, Travis had no intention of returning home to wait out the five hours before meeting Danny for the sale. Saturdays his mother lounged around the house smoking cigarettes and swearing up a blue streak, and he had no desire to share the experience. Plus, he really didn't think he would have a problem filling the empty hours. After all, how may purposeless Saturdays had he wasted before?

But for some reason, today was different. That empty feeling that had been plaguing him all week seemed to be stalking him, and the cold, bitter Detroit wind that came with the brunt of autumn seemed to cut right through him.

Why is that? he wondered. Before, he had always been oblivious to it, immune to it, but not today. He lit a cigarette to try and warm himself, and then he glanced at his watch. One o'clock.

He swore under his breath. Why was time hanging so heavy on his hands today? He had managed to waste three hours, but he wasn't about to spend another two in the same state of boredom. Travis ran through his options. He could roam the streets, checking out the scene, find out who was doing what. He could go to the warehouse and hang out with some of the gang. Or he could drum up a little more business.

In the past, any or all would have been perfectly satisfying to him. Nothing he did really needed to have a purpose; it just needed to fill time. Now it all seemed so empty. He glanced at his watch again. Five after one.

This was driving him crazy. Maybe he should have stayed at the *Press* office. At least that would have given him something to do, but he knew it wouldn't fill the black, empty void that just seemed to be growing within him at a cancerous rate. He needed to get his mind off of this nothing and onto something.

"Reba," he said suddenly, and just the mention of her name, and the solidity that came with that family seemed to send a spurt of something through his body. Hope? Relief? He jammed his cold hands into his pants' pockets and headed with renewed purpose back to his neighborhood and the Washington home.

"Why, Travis," Mrs. Washington said with surprise. "This is a nice surprise. We haven't seen you around here for a while. Come in. How's your school year going?"

"Fine, thank you," he said politely and stepped into the neat, warm little apartment and immediately felt the rush of peace that always seemed to envelop him whenever he was here.

He looked around, hungrily taking everything in: the old and worn but clean and polished linoleum. The dust-free table with a bowl of apples and squash on it. The threadbare couch with the aged afghan that Mrs. Washington had knitted years ago, carefully folded over the back so as to hide the bare spots. He could smell furniture polish (lemon he was sure), but even more so he could smell something baking in the oven. He drew in a deep breath and closed his eyes, wanting to savor it and keep it all. Finally, he opened his eyes.

"Is Reba around?" he asked.

"She and Willie and Jake and their father went to the football game about an hour ago," Mrs. Washington replied. Travis's disappointment was tangible.

"Oh," was all he said, and he stood awkwardly in the middle of the room, not knowing what to do next. Despite her flurry of activity in the kitchen, Mrs. Washington watched him closely out of the corner of her eye. *He looks like a caged animal,* she thought and felt for the young man.

"I hope you're not too disappointed," she said, "and that you're not in too big of a hurry. I could use your help."

He seemed more than a bit relieved about staying, almost excited, she thought. But within seconds, he had managed to hide it. "No hurry," he said coolly. "What's up?"

"Two things," she answered. "I need a taste tester on this cake here … new recipe," she explained. "And more importantly, Jocelyn and Chris will be up in a minute, and if you could keep them occupied for about an hour till I get the last cake baked, I would be eternally grateful."

The thought of babysitting would normally have caused Travis's nerves to bristle and his stomach to revolt, but not today. There was something in this house he wanted to hang on to. Something he never wanted to let go of. At least not until three o'clock.

Travis found himself almost whistling as he strolled onto the Wayne State campus. He couldn't ever remember feeling this good, this light, this … well, almost free. The closest he had ever come to feeling this good was feeling nothing … when life just sort of slid by without any waves. And then there were the times when physically, he felt … well … felt pretty good, after the girls and all. Then there was the rush he got after surviving a raid or ambush, but that was all different. This feeling was something new.

"Happiness," he murmured and surprised himself and then grinned a little. *Yeah, that's what it is,* he thought. *This is what it feels like to be truly happy.*

His step picked up a little as he thought back on the two hours he had just spent with Mrs. Washington, Jocelyn, and Chris. Nothing exceptional had happened. Mrs. Washington had just talked in that soft, fluid voice of hers and soothed Travis into opening up and talking about himself, and then she listened, really listened.

He knew she was listening because she didn't just "mm hum" and nod, but she would interrupt him for clarification or ask questions. He had remembered thinking how lucky Reba was to have someone so interested in her. After all, if Mrs. Washington was this interested in *him*, then she *must* be even *more* interested in her own kids.

They talked and he tasted, and then Jocelyn woke up and demanded to be read to, and he obliged. At first he just read the words to *The Spider and the Fly*, but she would have none of that, and precociously turned the pages back to the beginning and vividly showed him how to enact the words. Then she turned back to him with hands on hips and head tilted and asked, "Okay?"

He couldn't help but laugh. "Okay," he agreed and then struggled through his inhibitions to get his body to "wiggle and tiggle and jiggle" when the spider did. Jocelyn coached him from the floor where she was going through all the motions herself. She made him read it four times and would have started on the fifth, but Mrs. Washington saved him.

"Enough," she insisted. "If Travis isn't tired of that spider by now, I certainly am. Go get your brother up."

Jocelyn readily obeyed, and in a minute came back dragging Chris, her arms under his arms and wrapped around his chest. She lifted him just high enough so that his dangling feet didn't scrape the floor. Now it was truck time, with Chris getting the dump truck, Travis the bulldozer, and Jocelyn the roller.

Again it was Jocelyn taking charge, dictating where the road should be built and supplying all the dirt (cotton balls) that would keep all three busy for days. By the time Travis had to leave, he swore they had laid five miles of cotton asphalt in that tiny apartment.

"You're late."

The voice startled Travis, and he realized that he hadn't been paying attention to where he was going but had ended up in the right spot anyway. He glanced at his watch and noticed Danny was right. He *was* late, and that was a first. He had never been late for a drop or sale in his career, and somehow he didn't mind one bit about being late for this one. In fact, he was a little irritated with the tone in Danny's voice. He erased the smile from his face and hid it deep in his soul. He began to feel the coldness of the wind under his skin again.

"Fifteen minutes is all," he said sharply. "You should learn to be patient."

But Danny wasn't patient, and Travis could see that. In fact, Danny wasn't even calm. He was fidgeting from side to side, his hands jammed into his jacket pocket and his eyes wild and frantic. For some reason, Travis shivered involuntarily.

He wanted to get this over with and get out of there. Danny Richards was bad news all over. The guy was dropping fast and hard and had no clue how to control it. Those guys were bad, the worst kind. He reached into his inside jacket pocket.

"Okay, give me the money and get out of here," he clipped, beginning to pull the baggie full of small pouches and needles, but he stopped when he didn't see Danny's hands move. He glared at him suspiciously.

"Where's your money?" he demanded.

Danny said nothing, just continued to shift from foot to foot and looked nervously about.

"I asked you, where's the money?" Travis spit again. Now the cold was cutting through him at a record pace. The peace was long gone.

Danny took one more nervous sweep of the scene and then confessed, "I don't have it."

Travis shoved the baggie back into his pocket, swore, and turned to leave. Danny put his hand on his arm to stop him, and Travis jerked it away.

"Keep your hands off," he warned, and Danny threw his hands up defensively. Travis straightened out his coat and again turned to leave.

"Hey, wait," Danny pleaded, but Travis was already walking. Danny ran him down. "Come on, listen to me."

Travis stopped and turned to face him, his face tight as stone, his eyes sparking even through the dark lenses. "What did you think? I'd give it to you for free?" he asked.

Danny shook his head. Travis turned away again. Danny started to reach for him and then thought better of it and pulled his hand back and ran in front of him instead, forcing Travis to stop.

"I—I just thought maybe you'd give it to me today and then let me pay you … Monday," he stammered.

Travis's mouth fell open for just a second and then it shut tight. "Oh, you did, did you?" he said very low and soft so that every hair on Danny's arms rose. "Well, you might as well get that lame idea out of your stupid little head right now because that will never—you hear me?—*never* happen."

"But I need it," Danny pleaded, and Travis's lips parted in a sinister grin.

"Then you'd better find the money to pay for it," he said in almost a whisper and turned to walk away again.

Danny felt like he would die or cry or something, not knowing what to do but knowing he absolutely had to do something.

"Then meet me here tomorrow," he finally shouted. "I'll have the money. I promise."

Travis stopped and looked at the frantic young man and slowly nodded. "Ten o'clock," he said, "and you'd better have it."

Chapter 24

Amanda Donahoe stood at the far end of the gym, the end closest to the school and furthest from the street, so that the football players, as they left, turned right, away from her, as they headed home. As each player emerged, her heart caught, thinking it might be Alex, yet praying it wasn't. She really didn't want to have to talk to him with the others around.

The sun had already dipped behind the building, causing the temperature to drop quickly. The wind had picked up even more speed, bringing some clouds with it and the smell of an early snow.

Amanda looked up at the sky and sniffed. *It could,* she thought. *It's snowed this early before.* Another two bodies emerged, and her eyes darted to them, and her heart beat faster. But neither had the broad, square shoulders of Alex.

She glanced at her watch. Four fifteen. The game had been over for more than an hour. Even if the coach had chewed them out for a half hour, they should all be showered and dressed by now, and she was sure she had counted over forty guys come out. Maybe she had missed him.

She slumped back against the side of the building and tried

to sort out what was going on here. Why Alex wasn't playing, and more than that, why the guys had all of a sudden and so obviously shunned him.

She glanced at her watch again. She would wait till four thirty and then go home. If he didn't come out by then, she had probably missed him.

Alex sat in front of his open locker and stared at nothing. He didn't know where he hurt worse: in his muscles, which had taken a brutal beating today from a pumped Central team; his ears, from Coach chewing them out not for getting beat but for losing, for playing divided, for giving it away; or in the very pit of his stomach from the realization that his world of football and friends was falling apart around him, and he didn't know what to do.

It was too late now to quit his tutorial—the damage was done. Central had beaten them; they now had two losses, and there was little chance of making up that ground to qualify as one of two teams for the play-offs let alone having a shot at the title. Madison would win, or Roosevelt, and Central, though they also had two losses, could take second because of their win over Montgomery in head to head. So quitting his tutorial, though he felt like flushing it right down the toilet, wouldn't fix anything.

Alex felt like slugging Richard for being such a fair-weather friend. Man, where was he now when all the other guys were ganging up on him? Didn't a true friend stick by a guy, stand up for him? "Thanks a lot, Richard," he said to the locker. Alex kept shoveling dirt on top of the fact that he had never confided in Richard, never trusted him enough to let him know what was going on. He denied the idea that he hadn't been a friend first by trusting Richard. No, it was all Richard's fault.

He was even mad at Coach Bower for his stupid rules. Surely his case would have been an exception, really. The guys would have understood. They wouldn't have had a problem with him missing a couple of days.

Alex heard the locker room door squeak open as yet another player left and then the room fell silent … so silent that Alex's ears rang, and he could hear the drip of a shower that hadn't been turned off completely. The *drip, drip, plop* of the water lulled him further into his pensiveness. *How can a guy's life get so screwed up in only a few weeks?*

He winced. It wasn't fair. *God* wasn't fair. It was all *his* fault really. That's what comes from praying. You're whole life spirals out of control faster than you can spit. He should never have done it. He was doing okay; he was still making it through his classes. He could have hung on.

But then another thought struck him. No, Mrs. Richards had caught on. She wouldn't let him slide. It was all *her* fault. Why did she have to be so pushy? If she could have just kept her big nose out of everything, then his life still would have been pretty smooth. Yeah, it was all her fault, 'cause hadn't she messed Reba's life up too? Yeah, *she's* the one.

Having found the perfect villain to lay his blame on, Alex stood up, slammed his locker shut, pulled on his coat, and headed for the door. His heels echoed as he strode through the empty locker room. The damp heat of forty-five showers only added to the steam rising in his own body.

Everybody had messed up his life, and, man, was he mad!

Lennis Bauer sat in his office with the door slightly open, just waiting for the sound of that last pair of shoes going out the door. *Forty-five,* he thought. *They're all gone.* He stared at the wall in front of him that housed pictures of various championship teams, but he saw none of them. He was only seeing his team that was on the field today, the team that scratched and clawed and played their heart out the first half, and the team that died the second. Died not from exhaustion but from suicide. Jealousy, pride, revenge, pettiness, anger. They were all the weapons of choice today, and they were all aimed at themselves and very effective.

He really hadn't had much to say after the game. He had said it all before the game and thought it had made a difference by the way they played that first half, but then the second half … when Alex went in …

He let out a long sigh. What was he going to do? They shouldn't have lost to Central, and he knew exactly where the fingers were going to start pointing … at him. The administration would be a little perturbed Monday morning, particularly the principal, Bob Smith, a former football coach himself, who would give him a little condescending stare as if to say, "What do you think you're doing?"

But then the phone calls would start coming from the parents, wondering what Bauer "thinks he's doing out there." They would begin second-guessing and sideline coaching and accusing him of playing favorites or of not being tough enough and by being so lax, causing division in his team. Yeah, he knew how it went.

And then after about five of those phone calls, Big Bob Smith would say, "I'll take care of it," and call Lennis into his office and ask him what he *was* doing.

Then what would he say? He could clear it all up by telling the truth, by explaining about Alex's illiteracy and how he wanted to read, and should read, and shouldn't be penalized for learning to read. After all, isn't that what school was for? … But that would be to save his own skin, and he had promised to keep it a secret, and so he would. But boy-oh-boy, what a costly secret.

Amanda glanced at her watch. A quarter to five. She released a deep breath and admitted defeat. Despite the extra fifteen minutes, there was no Alex, and it was getting pretty dark. She needed to be going.

With her arms still crossed in front of her for warmth, she pushed herself away from the building and started toward the street when she heard the locker room door open once more, and both she and her heart stopped.

The unexpected blast of cold air that hit Alex as he opened the door just blew all the steam right out of him and left him feeling cold and empty and very much alone. He stood in the doorway, hidden from the world by the brick wall that offered the locker room a little privacy, and stared at the dark ground in front of him. It really wasn't much help having all these people to blame. It didn't fix anything. He headed out into the darkness, his head bent toward the ground, his mind miles away and deep in thought. What was he going to do?

"Better watch where you're going there, stud."

Alex's head popped up just before he ran into that same hip-high cement post that had almost emasculated him earlier in the year. His heart both quickened and fell when he heard the familiar voice. He needed a friend right now, and Amanda was twice as good as a friend, but at the same time, a part of him didn't want her there. She was a danger. She was perceptive and bright and persistent, and in his present state, he didn't feel like trying to spar with her.

Initially, Amanda had every intention of going straight for the jugular, directly after the truth with no gloves on. That was how she approached most situations, by being assertive. But whether it was standing for almost two hours in the chilling wind or seeing Alex's utter dejection as he walked out of that locker room a half hour after his teammates, or both, something inside her told her to back off. Now was not the time.

"Rough game," she said and fell in next to him.

He looked up at her briefly and tried to smile, but he could not get rid of the pain fast enough, and before he dropped his eyes and mumbled a response, she caught it, and Alex knew she had caught it, and he felt himself shudder slightly at his vulnerability. Then all his defenses went up.

They walked along silently for a while, Alex staring at the ground, waiting, just waiting for the first question, alert as a cat though his body and mind wanted to settle into a comfortable numbness. Amanda felt just as uncomfortable. For a person who always knew her mind and spoke it, she was at a total loss, not knowing which tact to try, not even knowing if she should simply be quiet. But somehow that didn't seem like it would solve anything. That would mean thirty minutes of uncomfortable silence.

"Where does that put you guys?" she finally asked, and Alex let out a long, pent-up breath, which to Amanda sounded like it rose out of anger, and she regretted asking the question. But for Alex, it was a breath of relief. *We're on statistics,* he thought. And though he really didn't want to talk about that either, at least it was safer ground.

"Out of it, basically," he said simply. "Unless a miracle happens … which is highly unlikely," he added, asserting his newfound anger at God.

"Now don't count yourselves out," Amanda protested, seeing an avenue where she could be supportive. "Central could lose. They have to play Commerce yet, and you guys barely beat Commerce, so they could knock Central off, and that would be three losses for them, and you have Washington next, and they're a nothing and …" She was babbling and she knew it. She was nervous and trying to fill up emptiness with air and … and … and Alex interrupted her.

"And then we play Roosevelt who has beaten everyone," he countered.

"They haven't played Madison," she countered right back.

"But if they win, then Madison's in second, and if they lose, they're in second," Alex retaliated.

"But if they lose to Madison and then you beat them, then your records are the same."

It was all beginning to sound so complicated, and their voices intensified.

"I don't think it will happen!" Alex yelled in exasperation.

"It would if Coach Bauer would play you the whole game!" she shouted back. It was out before she could pull it back in. She hadn't meant to say it, really, but out it had come.

Alex turned to her in anger. "Well, I wouldn't hold your breath!" he blurted.

"Well, why not?" she yelled. "What's going on anyway?"

Alex fumed and fumbled over something to say but couldn't come up with an adequate answer. "You—you just wouldn't understand," he said forcefully and then turned and walked away, leaving her staring after him in the growing darkness.

"More potatoes, Reba?" her mother asked. Reba shook her head. She wasn't very hungry tonight. Her mother put the bowl back down and regarded her daughter quietly. "How was the game?" she asked. "Did you enjoy yourself?"

Reba nodded halfheartedly. "It was okay … we lost."

"Oh, I see," said Mrs. Washington and let the conversation drop, figuring she had a hold on what was troubling her daughter. Though she had never known her to be so concerned with football before, she did know that Reba was competitive, and these high schoolers could get pretty involved with their school teams.

But Reba's thoughts were far from the status of the team. She was thinking about Alex. Even though she didn't know a lot about football, she could tell he was good, really good. But when he finally did get to play, it was obvious even to her that though they threw the ball to him and blocked for him, the rest of the team wasn't behind him.

They didn't congratulate him after a fine catch. They didn't give him any high fives or pats on the back. And loving the theater the way she did, she had learned to read body language, and it was obvious when they huddled up, that Alex was the odd man out.

Alex is paying the price, too, she thought sadly, realizing that their twice weekly meetings were more costly than either had imagined.

"What do you mean he didn't show up?" Martha questioned.

"I mean just that," Greg said over the telephone line. "Travis Johnson did not show up for his interview." Martha let out an exasperated sigh.

"Hey, don't worry about it," Greg said. "I didn't call to complain. It's really no skin off my nose. I just thought you'd like to know."

Martha tried to calm herself. "Yes, I did want to know," she replied. "Thank you for calling, Greg. I'm really sorry this happened. I know you had put in some time preparing something for him."

"Hey, like I said," Greg said cheerily. "Don't worry about it. I'll just keep it all together for the next time."

If there'll be a next time, she said silently.

"Well, thanks again for calling," Martha said, "and again, I'm sorry."

"No problem. We'll see you." And the line went dead.

Martha hung up the phone slowly, her jaw tight as she came to a slow boil. Irresponsibility. That's all it was. And because of this fifteen … sixteen-year-old kid, she had been hung out to dry with one of her professional associates, and she didn't like the feel of that. And to top it off, it was Saturday night, and she couldn't remedy the situation until Monday, which meant she had the rest of the weekend to stew about it.

No, she didn't like this one bit. She was used to being in control of the situation, and this was the second time today that things had kind of slipped through her grasp. It wasn't going to make for a restful weekend.

Alex sat alone in his room, staring bullets at the wall and taking quick, controlled breaths. He was mad. Mad at everyone and everything. First, Richard and the rest of the team, then Amanda. His whole gut twisted inside at the thought of her. Man, why did she have to push? Why couldn't she be like those dumb girls who just ogled you if you put on a uniform? Why did she have to be so stinkin' knowledgeable about the game?

He swore under his breath and felt himself redden at his use of profanity. He used to never cuss. Now it was turning into an almost everyday occurrence. He let out a low breath. Well, it wasn't *his* fault. It was everybody ganging up on him. Even his parents, asking all sorts of probing questions, making eating much less enjoyable and dinner almost impossible.

"But why isn't Coach Bauer playing you as much as before?" his father had asked. "Are you in some sort of discipline trouble or did you get beat out of your starting position?"

"Yeah, that's it, Dad," he had lied out of anger. Why couldn't everyone just leave him alone? "I got beat, and I'd really rather not talk about it." With that, he shoved his chair back and walked out of the room, not even asking to be excused, while his parents, in shocked surprise, watched him disappear.

Now he sat in his room, jaw tightly set, eyes still shooting bullets at the wall, and his breathing still coming in short, angry spurts. Out of the corner of his eye, he caught something shiny lying on his bed and turned to see what it was. The laminated flash cards Reba had made him had slid out of the neck of his backpack and now lay half exposed. He stared at them a moment, his eyes hardening and his breathing growing faster.

Then he stood up and walked deliberately toward them. He

stood for a minute over his bed and gazed at the pile of juvenile pictures of a house, road, cat … he slid the cat to the side … jar, girl, vase. He just stared and breathed and then finally reached down and carefully shuffled the cards into one neat little pile, then picked them all up, and straightened them out in his hand. In the next moment, he heaved the entire lot of them against the far wall.

Amanda could have kicked herself all the way home from Montgomery High School. Why had she said that? Asked that? When would she just learn to keep her mouth shut? What was that verse? "Be quick to hear, slow to speak, slow to anger," something like that.

She had always been quick to speak her mind, and more times than not, it had gotten her into an awkward situation. Well, this time it wasn't only awkward but painful. She shouldn't have pushed. Alex was obviously hurting, and all she had managed to do was stick another knife in the wound.

Amanda chastised herself in the privacy of her dark room yet still couldn't get rid of that sense of disquietude that had plagued her all day. As much as she blamed herself for what had happened, she still couldn't shake the feeling that Alex was hiding something … and it was something that was just eating away at him. What was that verse in the Psalms? She quickly went over and picked up her Bible and shuffled through the pages until she found the psalm and then skimmed through the underlined verses until she found it: Psalm 32:3–4.

> When I kept silent about my sin, my body wasted away
> Through my groaning all day long.
> For day and night Thy hand was heavy upon me;
> My vitality was drained away as with the fever-heat of summer.

She nodded to herself. That was Alex. He definitely wasn't playing all his cards, and it was eating him up. Well, she wouldn't push again, but she would be there for him when he might finally want to talk.

Travis lay on his bed and listened to the loud ticking of his clock and cursed Danny Richards. After his afternoon, he had been feeling pretty good and then that idiot had to ruin it all. Had Danny just had the money, the sale would have taken only a minute, and he wouldn't have even had to think about it. But he *didn't* have the money, and Travis *did* have to think about it. In fact, he had to get mad, confront, lay it on the line, make the guy face reality. And that just burst the happiness bubble, letting that empty, hollow, and cold feeling suck all that Washington warmth right out of his being.

He stared angrily in the darkness, trying to ignore the ticking that seemed to grow louder and louder. He cursed at it and raised up to see what time it was. Midnight. And he wasn't even close to going to sleep. Travis heard a high giggle that he recognized as his mother and then a lower laugh that he didn't recognize at all, and he felt his stomach turn. Now he cursed *her* and wished the clock would tick louder.

Chapter 25

"What do you mean you're not going to church?"

Martha stared at her son incredulously. This was the first time in nineteen years that he refused to join his parents in attending church Sunday morning, and it only served to further shake the family foundation that was already beginning to be stressed.

"It's not that I'm not," he answered, licking his lips and trying hard to hold her gaze. "It's just that I can't. I have so much studying to do, and I promised Carl that I'd meet him at the library."

Martha stared back, trying hard both to understand and to think of something to say.

"I thought the library didn't open till twelve on Sundays," Graydon stated quietly.

Danny almost jerked, but he worked hard to keep a calm profile. "It doesn't," he confessed," but we were going to meet in the Union around ten and just study together until it opened."

Now it was Graydon's turn to stare, and he looked hard at his son, tearing away the pieces of flesh until Danny felt like all his lies were laid open for everyone to see.

"It's when you are the most stressed and have the least time that you really need to spend time with and rely on the Lord," Martha said, having finally composed herself and formulated an argument. "You know the saying that you have so much on your plate that 'you haven't got time *not* to pray.'"

Danny smiled. "I know, Mom," he replied quietly, "and you can bet I'll be praying. It's just that I have one more midterm that I really need to pass, and with a good grade."

Martha sighed in resignation. Danny was a big boy now, an adult actually, and as such welcome to make his own decisions. *Train up a child in the way he should go, and he will not depart from it,* she thought and then smiled at her son. "Study hard then, and we'll see you when we get back this afternoon."

"Thanks, Mom," he said, and for the first time that morning he felt his heart return to a normal rhythm. "See you later, Dad." He looked up into the eyes of his father, only to be met with that same hard stare of earlier, and he felt his blood congeal in his veins.

"Let's go, hon," Graydon said softly to Martha as he turned his back to his son and guided her toward the door.

Though Danny couldn't shake the chill induced by his father's icy stare, he had no time to waste thinking about it. It was already nine o'clock, and he had to get sixty dollars by ten. He pulled out his cell phone, punched in some numbers, and listened to the ringing beginning on the other end.

"Come on, come on, be there," he hissed into the phone, tapping his foot impatiently. After the fifth ring, the voice message clicked in. "*Nooo!*" he yelled and was just beginning to hang up when he heard a garbled voice come on over the recorded message.

"Hello?"

"Mike?" Danny yelled over the message that was still playing. "This is Danny Richards."

"Danny, hold on. You called the house phone. Let me call you back on my cell."

Danny hung up and silently cursed himself while breathing a sigh of relief that at least Mike had answered and not his parents. In a second, his cell rang and he answered.

"Sorry about that, Dan my man, but I was in bed. What are you doing calling so early?"

"It's nine," Danny replied, and Mike laughed.

"Nine on a Sunday morning after a great Saturday night," he said. "So what's so important?"

Danny tried to sound both calm and apologetic and issued a self-effacing laugh. "Oh, I just need to get out of a little hot water is all," he said.

"Yeah, like what?"

"Like forgetting my parents' twenty-fifth wedding anniversary," he lied and waited.

"You're kidding," Mike said. "Man, you're an ingrate, you know that? When was it?"

"It's today."

"Well, say, that's not too bad. Then you really haven't forgotten it—yet. You're still kicking. So why are you calling me?"

"I'm dead broke, man," he confessed, "and I was wondering if you could spare me a little cash so that I might take them out to a nice dinner and then buy a little something silver. That is what twenty-fifths are, isn't it?"

"Heck if I know," Mike answered, "but it sounds good to me. How much do you need?"

Danny had already thought this part through. If Mike bought in early like he had, he was going to up the price. That would keep him in heroin for a couple of weeks longer. "About one-fifty."

A low whistle carried back across the line. "Where are you planning to take them, *Chez Cherie*?"

Danny held his breath but didn't back down. "No, just someplace nice. I thought about Rex's."

"Mmmm, nice spot," Mike said. "Yea, I guess I can lend you the money. When do you want it?"

Danny didn't want to sound too anxious. "I'm on my way out now, how about if I just stop by?"

"Now? I don't have that much cash here. I have to go to the Ready Teller at the bank. How about one?" Danny felt the blood start pounding in his brain. Now what?

"I really need it now," he insisted. "I called Rex's and they said they're booked, but if I show up around ten with a cash deposit, they'll hold a table for me." He winced. It was the most feeble, see-through, unbelievable story ever.

"I've never heard of a place doing that," Mike said, and Danny felt his heart sink. He was dead. "But, hey, what do I know. I don't get to Rex's too often. ... All right, bud. You better realize that I don't get my rear out of bed this early for just anybody. You owe me one. Meet me at the Commerce Bank on the corner of 58th and Mistletoe in about half an hour, and I'll save your bacon."

He laughed and Danny joined in, albeit a bit weakly. He had managed to avert another disaster. He would have his drugs for another couple of weeks ... but then what?

Alex stared at his waffle while his father shook his head sadly over the Sunday morning sports page.

"Did you see this, Alex?" he asked, folding the paper so that only the offending article was visible. "Why does the news media insist on riding high school coaches so hard?"

Alex stared at the muddle of large letters on the quarter page in front of him. He noticed a *C* and felt his heart lift. It was the first letter he had ever really recognized, and he immediately thought of "cat" and that hard sound. *What word would begin like cat?* he thought. Central High eluded him on the page, just as they had on the field yesterday.

"Well?" his father insisted, "is that a crime or not?"

Alex just shook his head, attempting to look like he was in full sympathy with his father and took the ambiguous approach. "I can't believe it," he muttered.

"Why? What does it say?' his mother asked from the waffle iron, and Alex was thankful for her interest. This way, he, too, would know what was going on. "Read it to me."

Mr. Kowalski took back the paper and slapped it firm. "It says and I quote," he said in a deep voice, "'The cool, collected, and respected judgment of Coach Lennis Bauer seems to be a thing of the past. Though his team scraped and hustled like his teams of old, the leadership from the sideline seemed to be missing.

"'The decision not to play young Alex Kowalski, who at the beginning of the year was looking very seasoned and like a potential star, has more than a few sportswriters and fans perplexed. If it's discipline, Coach, then take care of it. If not, then let us know what you're doing.' … Not exactly unbiased, objective reporting, is it?" he concluded and then laid the paper down and looked at his son.

"Why isn't he playing you more, Alex?" he asked. "Did that Marshall kid really beat you? You looked better yesterday." The waffle lodged deep in his throat, and Alex grabbed for his glass of milk to help wash it down.

"Don't know, Dad," he said simply, never letting his eyes waver from his waffle.

"You're not a troublemaker, are you? It's not a discipline problem like the paper said, is it?" his mother asked worriedly.

"No, Mom," he said, grateful that he really didn't have to tell an all-out lie. "I haven't been causing trouble."

His father picked the paper back up, looked again at the article, reading the rest with his head slightly tilted back so as to get full use of his bifocals, and then finally set the paper down and removed his glasses.

"So you think Coach Bauer is being fair?" he asked suddenly. "Do you feel confident that he knows what he's doing? You haven't lost faith in him, have you, son?"

Alex felt his stomach turn inside out. *Was this just the beginning? Was Coach going to be taking a lot of heat because of him?*

"No, Dad," he answered honestly. "I haven't." But at the same time, he thought he heard the creaking of more beams splintering in his world that was already falling apart piece by piece.

The sunlight streaming through the curtainless kitchen window was the only bright spot in Travis Johnson's morning. He hadn't slept well at all. Danny Richards had taken care of that yesterday. He had thought he could forget it all by playing the gang role last night, so he had surrounded himself with the alcohol and dope and girls and gang members that came with the territory, but he only felt himself feeling more and more alone.

With as many people as there were crammed into that warehouse, and with as much stuff as was lying around, and with as loud as the music was playing, a guy would think that he wouldn't have room to think about anything else or feel lonely. But that was not the case. Never had he felt so isolated and … he hated to admit it … scared. And what scared him most was that he didn't know what he was afraid of. All he knew was there was a growing hollowness inside him and an ever increasing vacuum surrounding him, and he couldn't account for either.

Yesterday at the Washingtons, all that emptiness seemed to be filled, by what he had no idea, but it had been gone and he had felt good, and happy, and … and something. But that was yesterday, and as the ancient Beatles' song said, "yesterday's gone."

Travis reached down and opened the door to the end table and pulled out the huge Bible. It was covered with its usual thin layer of dust. Both his writings and his money were hidden within the pages of the book. He had no intention of looking at his writings. It had been weeks since he had even attempted anything.

No, today would be a money counting day. He sat still for a

moment and listened to the sounds of the house. Nothing. He listened closer. Only a slight snoring from his mother's room. That would go on for another couple of hours. He turned an ear toward his brothers' and sister's rooms. No sounds. All was safe.

He let the Bible fall open at will and was greeted by a crisp one-hundred-dollar bill. He smiled. Yeah, this was better. Then his eye caught a word on the page beneath it and as much as he willed himself not to read, his eyes wouldn't let go.

> He stretches out the north over empty space,
> And hangs the earth on nothing.

He felt a panic. Then he turned again and this time the money was forgotten. All he could see were the words on the page.

> For what does it profit a man to gain the whole world,
> And forfeit his soul?

The room was so tight it was suffocating him, yet too large to give him any security. Travis slammed the Bible shut and shoved it back in the end table. The noise caused the snoring to skip a beat, and a groan erupted from his brothers' room. For once in his life, he was grateful for both. It meant he wasn't alone.

"So do you have the money?"

"Yeah."

"Give it."

Danny handed Travis the three bills, which Travis glanced at briefly and then stuffed into his pocket. Then he pulled out the baggie containing the needles and heroin and almost threw it at him before turning to leave. The buy had been completed. He wanted out of here as fast as possible but not without a final word.

Danny watched and felt an unaccustomed fear.

"If you *ever* come without money again, you can find yourself another nanny," Travis said sharply, and with that, he turned on his heel and strutted away. Danny watched him leave. He had no reason to doubt his word. The remaining ninety dollars would get him through a few weeks, but then what?

He swallowed. Like everything else, he didn't want to think about that just now. He wanted to escape. He glanced at his watch. He needed a fix now, but where? He couldn't go home because he told his parents he'd be here. He looked around frantically. Maybe there was someplace close where he could find a little privacy. He'd look.

Alex had merely gone through the motions of the service: standing, singing, praying, and now as the pastor began his sermon, he let his mind wander a million miles away. *What happened to all the good that was to come out of this sacrifice? Where were the benefits?* he silently complained. It was amazing how something that had been so highly touted a few weeks ago could end up destroying so many lives in so short a time.

First, Reba's play chances, which he still felt bad about, then his football, then his relationship with Amanda—whatever it was before this whole thing started—then Coach's reputation. And add to all that all the lying and deceiving he had had to do. He shook his head. How did it go so wrong, so fast?

Alex vaguely heard the pastor mention a passage in Proverbs.

> Pride goes before destruction.
> And a haughty spirit before stumbling. (Proverbs 16:18)

He felt a jolt of guilt rock his body, and he swallowed hard. Why did the verse bother him? His problem wasn't pride—he wasn't being proud or haughty. In fact, if anything he was being pretty downright humble, giving up football and allowing God to make an all-out mess of him just for the chance to learn to read. And really, that's all it was—a chance. After a stinking week of those flash cards, he hadn't seen much improvement.

As much as he didn't want to, he listened to the pastor as he moved to the next proverb.

> Before destruction the heart of man is haughty,
> But humility goes before honor. (Proverbs 18:12)
>
> The reward of humility and the fear of the Lord
> Are riches, honor and life. (Proverbs 22:4)

Alex wanted to scream that it wasn't his pride that was causing all of these miserable things to happen, but he couldn't even convince himself. He didn't want anyone to know he couldn't read. He didn't want people to think he was stupid. He didn't want people looking down on him or judging him. And so his *pride* had sworn himself and others to secrecy. Now he had one more burden to add to his misery.

Suddenly, another verse rose out of the reservoir of his memory.

> When I kept silent about my sin, my body wasted away
> Through my groaning all day long.
> For day and night Thy hand was heavy upon me;
> My vitality was drained away as with the fever-heat
> of summer. (Psalm 32:3–4)

He had no idea why or how it had come to his mind, but with as much conviction as it brought to his heart, it brought an equal amount of peace to his soul.

Amanda sat quietly in the church pew with her family and barely listened to the minister's sermon. Her mind was still on Alex. She had decided she wasn't going to push, but she didn't want to do nothing either.

What does that leave me? she wondered and almost as quickly the Holy Spirit answered: *Pray.*

She chewed on the thought while the word flowed past her. She had never been much of a prayer warrior. It just seemed too passive. She would much rather *do* something, get her hands dirty, but look where that got her yesterday. She had alienated Alex, the first boy she had ever really liked, and all because he was keeping something from her, and she didn't like it.

Yeah, but what do I pray for? she argued.

For Alex, came the answer just as quickly.

But about what?

Just pray for Alex.

She released a long, slow breath.

All right, you win, she surrendered. *I'll just pray for Alex and let you take care of the particulars.*

She felt funny, awkward. In the past, her prayers had been hurried lists of wants, dashed off on her way to school before she met the demands of the day. And all of those she had pretty much had a handle on to begin with anyway. It was more like just asking God to bless what she had already planned.

This was different. This was going to be all God and very little of Amanda. Her part would come from the sideline. Praying, watching, and waiting—with no timetable. This was definitely not her modus operandi. She let out another low sigh. She didn't like it, but she would do it—simply because there didn't seem to be any other course of action.

Lord, she began and then stopped. Now what? *Lord,* she began again. *I turn Alex over to you. Something is dreadfully wrong, and I just lost whatever relationship I had with him. Take care of him and let him know that he can trust me.*

Was that last part selfish or selfless? She wasn't quite sure, but at least it was the truth. Next time she would be there—not to talk but just to listen.

She smiled ironically. *I wonder whose prayer request was just answered by* that *vow?*

"Martha! Graydon! So good to see you two. It's been ages!" Beatrice Carmichael waved her handkerchief and waddled as quickly as she could toward the two. "Where have you been keeping yourselves?"

Martha and Graydon looked at each other knowingly and smiled.

"We've been here every Sunday," Martha said, smiling. "It's you who has been missing."

"Oh, I know," Beatrice admitted, shaking her head and twisting her handkerchief. "I have just been *so* busy, you wouldn't believe it. Two weddings … a funeral … then my brother came up for a weekend, and you know he doesn't go to church, so I felt obligated to stay home with him … I haven't seen him in five years, he's been out in California, you know …"

Martha and Graydon looked at each other again; this time their smiles were a little more strained. Beatrice hadn't come up for air yet, and probably wouldn't for a good ten minutes if they didn't find an escape. Graydon cleared his throat loud enough to cause Beatrice to pause to look at him, and Martha took advantage of the respite and jumped in.

"I'm afraid we'll have to catch up another time," she said. "Danny's studying, and we'd really like to spend a little time with him. He's just been so busy himself with college and all."

The subject of Danny made Beatrice's eyes glow. "I saw him the other day," she said. "At the bank. Called for him, but I guess he didn't hear me or was in a hurry or something because he just hustled out the door."

"When was this?" Graydon asked, an unaccustomed iciness in his voice that caused Martha to glance up at him abruptly.

"Oh, a week, two weeks ago?" Beatrice said. "Somewhere in that time frame."

Graydon's lips pulled into a tight line, and his eyes grew hard. Martha felt her heart speed up.

"Are you sure it was Danny?" she asked. "After all, you did say he was hurrying out." She prayed Beatrice was mistaken. She didn't like the look on Graydon's face and all it might mean.

"No, no, no," Beatrice said smiling, shaking her head and hands. "It was Danny, I know, because he was wearing that nice jacket you and Graydon gave him for graduation. You know, that leather one."

Martha felt her heart sicken. But why? What was wrong with her son being at the bank?

"Well, he must have been putting some money in," she said lightly, but remembered all the pleas for money in the past month, so that really didn't seem too likely.

"I don't think so," Beatrice countered. "I think he was putting money into his wallet, but I really wasn't in a position to see," she added smiling, her eyes almost hidden behind folds of skin around her eyes.

Martha felt Graydon's grip tighten on her elbow. "Well, you'll have to excuse us," she said lamely. "We really do need to be going." And she allowed herself to be led away.

"Well, you tell that handsome boy of yours that I wish he'd say hello next time," Beatrice said.

"You can bet on that," Graydon clipped, and Martha felt a most ominous foreboding. This was *definitely* not going to be a good end to the weekend.

Chapter 26

Martha drove through the early morning deserted streets in a daze. For the first time in her life, she approached work with a sickening feeling, like a pit hung heavy somewhere within. It was hard to determine exactly where, but then that really wasn't important. The effect was the same. It weighted her down, made her feel leaden. And it had nothing to do with what lay ahead of her at school. It had everything to do with what had happened yesterday afternoon. She subconsciously stopped at the signal and waited for it to turn green, her eyes vacantly focused on nothing, just glazed and staring straight ahead.

Graydon had been livid when they returned home from church. He rapidly paced up and down the living room floor until she thought he was going to wear out a strip of carpet. She tried to settle him down, but he wouldn't be appeased. He wouldn't even answer her. He was locked in his own thoughts.

Every few minutes he would head toward the hall, and once even got as far as Danny's door, but each time he would stop himself and come back to the living room, fuming more than before. By the time Danny returned home, Graydon's anger had risen to a slow boil. Danny stepped into it unaware.

"Where have you been?" The words lashed out the minute Danny closed the front door.

"What?"

"I said, where have you been?"

Danny looked at his father like he was crazy. "At the library, studying, where I said I'd be."

"Can you prove it?"

"Whaaaatt?"

"Can you prove it?" Graydon repeated, his volume rising.

Now Danny was beginning to get mad. Having been ambushed and pushed into a corner for no apparent reason, he came back the only way he felt he could and keep his secret—by taking the offensive.

"Why should I have to prove it? Since when do I have to account for every minute of my life? I thought I was an adult now."

"Not as long as you're under this roof, you're not," Graydon threw back. It was the age-old parental adage, and Danny was offended.

"Then maybe I should just find another roof to live under," he said and moved to walk past his father.

"I'm not through with you yet," Graydon yelled.

"Yeah? Well, I've had about enough of you," Danny yelled back. "Why am I being given the third degree here? All I did was walk in the door!"

Martha had been watching in horror as the two faced off against each other, and she tried to think of something to do. They had never fought before. Graydon was Danny's hero, and Danny, Graydon's cherished son. Where had all this hostility come from? And when did it start? Judging by Graydon's anger, it was apparent that it had been building for some time, that the pent-up emotions were using this opportunity to release themselves.

And Danny? Since when did he become so belligerent? She had *never* heard him talk to his father this way. Worse yet, with whom did she side? She looked at the two men in her life as they faced off and thought she saw Graydon waver slightly.

"We saw Mrs. Carmichael at church this morning," he said simply. Once it was said, it really didn't seem to be much of a thread to hang their son on.

Martha looked at Danny and thought—had he balked? Blanched? She looked again and decided not.

"What does that have to do with anything?" he asked cautiously.

"She said you were at the bank a couple of weeks ago." Another cautious pause? No, maybe not.

"So?"

"She said you were withdrawing money."

Danny let out a laugh of disbelief. "She didn't even wait on me. How would she know what I was doing? Man, all that lady is is a busybody and a gossip."

Now Graydon looked like he had bitten off too much. That maybe a trip to the bank *wasn't* worth all that he was thinking.

"Then what *were* you doing there?" he asked, hoping to salvage a little face.

"I was cashing a check."

"Where'd you get the check?"

Danny let out a loud breath of impatience. "I work at a computer store, remember?" Now Martha was sure she saw Graydon turn pale. He licked his lips.

"She said you were putting cash in your wallet," he continued weakly.

"Yeah, that's true," Danny said and felt his advantage strengthening. "I thought I'd keep a little out for spending money. I've had to come to you for books already. I really didn't want to hit you up for petty cash."

Now Graydon looked like he had been hit in the stomach. He stood there staring at his son and feeling the security of his position slipping. Danny sensed it too.

"Anything else I can answer for you?" Danny asked sarcastically. "I don't know what you *think* I've been doing, but you're welcome to search me, my room, my bag."

It was a bold move, and he knew it would only serve to make

his dad feel worse. He had been raised in an atmosphere of trust and knew his parents well. They wouldn't search.

His father stood and stared at him evenly, watching, looking for a small crack in Danny's armor. He could have been wrong. Every instinct in his body said "search," but he knew if he came up empty-handed, he would only look more the fool.

"That won't be necessary," Graydon said in an even voice, and wanted to add the word *yet*, but held his tongue.

Danny stifled his own smirk of victory. "Then is it okay if I go get a bit more studying done before dinner?" he asked with more energy than he had expressed in weeks. Graydon didn't answer.

"Sure, hon, you go ahead," Martha finally said, nervous from the vacuous silence.

Danny smiled and waved in victory, then disappeared down the hall with Graydon's eyes still on his back.

Now, as she pulled her car into the Montgomery High School parking lot, Martha shivered involuntarily. She came to a stop and turned off the motor, but continued to stare straight ahead.

True, Graydon's suspicions proved unfounded, but that did little to alleviate the tension that had suddenly emerged in their household. Danny had been more friendly and talkative than he had been in weeks, but this only served to push Graydon into deeper silence. When they were finally alone in bed later that night, she moved toward him, hoping to get him to open up, but he said nothing, and she could feel his body tighten next to her.

She sighed and brought herself back to the present. Well, she couldn't worry about it now. She had a full day of classes to teach and a play to get ready. Like Scarlet O'Hara from *Gone with the Wind*, she would just have to think about that tomorrow.

In the early morning, Danny rechecked his room to make sure there was no evidence at all of heroin or drugs, loose cash or failing grades.

Yesterday had been too close of a call, and had his father chosen to search him or his room, the teaspoons of heroin would have been there for the finding.

From now on, his room was out. He would have to find somewhere else to shoot up if he hoped to keep his extracurricular activities a secret.

Travis stared at the Patrick Nagel print with little interest. He was supposed to be in the process of copying it: stretching his canvas, mixing his colors, all that. He knew he could do it. Copying Nagel didn't require any shading. It was all straight lines, and he had always kind of liked the style. Two weeks ago he probably would have jumped at the chance to hang one—even a copy—up in his room. But that was two weeks ago. Today he couldn't see the importance of it. In fact, he couldn't see the importance in anything.

Why was he here at school? What did it matter anyway? Everyone was going to die and then what? What did it matter what you knew, what you studied, what you did with your life? It was all for absolutely nothing. What was it he had read in the Bible that morning?

He had only snuck a peak before he left to see if the same foreboding verses would surface to haunt him, and sure enough, one had. The Bible had opened up to a page that didn't even have money in it, and the verse that stared him back in the face was hard to forget: "'Meaningless! Meaningless!' says the Teacher. 'Utterly meaningless. Everything is meaningless.'"

"Then why try?" muttered Travis under his breath. "Why *live* for that matter?"

Creeeeaaaaakkkkk!

For the third time that period, the door to Mrs. Richards's first period class opened and a student aide from the office entered.

Martha stopped her introduction—for the third time—and let out an exasperated, and very audible sigh.

"Yes?" she asked irritably.

"Marcus Jasper's supposed to go to the office," the aide said, waving a yellow off-campus pass. "His mother is here to take him to a dentist appointment."

Marcus Jasper gathered his books together and headed for the door.

Why had he even bothered coming to school, she wondered, *if he was just going to turn around and leave fifteen minutes later?*

Once the door closed behind him, Martha turned back to the class. "Now, let's try this for the *fourth* time," she said, all the while deciding that this was not going to be a very good day.

First period finally came to an end without another interruption, and second period suffered only two, but Martha had much more to worry about third period. Travis Johnson strolled through the door and gave her a casual grin before plopping in his seat with more ceremony than usual.

She watched him closely and found his behavior odd. Usually, he tended to ignore her and the rest of the class, choosing not to draw attention to himself. Why the change now? Especially after he had purposefully stood up the job opportunity she had set up with Greg Patton at the *Press*. Had he played her for the fool and now was telling her that he had succeeded?

Martha felt her ire ignite. There was no way she was going to let this sixteen-year-old make her life miserable. Despite the fear that he and every other gang member put into the faculty and student body, she was not going to let this little punk run her life.

"Mr. Johnson," she said sweetly once everyone had taken their seat. "I'd like you to stay after class." Then she turned her back on him to address the rest of the class, not allowing him a chance to counter.

For some reason, Travis felt his heart pumping harder than usual. Surely he wasn't scared, he thought. Of a teacher? A woman teacher at that. But then again, he wasn't sure of any of his feelings or actions right now. For instance, why the smile? Normally he wouldn't have given her a second thought, but instead, today he took the aggressive role. Why? Where had that come from? Was he feeling guilty for bailing out of the newspaper? Boy, that would be a new one. Whatever. He slouched down into his seat to wait the period out. Whatever she thought she was going to dish out would be of little consequence.

"Travis, please remove your sunglasses."

Mrs. Richards's voice startled him, and he glanced up at her. Her eyes were blazing fire, daring him. He had never seen her like this. He chewed his gum slowly and contemplated what to do. In the past, he would have obeyed without a second thought. He really wasn't much of a troublemaker, but this was a showdown. Finally, he slid them off and laid them carefully on the edge of his desk.

"Thank you," she said, nodding toward him. "And now would you please get your book out?"

Those same daring eyes. He returned her stare coolly, only this time he smiled ever so slightly. *She has no idea that I really control* her, he thought cryptically, *through her little golden boy, Danny.* Yet for some reason, he felt an unaccustomed sense of dread.

When the bell rang, the rest of the class filed out. Martha stood next to the door waiting for Travis. He sauntered up to her as members of her fourth period class started to stroll in. She put her hand up to halt them and then moved toward Travis, who had only managed to get to about midroom.

"I want to see you at the beginning of lunch," she said firmly. "In this room. We have a few things to discuss." He only returned her gaze and then pushed by her and left. She had no idea if he would show up or not.

Chapter 27

"Have a seat, Lennis," Bob Smith said congenially and extended his hand toward an open chair. "Make yourself comfortable."

Lennis watched the principal carefully as he took the offered seat. Bob Smith was anything *but* comfortable. Little drops of sweat were already beading on his brow, and he had run his forefinger around his collar four times already. The man was definitely a little nervous, and Lennis was more than sure he knew the content of the conversation that was to follow; he was just surprised it had taken till fourth period for him to get the call. The phones must have really been jumping off the hooks this morning.

"Lennis, you know I've always respected you as a coach and stayed clear of interfering with your program," the principal began.

Lennis nodded and waited. The principal cleared his throat, stalling, trying to determine the best route of approach.

"But I'm a little concerned about the way this season is going," he stated lamely.

"Why is that, sir?" Lennis asked.

"What?" Bob Smith asked, a little surprised.

"Why are you concerned about this season?" Lennis repeated.

"Uh, well, you're not winning like you normally do," he said.

"You told me winning really didn't matter in your book," Lennis answered calmly.

"Well, normally it doesn't," Smith replied and was all set to continue, but Bauer interrupted him.

"Then why does it now?" he asked sharply. He wanted to get to the crux of the problem and be done with it. He had a class to get back to. He only gave the boys ten minutes to get changed and into the gym, and they would only wait a few minutes before they came up with their own forms of entertainment.

"Well, uh, because … because you have the potential to win," he finally spit out. "You *should* be winning." Lennis stood up. He had heard all he needed.

"Mr. Smith," he said calmly and without hostility. "You hired me to coach this team the way I saw fit. I know you've probably been inundated with phone calls this morning, questioning my coaching decisions last Saturday, but the boys played hard, and it was a good game. But I have my reasons for what I'm doing, and I don't feel I need to explain myself, especially to a bunch of parents.

"However, if at any time you feel someone else could do a better job, then you have the power to correct that situation. Now, if you'll excuse me, I had better return to class before something happens to the gym."

He stood up to leave. "Would you like me to return later to finish this discussion?"

Bob Smith managed to pull his lower jaw closed to keep from gaping and thereby maintain a little of his dignity. He needed to regain control, and he knew it.

"I'll let you know," he said firmly, to which Lennis nodded and walked out the door.

It was tough to guess what the principal would do. He hadn't given Bob a chance to really speak his mind, which always irritated the man, and there was no telling how much pressure had come in over the phones that morning. If the boss really did want to assert his power, then there was little Lennis could do and he knew it. He could be out of a coaching job by two thirty.

"You didn't show up at the interview Saturday," Martha began icily. Normally she would not come across this angry, but the morning had progressed just about as miserably as it had started, and she was not in a good mood. "I'm not used to going out of my way to set up opportunities for my students with my professional contacts only to be stood up."

Travis had spent the better part of fourth period devising the best plan of attack. Despite Mrs. Richards's anger, he knew that she really did care about her students, probably even him, and that she would bend over backward to help them. Therefore, he would push all the right buttons and pull all the right strings.

"I got a little nervous," he said meekly. "I've never gone for a job interview before. I just got scared."

Martha stared at him hard. She could hardly believe this kid could be scared of anything. He seemed impervious to pain. But then again, some of his writing, when he did it, seemed to have some sensitivity to it, so then … maybe he was telling the truth. Hadn't she also read somewhere that a tough outer shell of rebelliousness was often just a facade for fear?

Her face began to visibly mellow, and Travis knew he had her. He had found her soft spot and played to it perfectly. It surprised him a little that a veteran drama teacher like her couldn't read through his little act. Either he was better than even *he* gave himself credit for, or she wasn't as bright as he had given *her* credit for. Or, like most teachers, she only saw what she wanted to see, and he was sure *she* wanted to see a young, inner-city gang member who was silently crying out for her to help him.

"Why were you scared?" she asked, her voice softer and a little coaxing. Travis felt himself gag inside. He needed to end this little charade quickly or he would be nauseous.

He shrugged.

"There's really nothing to be scared about," she said reassuringly. "Mr. Patton is a fine man. He would give you a fair break. And remember, you *are* a good writer," she added with a smile.

The last comment, he knew, was to build up his self-esteem. *All teachers were alike,* he thought cynically. He nodded to show he was listening.

"Would you like me to call him up and set up another interview?" she asked.

Travis shook his head. No use stepping into that trap again. "Not yet," he said, trying to sound uncertain. "I really don't think I'm ready."

Martha let out a small, discouraged sigh. *He needed to get into* something, she thought, but she decided to be patient. She would wait.

"Very well, then," she said, standing and giving him a motherly smile. "Let me know when you're ready."

He nodded again and stood up with his head bowed a little in an uncustomary look of contrition. "I'm sorry if I caused you any problems," he said and felt himself wince inside. Never in his life had he apologized, and even though this one wasn't sincere, he didn't care for the sound or feel of it.

Martha's eyebrows rose in surprise. Maybe this kid wasn't as bad as everyone made him out to be. Maybe there *was* hope. She would pray hard over the weeks to come and look for ways to help.

"I'll convey that message to Mr. Patton," she replied smiling. Travis looked up at her like a whooped puppy waiting for permission to leave.

"You may go," she said and felt a warmth inside. *I knew it!* she thought with exuberance. *He can be saved!* But she failed to see the smirk on Travis's face as he exited the door.

Alex tried to concentrate on the pictures in front of him, but his mind was filled with more than just backward letters and juvenile pictures. By the end of fourth period, word had already gotten around school that Coach Bauer had been called into Mr. Smith's office, and as the day wore on, the rumor grew that his dismissal as head football coach was imminent. Alex twisted and turned in his seat. This was all his fault.

He looked over at Reba, who was patiently waiting for his answers. He was responsible for her missing out on the play. He thought about Amanda. He was responsible for her frustration, too, in some way, but wasn't exactly sure how. What it all boiled down to was that he was basically responsible for just about all the woes of the world right now.

Alex looked down at the pictures: ball, baby, barn, bat, bath; then at the series of cards. All the cards began with the same letter. The problem now came after that first letter. He was learning the sounds that followed, but sometimes, and for no apparent reason, his brain flip-flopped the letters so "bath" to him looked like "btah." But not all the time. That was his frustration, but at the present it was nothing like the frustration that his world and the worlds of all those he came into contact with were quickly spinning out of control.

"All right, gang, that'll wrap it up!" Amanda yelled, and immediately the atmosphere in the auditorium went limp. The rehearsal was exhausting. Scenes were run through time and time again, working on the blocking, the moving, and the speaking until it all meshed.

Amanda found the closest thing to sit on—a sawhorse left by the stage crew—and dropped herself unceremoniously on it and released a deep breath.

Sure acting looked like fun and an easy way to make a living, but it was mostly hours and hours of grueling practice. She was spent. The nonstop activity and constant problem solving had one benefit, however, and that was it kept her from thinking about Alex. Now with her mind free, his image came rushing back.

I don't think I'll meet him, she thought. *But it might be better just to give him some time to himself. If he sees me, he'll only tighten up and get defensive.*

For Amanda, this was a tough decision. Her natural inclination was to confront, to resolve. She liked nothing unfinished, nothing left in limbo, which was one reason Mrs. Richards had selected her as student director. Things would get done, and practice wouldn't end until they were done right.

But such a persistent, "I want it now" approach did have its problems, two of which she was experiencing right now. One, it allowed little space for anyone else, and two, it wrecked havoc on a person's prayer life. God's timing and her timing were not even close. So her decision to give Alex room and time was a tough new concept for her to stomach.

Amanda stood up, resolved, and started picking up some of the loose props that were lying around. She figured it would be easier to stay and work until she knew she had missed him. At least it would offer her an excuse if he should ever ask.

Alex showered and dressed alone, the others long gone. Today had been worse than all the other days put together. The entire team knew that Coach Bauer had been called in and something was brewing. And they all knew why too, and when Alex set foot on the practice field two hours late and began his compensatory stairs, he could feel every eye on him, and each one carried poison. He had hoped his last-minute decision to start attending practice after his tutorial would help mend some of the broken fences, but after only one day, the gaps seemed even wider.

Coach Bauer ended practice with his spiel about how the season wasn't over and that the play-offs weren't out of the picture yet. But they could not worry about what the other teams did. They had to do everything *they* could do to put themselves in position. Then regardless of the outcome, they could take pride in the fact that they had not given up. And above winning, yes far above winning, taking pride in your efforts was most important.

It was a nice speech, and for most teams it would have pumped up the ole adrenaline again. But not this team. They were defeated from within. Alex could see it; he could feel it; in fact, he could even taste the bitterness in his own mouth. But he didn't know how to help. Coach was keeping his end of the bargain to protect Alex's secret, but at what cost?

Yesterday's verses came flooding back. Was it his own *misplaced* pride that kept him from coming clean with his teammates? Did they really have the right to know about his own personal struggles? He packed his bag and headed out the door. The air was nippy, and Alex welcomed its freshness. He automatically looked around for Amanda and felt a sharp sting when he didn't see her.

I've run her off too, he thought morosely, yet he was somewhat glad she wasn't there. He needed to talk right now, but not with her. His business was with God.

Chapter 28

Alex closed his book locker with the calm of a man who had made up his mind. The last two days had been the worst he had ever experienced. After Monday's icy reception by the rest of the team when he arrived late, Tuesday's full practice was full of fire and vengeance. None of the players, not even Richard, tried to hide their anger at him for his mysterious on-again, off-again appearances; at Coach Bauer for his apparent, and unprecedented, favoritism; and at the world in general for all the factors they couldn't pinpoint.

He was angry himself. The other players had no right to be mad. Coach hadn't pulled him any favors. The rules had never changed. He was paying the price for his decision. He wasn't getting the playing time he wanted, and he was running the equivalent of the national debt in stairs, but all they saw was what should have been, what even *could* have been had their focus not been twisted all out of shape. Couple that with the guilt he felt about the raging rumors of Coach Bauer's imminent firing as head coach, and he was about as miserable as he ever thought he could be.

But all that changed this morning—late last night, actually. After struggling through all the options—of which there were really only a relative few—he decided to shove his pride in his pocket and confess to the team what was happening.

Actually, that decision had been the easy part. It grew more difficult from there. Should he tell more than the team? There was no guarantee that they would keep his secret even if he asked them too, but he could pretty much count on massive distortion if the story swept across the campus. He had always feared himself an idiot, slow, retarded. Now those very rumors could beat him back to school tomorrow and seal his fate.

Should he quit? Would the team and coach be better off at this time without him, or would they read that as bailing out of a sinking ship? Should he tell his parents? Amanda?

The last one was the hardest of all to deal with. He had no idea what she really thought of him, but to lower himself voluntarily in her eyes seemed to be the kiss of death. She was a scholastic standout, he a struggler. Somehow the match didn't seem to fit too well.

In the end, which was about twelve thirty that night, he had decided to face them all: his parents, his teammates, Amanda, in that order. With his mind finally at ease and his body filled with a sense of peace that he had never before known, he had drifted off into the most restful sleep he had experienced in a long time.

When the bell sounded ending another school day, Travis was out of the main doors before it finished its wail. Agitated, he walked purposefully, briskly retracing the route he had taken that morning. His body was pumping with an extra dose of adrenaline. He had to get out, do something, or he felt he would go crazy.

All day his mind drifted, or rather it was pursued. That's what it was. It was as though someone was after him, hounding him, pounding on his brain, peeking over the edges—hunting him and just waiting to pounce. He had to find something to keep himself busy and his mind occupied.

Sooner than he realized, he found himself back in his neighborhood, and he walked straight past the deteriorated apartment building that doubled for his home. Five minutes later, he was at the Marauders' warehouse. At this time of day it was almost abandoned, except for the few extreme deadbeats who stayed stoned all day. Most made an attempt at showing up at school, though not for the educational value, but mainly to display muscle.

While Travis waited impatiently, pacing the floor, waiting for the others to arrive, he planned. He glanced at his Rolex. They would be here soon. He fashioned his strategy in his mind. The others would be surprised. First, because, despite his notorious reputation, he had always been a fringe player, hanging around the edges and not one of the more involved leaders. And second, because it was Wednesday. Midweek hits weren't in vogue. Most gang activity took place on the weekends. He wasn't sure why except that maybe it was a release from a week of dope and boredom. More show of muscle.

Others began trickling in, flopping down on sofas with springs and stuffing bulging out. A few seemed totally oblivious to him, but most seemed surprised to see him there. When Travis was sure that he had a number he could work with, he moved to the center of the room. He didn't have to say a word. The hush merely followed him.

"Who has a van handy?" he asked. A couple of hands rose. "Sliding side door?" One of the hands was pulled back down. "Any of you have some heavy gear with you?"

"Can get some," came a reply. "Whacha have in mind, Stone-bone?"

Travis turned toward his questioner without malice. "Just promoting business," he said simply. "If you don't keep reminding people of the rules, they begin taking a few liberties. I've just heard talk," he stated, "and thought a little reminder might be in order."

"You doin' the shootin'?"

"You doin' the drivin'?" Travis replied, and the face in the growing dim grinned.

"Wouldn't miss it for the world."

"Ahhhhh, I can't believe I left the rehearsal schedule in my room." Martha groaned through clenched teeth. "Amanda, will you run up and get it? It should be right on top of my desk. Here are my keys."

Amanda grabbed the keys on the run and headed out the door.

Typical, Martha thought. *So far, this week has been the most disastrous of my life!* At school the interruptions had come nonstop throughout the day, and the students were losing that beginning-of-the-school-year glow and enthusiasm. Everyone had become sluggish. Then at home, Danny was as secretive and defensive as ever, and Graydon just as suspicious. Nothing was flowing smoothly anymore. Not even play practice.

"C'mon, Amanda, hurry!" she whispered tensely and glanced at her watch. "We're already ten minutes behind."

Then her heart did a sudden flop and dropped to the pit of her stomach. She looked at her watch again—3:10. *What day is this?* she thought frantically. *Wednesday.*

"Oh, no," she muttered, shaking her head and getting a deep sense of foreboding. Another nice little compartment of her life was about ready to tumble.

"It's kind of stuffy in here. Do you mind if I open the door?" Reba asked.

Alex shook his head, his eyes never leaving the papers in front of him. "No, go ahead." He was past first letters and beginning to see patterns in entire words.

"Did you find the three that rhyme?" Reba asked from the hallway. Alex grimaced over the words.

"Use the pictures if you have to," she encouraged, but Alex refused. He knew which three rhymed because they all looked the same. His problem was remembering the sounds all at once—putting all three of the letters together at once. His upper lip folded under his bottom teeth as he pushed his jaw forward in determination, and his forehead creased till his eyebrows almost met.

"Cat," he said slowly, "bat and hat."

"Perfect!" Reba shouted excitedly.

"And I didn't use the pictures," Alex added before she could say anything else.

Reba smiled. "I didn't think you would."

Amanda took the three flights of stairs two at a time. When she reached the top, she doubled over to catch her breath.

"Maybe I should reenroll in PE," she gasped. "This is pathetic." She stood up and walked toward Mrs. Richards's room as quickly as she could while still under the effect of oxygen deprivation. When she was about fifteen feet away, she stopped.

"Why's the door open?" she wondered aloud and then shook her head. *Mrs. Richards is really preoccupied these days. She hasn't even bothered to lock her room and then forgets she's left it open.* She started toward the room again but stopped as a squeal of delight escaped through the open door.

"Now read these," said the high-pitched voice enthusiastically. Amanda recognized that voice.

A low, deep voice stuttered and then started again. Amanda instinctively tilted her head, her ear toward the door to catch what he said.

"Sun … f … fun … rrrr … run," the voice announced with pleasure.

Another shriek of approval. "You are doing so well!" the first voice, the girl, said excitedly.

"Thanks," came the reply. Amanda froze. She knew that voice too. Without thinking, she moved cautiously to the doorway, trying hard not to be noticed.

"Now one more set of words before we move on," the girl said. "And this group has ten words, five of which rhyme … and no pictures."

"I haven't been using the pictures," the deep, rich voice reminded her.

Amanda felt a chill run up her back. That voice was much too familiar. Why couldn't she place it? Both of them.

"Ready?" asked the girl.

"Ready," came the reply.

"Go."

There was what seemed an eternity of deafening silence before the deep voice began. "Hill … fill …" he said slowly. Amanda inched her way to the door. "Pill … pi—no—sorry. Bill … There's pill." A long pause. Amanda peeked around the corner just as the blond head pulled up from his paper and smiled widely for his mentor. "*Kill!*" he said emphatically and raised both arms in triumph.

It was at that moment that he caught sight of the figure at the door, and the smile and arms and Amanda's jaw all dropped in unison.

"How much you payin' for those needles?"

Danny looked down at the syringe in his hand. "It's free," he said. "Every time I buy a teaspoon, he throws in a clean needle."

The young man sitting across from him let out a laugh filled with pity. "Man, nothin' in this world is free," he countered. "Least of all drugs. You can bet you're payin' for it. How much is your supplier charging you a teaspoon?"

Danny swallowed hard before answering. He really had no desire to look the fool. "Forty dollars."

The other young man let out a low whistle. "Not only is it not free, my man, but I'd say you're paying for someone else's habit as well."

Danny felt a lump rise in his throat, and his face grow red. Travis had taken advantage of him. He felt his anger churn and then realized he had no one to blame but himself. Not once had he questioned the price.

"You sure your needles are clean?" the other asked.

Danny felt his blood run cold. "Sure," he said, though not at all sure. "They come vacuum wrapped."

"Let me take a look," the other said, waving Danny to pass the needle to him. Danny handed the package over, and the young man scrutinized it carefully and then pushed his lower lip out.

"Yeah, it's clean. Your man did you right there," he said and handed it back. Danny felt his blood begin to flow once again. "But I think you'd better find yourself a new dealer. This guy's pumping you dry."

"Would someone else give me clean needles?"

The young man shook his head. "Doubtful. But hey, man, you can shoot up here. We share, but we're all clean, and we sterilize the needles out in the kitchen. Nothin' to worry about."

Danny rolled his tongue across his dry lips. Money was short, and Travis really didn't seem too thrilled about working with him anymore. And besides, he was a little scared of the guy anyway. Plus, these guys were college students, some in tough premed classes. They were educated, smart. They wouldn't do anything that could really do harm to themselves.

He felt his body shiver from want, and he ripped the needle from its wrapper and dipped it into the solution.

"I think I might do that," he said as he wrapped the rubber hose tightly around his arm. After all, his need was becoming much greater than his fear.

Chapter 29

Though he couldn't define it, Alex couldn't shake Amanda's look from his mind. She had stared at him confused and embarrassed, then excused herself and walked quickly to Mrs. Richards's desk and almost in a panic searched for something, only to pick up a piece of paper and then retreat to the door. It happened so quickly that all Alex could do was stare. Once she was gone, he and Reba sat in stunned silence for a few minutes.

"I'm sorry," Reba finally said quietly.

Alex shook his head. "It's all right," he said smiling weakly. "I was going to announce it to the team this afternoon anyway … too many problems, you know, trying to keep it a secret and all."

He stared back at the empty doorway. "I was going to tell Amanda too, eventually. I guess this saves me the trouble."

Reba watched him out of the corner of her eye and couldn't believe how much she hurt for the boy. *Lord, he thinks his world is crumbling around him,* she prayed silently.

"Do your parents know?" she asked.

He nodded. "Told them this morning."

"And?"

He shook his head and smiled. "They were terrific. No 'why didn't you tell us before?' or 'that can't be true.' They just listened and asked how they could help." He shook his head again. "I can't believe I was scared to tell them."

Reba fell silent again. She knew that Alex's major confrontations were still ahead of him. She glanced at her watch.

"I know we've only been working a few minutes and all," she said, "but would you like to cancel today and go on out to practice and take care of it?"

Alex pursed his lips and thought over the offer, but finally shook his head.

"No," he said and took a deep breath, and she could see a peace fill his eyes. "No, I'm finally learning that God does have everything under control and that I really don't need to waste all my energy worrying about it. I think I'd like to stay."

He smiled at Reba warmly, and that part in the play that had meant so much to her only a month ago now seemed like a meaningless trinket.

Amanda was not dumb. By the time she had returned to the auditorium, she had the whole puzzle pieced together. Mrs. Richards's look of conspiratorial concern only confirmed her conclusion. She said nothing as she handed her the practice schedule and then returned to her duties, knowing all the time that Mrs. Richards's eyes were filled with curiosity and focused on the back of her head.

It all fit. Reba not making the play. Alex not playing. Alex not talking. Coach Bauer under fire. *Were they all in this little scheme together, and how many by choice and how many by draft?* she wondered, her mind wandering back to Reba … maybe even Alex. She glanced back over at Mrs. Richards. She was sure she had masterminded the whole plot, but with how many volunteer accomplices?

Amanda took a deep breath. She was being unfair because she was mad. Not mad that Alex couldn't read, but mad because she hadn't been included. Why hadn't Alex told her? *Why should he?* a small voice whispered. *Why* would *he?* Would *she* have confessed that she was a sixteen-year-old illiterate, especially to the boy she most wanted to impress, most wanted to think highly of her?

She stopped and thought about that one. Was he trying to impress her? Was that why he shielded his secret from her? The thought brought her a sense of warmth. She may be jumping, may be hoping, may be pushing—which she did very well, and often—but it was what she wanted to think.

But a problem still lurked. The secret was out. Now what?

Alex sprinted up the stairs, pumping his arms and gasping for breath. When he reached the top, he let his arms fall limply to his side, jogged in place momentarily, and then started back down. When he reached the bottom, he turned and repeated the routine. No one needed to yell at him to do six more, or ten more, or one more. After three weeks, he knew the routine. And after three weeks, it didn't seem to get any easier. Today, he carried that extra weight of confession.

He finished his last set of stairs and jogged back out to practice, taking his usual position next to one of the assistants. Coach Bauer called a few more plays, watched them executed pathetically, and ran his hand through his hair in frustration. Finally, he blew the whistle in exasperation and waved the team off the field. They responded in slow motion.

Alex watched him closely. His eyes, though always bloodshot from the endless hours of watching game tapes, had always been full of fire. Now they seemed defeated. Alex felt for the man, and that sense of nagging guilt plagued him again.

Coach Bauer turned away from the playing field and motioned

for the players to sit down before him. They complied and removed their helmets. Again, he ran his hand through his hair as though hoping to pull out a trick card. When everyone was settled, he turned to address them but seemed at a loss as to what to say.

"Coach," Alex said, standing up. "Can I say something?"

Coach Bauer looked at him with surprise, but backed away and relinquished his spot at the front. For a moment, Alex thought he saw a look of relief, but a quick second glance revealed a closed, cautious air. Alex worked his way around and over his teammates who made no effort to move an inch for him. When he reached the spot vacated by Coach Bauer, he turned, only to look into a sea of hostile faces. He swallowed hard and prayed all in the same moment.

"I know you blame me for a lot of what's happened this season," he began. "I know you think I'm treating this football team as secondary, unimportant. That I have more important things to do." He paused, more to keep his voice from shaking than to think about what to say. He had rehearsed the speech over and over in his mind until he could recite it in his sleep. The audience, however, was now present.

"I know you also blame Coach Bauer. You feel he has given me special treatment because he thought I was some star or something, and he didn't want to lose me."

He paused again. Every face confirmed his words.

"Well, I'm here to tell you that this team is *not* secondary to me, though right now, football is. And Coach Bauer is *not* to be blamed for anything."

A few of the faces lost their hostility and looked confused. He forged on.

"My being here and playing has caused a lot of friction, and I'm here to say that if it will help the team, I'm willing to quit. That's up to you. I'm not bailing out, because I think we can still win this thing. But before you make up your minds, I want you to know the whole story.

"I'm not missing practice for tutoring that could be done any time. I'm missing practice to learn how to read. I am a high school sophomore, and I don't know how to read one single word, or I didn't until a few weeks ago."

Now the looks changed to disbelief.

"I don't need to go through the entire story, but a teacher found me out—finally—and another student gave up a chance at a lead role in a play to tutor me, and Coach ..." he glanced over at Coach Bauer and smiled weakly but sincerely, "... well, he kept my secret ... much to his own discomfort."

Alex looked back at his teammates.

"I think most of you know that football is one of the most important things in my life, but if I don't know how to read, football won't be an option. I don't want this year to end badly, with hard feelings and a divisive spirit. That's not Panther football. So ... if you want me to quit, I will."

He stood there silently for a moment with all eyes on him. No one moved, and he wondered what he should do next. He hadn't planned for after the speech. Coach Bauer cleared his throat as though stalling for time. He didn't know what to do either.

In the back, a player rose. It was Richard. "I vote Alex stays," he said. Alex glanced at his friend and thought he saw tears in his eyes. It was probably just sweat.

Another rose. "I vote he stays."

One by one the players rose to their feet, announcing their support. When all were standing, Coach Bauer stepped forward, the fire in his eyes rekindled.

"All right then!" he yelled. "Let's get back out on that field!"

Amanda waited in the dark, swaying back and forth in an effort to stay warm. Every other minute she second-guessed her decision to be where she was. *Maybe he doesn't want to see me right now,* she thought and started to walk away, only to stop herself. *No, I need to talk to him,* she would convince herself, and so she would stay.

As the players began to file out, her heart started pounding in her chest. *This was* not *a good idea,* she thought, but there was no escape now.

Alex finished dressing slowly. His body hurt, but it was a good hurt. Friendly pain, from teammates pumped up about the future. The change on the field had been almost instantaneous. No one had talked to him directly; it was too soon for that. One can't turn from three weeks of shunning to immediate and open acceptance; it just wouldn't ring true. There had to be that silent and awkward feeling-out period first.

After dressing, a few of the guys had shyly glanced at him and smiled on their way out, a couple saying, "See ya tomorrow," but most just slipped out quietly, unnoticed. It would take a few days, Alex knew.

He finished buttoning his shirt and looked up to see Richard at the end of the row. The two looked at each other for a few seconds, then Richard breached the distance between them and stopped, placing his hand on one of the lockers.

"I'm sorry I rode you so hard, man, but I wish I'd have known," he said. "I could've helped."

Alex glanced down at his shoes and then back up, and he could see that Richard was both sincerely sorry and hurt.

"I'm sorry, too," he said softly. "My pride hurt a lot of people."

Richard waved him off. "Water under the bridge now," he said and then added with a wry smile, "but you're not gettin' me to read your schedule for you anymore."

Alex smiled. "You see through that now, huh?"

Richard shook his head. "Like glass, man, but you had us all fooled there for so long."

Alex nodded slowly. "Me, too."

Amanda had given up. *Maybe he never went to practice today,* she thought. *Maybe her sudden guest appearance had affected him more than she realized.*

She moved out of the darkness of the building and headed for the street. She would think of another way to meet up with him. Right as she paralleled the locker room door, Alex emerged. The sight of each other startled them both, and they stopped and stared. Amanda's hand flew involuntarily to her chest.

"I'm sorry," Alex said. "I didn't mean to scare you." He shrugged his shoulders by way of explanation. "I just didn't expect to find you here."

For the first time, he was looking straight into her eyes, searching and waiting, and she noticed in the light of the street lamp that they were a lustrous, light blue. Clear and strong.

"Why not?" she asked softly.

"I *was* going to tell you," he said by way of defense, but she raised her hand to stop him and moved toward those determined yet vulnerable blue eyes.

"I know," she said in almost a whisper. She felt herself drawn to him. Her heartbeat quickened. *What am I doing?* she wondered. This part wasn't rehearsed—*none* of it was rehearsed. But she found herself wrapping her arms around his neck and pressing her face into the warmth of his shirt collar as she let the tears flow. It didn't matter that he didn't know what to do. She raised her head to whisper in his ear.

"You are the bravest, most admirable man I know," Amanda said and kissed him on the cheek.

Chapter 30

The *Detroit Press* had a small article about the fatal drive-by shooting in West Detroit, but it was hidden among a flock of other violent deaths on the fifth page of the second section in Thursday morning's edition. Other than that, the incident was forgotten, except, of course, by the victim's family. But it seemed anymore that daily there was a new victim, and consequently, a new victim's family. The numbers were too much to cope with, both emotionally and legally. Police investigators appeared, took notes, wrote a report, and attributed it once again to gang violence.

For Travis, the night provided both the relief and the control over his life that he had been yearning for. For two hours his blood flashed through his body, making his mind sharp and his senses acute.

They had cruised the streets for almost two hours looking for Jamal "D-Man" Hicks, leader and ghetto "war lord." For weeks now, D-Man—"Death Man"—had been inching his way into Marauder drug territory. A few skirmishes pushed his people back, but the trespassing had become more blatant, the movement more casual, more arrogant. Travis, like the other gang leaders, took it as a major slap in the face, and so when he requested a van Wednesday night, there had been no objections.

The headlights of the van finally caught up with Jamal right where the Marauders wanted him—trespassing on their own home turf. Travis signaled for the van to slow down so that he could get a closer look, an accurate identification, and when the small group turned and shielded their eyes to see who was coming, he was sure.

He motioned to move on, and when the driver jammed the pedal to the floor, the tires squealed as they tried to gain traction. The van pealed toward the victims. On command, the van door slid open, and Travis braced himself in the doorway, the AK-47 held tight against his body. As they sped past, he sprayed a round of bullets into the crowd and saw three go down immediately. He smiled wryly to himself. One had been Jamal.

In a more dangerous move, for the others could have prepared themselves to return fire by now, Travis had the van turn around and head back toward the fallen victims. He wanted to make sure Jamal was dead. The van weaved and careened toward the group and got its intended result: the survivors scattered, leaving their fallen to the merciless slaughter of the Marauders.

Like Brutus of ancient Rome, however, Travis didn't consider himself a butcher, so he only aimed at Jamal and spared the others. Four or five bullets riddled the body, bouncing it up and down with each impact. Satisfied, Travis waved the van on down the street and back toward the warehouse.

That was Wednesday night, and the adrenaline high kept Travis's head clear and lucid. But nothing lasts twenty-four hours, and though the warehouse never emptied completely, one by one, members either fell asleep or passed out, and Travis again felt himself alone and empty. Soon those haunting verses crept back into his mind to fill the void.

For you are dust and to dust you shall return, a calm voice whispered in his ear. *For what does it profit a man to gain the whole world and forfeit his soul?*

"*No!*" he screamed and raised his hands to his ears, trying to stop the voices, but it was no use. More accompanied the first, just as calm and powerful. What could he do to escape? he wondered. Where could he go?

Alex pulled his shoulder pads over his head, pulled and tied the string in front to secure them in place, and smiled contentedly to himself.

Man, it's good to be alive, he thought and then chuckled. Four days ago he wouldn't have said that with any enthusiasm, but a lot had happened in four days—in one day actually, ever since he had heeded God's command and humbled himself. What could he have been thinking before?

Though the football game against Washington should have been the first thing on his mind, and would have been a year ago, Amanda was the first image that popped up.

She's incredible, he thought. His fear that she would think him stupid was in itself stupid. Wednesday when she had met him outside the locker room, she promised not to say anything. She said she wasn't going to pry or push, but in the end she just couldn't help herself.

"I guess I just can't leave well enough alone," she confessed as he walked her home, his arm, for the first time, wrapped around her shoulders. "I want to know all about it. How did you feel about not being able to read? How did you get as far as you did?" she asked with real astonishment.

"And why is it you couldn't read?" She had asked this last question forthrightly, without any condemnation or judgment that he might be mentally deficient. But in her eyes, it really was a mystery that someone hadn't been able to learn to read.

At total peace with himself now, Alex, as best as he could, tried to answer all her questions. How he had felt for the longest time that there was something wrong with him, that his mind was somehow defective, that he was retarded, or stupid, or all of the above.

"But you know so much!" she countered, pulling away from him momentarily and placing her hands firmly on her hips to take that adamant and determined stance he had really grown fond of.

"How could you think you were stupid?" she questioned. "You knew … excuse me, *know* more than half the kids in my science class do, and they *know* how to read."

"That may be true," Alex had replied, "but I didn't know I knew more than they did. Remember, I'm in classes with quite a few kids who don't care *what* they know."

"That's the system's fault," Amanda had said with indignation as she slid back under Alex's arm. "They should do away with compulsory education. If students don't want to be here, don't make them. It just ruins learning for those of us who want to and turns school into a day care center."

Alex had smiled to himself. Amanda had another cause. He decided to speed up some of his explanation before she got too wound up.

He detailed to her all the methods he had used to get out of reading, all the schemes he had used to remember and glean information, all the patterns he had set up for getting the necessary homework done and turned in, *and* all the people he had used to get where he was. Amanda had shook her head.

"That only shows how bright you are," she said with conviction.

Now, even the memory of her compliment caused the grin on Alex's face to grow wider.

"Hey, Piston, got a girl on your mind?"

Startled out of his daydream, Alex looked up and into Richard's grinning white teeth. He found himself blushing, remembering Richard's same little chide at the beginning of the season and how far from the truth it was then, yet how right on it was now.

"Actually, yeah," he said, feeling the warm blush of his face. It was good having Richard back as a friend.

"Well, see," he said, giving Alex a pop on the shoulder, "that shows you're getting smarter every day. For a while there all that little brain of yours could focus on was football. I was really worried about you, Polish."

Alex grinned wider. "Yeah, but I think Coach would rather I be thinking about football right now, don't you?"

Richard snapped his fingers as though in remembrance. "Oh, yeah. That's why I came over here. To get you. Coach said for you to get that Polish hind end of yours in motion and into the team room or you'll be seeing more of those stairs on Monday than you ever dreamed possible."

It really was totally unnecessary. After all, Mr. Washington was with them, but Travis still escorted the entire Washington family to the high school stadium to watch the football game. But there were multiple reasons for doing it.

One, it gave him something to do, and God knew he needed to keep his mind busy. After the drive-by, it had been drinking and smoking, then girls, then parties, and almost drugs, but again, his inherent self-protection device had kicked in and stopped him. He wished it hadn't because after each diversion, whether at twelve midnight or ten the next morning after the hangover wore off, the vacuum returned and sucked his soul clean out of him, leaving him feeling emptier than ever before. So one, he wanted to keep busy.

Two, he actually worried about them. Jamal's gang, the Raiders, had been seen in the neighborhood, looking and waiting for a chance to seek revenge, and he didn't want the Washingtons hurt. He would recognize the Raiders and be able to warn the family or get them out of danger.

Finally, though he had never been able to lay a finger on why, he loved being around this family. Despite the poverty that surrounded them, they had such a sense of peace that was so palpable it made him ache with envy and desire. And somehow that dull and painful ache was much more desirable than the hollow vacuum that followed him around the rest of the time.

Lord, thank you for bringing Travis along. I know you are working on him, Lord, because he looks terrible. Please use my family and me in any way you can. Amen.

Reba finished her prayer and sighed happily. God was good, and she knew he would eventually bring Travis into his fold despite all the odds against that. After all, hadn't he just worked a miracle solving Alex's problems? she thought satisfactorily. And that was pretty messed up.

She took in a deep breath of the crisp, cool air of early November. She loved this time of year. The awful summer humidity was gone, and the air was nippy and dry according to Midwestern standards. A pallet of brown, gold, bright yellow, and brilliant red floated to the ground or was rustled slightly by the fall breeze as the trees casually shed their leaves.

Instinctively she pulled her wool coat snugly around her. *It's a good coat,* she thought happily. *Not new, but warm and pretty.* But not as warm and pretty as the family that surrounded her. *Thank you, Lord,* she said silently, *for making me the luckiest girl in the world.*

Amanda let the crisp autumn wind bite at her skin and whip her strawberry blonde hair about her face. She was enjoying the freshness of the day. In fact, her life seemed to have had a fresh start or at least a sudden push to a new level of happiness.

She looked down at the field and scanned the players for number eighty-four and then felt her heart beat harder and deeper and fuller than it had.

I don't know if this is love or not, she thought, *but whatever it is, I want to keep it.*

Since she had learned Alex's secret, she had become a one-woman research department on dyslexia, trying to find out all she could about it, and how to fight it. It was amazing what she had learned in just three days, like almost all dyslexics were above-normal intelligence, and, in fact, some geniuses suffered from the reading disorder.

She read the material and marveled over it but did not share it with Alex. Though hard for her to keep her mouth shut at times, this was one time she was using all her forbearance. This was Alex's war, not hers, and she knew he would include her when he felt the time was right. Still, she was subtly probing for ways to help or encourage without being too obvious.

A whistle sounded down on the field calling both teams to the sidelines. Amanda watched number eighty-four jog to the side and take his spot along with the other thirtysome nonstarters. But this time, it didn't bother her. This time his position on the sideline was something to be proud of.

It had not been a good day for Washington. The underdogs by three touchdowns to begin with, they were no match for a revitalized Montgomery team. The starting offensive lineup had scored on its first series of downs, and then the defense had caused Washington to cough up the ball on the second play of their possession, and the offense converted another touchdown three plays later. By the end of the first quarter, the score was already twenty-one to nothing.

Coach Bauer didn't hesitate. He pulled out his first string and put in the second. They hadn't had much playing time all year, and if the uncertain turn of events happened this weekend, and

Montgomery was still in the play-off hunt, they might not see too much action next week.

The first string relinquished the field graciously and then cheered wildly from the sideline while the second string, pumped up by the unaccustomed support, scored twice more, while the defense allowed Washington only a hard-earned field goal.

At halftime, there was no need for a Coach Bauer pep talk or morale boost. Helmets were smacking against each other, pads were being pounded, chest bumps abounded. And when the Montgomery Panthers took the field for the second half, it was the remaining third stringers in their pristine white uniforms that halted the early drive of the Patriots by picking up a fumble and then cashing it in twelve plays later.

Neither team scored for the remainder of the third and half of the fourth, and only one player on the Montgomery squad hadn't seen any action—Alex. As the clock ticked away, the other players seemed to get antsy, nervously shifting from foot to foot. They cast anxious sideways glances at Coach Bauer, then looked at each other, and finally they gave a furtive glance at Alex, all the while wondering if Coach Bauer would play him at all.

It seemed such an odd thing to do to leave him on the sideline, especially after all had been resolved. But Alex didn't worry. He knew Coach Bauer hadn't forgotten him and that there was always a reason behind his actions.

He was right. Not only was Coach Bauer in tune with what was happening on the field, but he was keenly attuned to what was occurring on the sideline. These young men, who last week were bound and determined to keep Alex Kowalski from touching a football, were now eagerly waiting for him to get his chance on the field. Coach Bauer wanted to use that change to its full potential.

Finally, when the Panthers regained possession and it looked like it would be the last time Montgomery would handle the ball, the entire sideline was on edge, hoping, praying.

"All right, Kowalski, get in there—"

Alex was off, and his teammates jumped and cheered and raised their fists in the air. Alex pointed at Marcus, the third string end he was replacing, and then gave him a high five as they passed.

"Good job, Marcus," he said.

Alex could see the young sophomore grin from behind his face mask.

Michael Gutierrez seemed a little nervous when Alex relayed the plays. Though a year ahead of Alex, he had never played with any of the first string, even in practice, and now he was supposed to pass into the arms of the star. Michael was not feeling too good. Alex lined up.

"Ready … set … hut … hut—"

Alex was off with the snap of the ball, sprinted twenty yards downfield, faked left, and then cut across the middle of the field and looked for the ball. Michael saw him and released, but it was a feeble attempt. The ball careened through the air weakly. Alex was forced to stop and reverse direction and dive for the ball. He managed to pick it up right before it hit the ground for a gain of fifteen.

Though he would have been down automatically, the nearby linebacker couldn't resist the temptation to release a little of his own frustration by making sure Alex knew he was down and slammed into him right after Alex hit the ground. The hit was merciless, and Alex felt himself chewing on grass, but he held on to the ball and heard a whistle screech right above him.

"Unnecessary roughness!" the ref screamed and pulled the linebacker off of Alex. "Fifteen yards!"

Alex shook his head to clear it, tossed the ball to the ref, and jogged back to the huddle. Michael looked miserable. He opened his mouth to apologize, but Alex cut him off.

"Nice pass," he said with a grin. "Got us an extra fifteen yards."

The young quarterback's face visibly relaxed, and he moved into the middle of the huddle to call the next play. This time Alex set up on the right. It was the identical play as the last one, only reversed. Alex sprinted twenty yards up, faked right, then cut back across the middle. He thought about slowing his speed in case Michael threw behind him again, but thought better of it. The play called for an all-out sprint, so that's what he did.

Michael fell back into the pocket, saw Alex cut, and then fired the ball right to the spot Alex was supposed to be. The pass and the timing were perfect, and Alex never slowed as he pulled in the ball, right on the numbers, and turned up field. Fresh from three quarters on the sideline, he outraced every defender and sprinted into the end zone. When he turned to head back to his teammates, he saw Michael Gutierrez going wild. It was his first touchdown pass—ever.

"Well, that was a regular blowout!" Graydon said with a grin as he picked up his and Martha's stadium seats.

"Oh, it wasn't that bad," Martha insisted.

"Forty-two to three is not good," he said firmly. "That is a blowout in my book."

Martha conceded. "Well, at least all the boys got to play," she said and felt a certain satisfaction with Alex's three-minute heroics. *He's a good boy,* she thought, *a good, Christian boy, just like Danny.* "Well, despite the score, you have to admit this was fun, wasn't it?"

Graydon gave her a quick squeeze. "Yes, it was. Very relaxing."

"Hey there! Mr. and Mrs. Washington!" The two looked up to see Mike Humphrey, Danny's friend, climbing over seats to reach them.

"Hello there, Mike," Graydon said smiling broadly. He had always been fond of Mike—a good athlete, polite. "What brings you out to a high school game? Old college guy like you."

Mike grinned at the teasing. Like Danny, he had only graduated last spring. "I like to keep up with the team," he explained. "Coach Bauer was always good to me."

Graydon nodded. Coach Bauer was good to and for a lot of boys.

"Anyway," Mike began. "The reason I ran over here was to say congratulations."

Martha and Graydon looked at him a little confused. "For what?" Martha asked.

"For celebrating twenty-five years of marriage?" Mike said, using his hands to prompt them into the importance of the achievement. Martha and Graydon just stared at him.

"We haven't been married for twenty-five years," Martha corrected him. "Only twenty-two."

Mike shrugged. "So Danny was off a few years. Still, twenty-two years is a pretty long time."

The smile faded from Graydon's lips. "Just when did Danny say we celebrated this anniversary?" he asked casually.

"Last Sunday. He called up Sunday morning all in a huff. Said he had forgotten all about your anniversary and wanted to take you two to dinner and all that—" Mike stopped when he saw the complete bewilderment in their faces. "You did go out to dinner last Sunday, didn't you? Rex's?"

Martha and Graydon slowly shook their heads in unison.

"Was it even your anniversary last weekend?" he asked, his voice weakening. Again, two slow shakes of the head.

"Not even this month," Graydon said softly. "More like April." Now it was Mike's turn to look completely baffled.

"Tell me," Graydon said slowly, and Martha could hear his effort to control the suspicion and anger growing in his voice. "Just why did Danny call you?"

Mike looked up, the perplexed expression still on his face. "Huh? Why, he said he needed to borrow some money."

Travis tossed his cigarette to the ground and crushed it with his feet the minute he saw the Washingtons exit the stadium, then turned his head away from them and exhaled the smoke. When they caught up to where he was, he fell into line and walked alongside, that feeling of power and importance rising once again.

"You should have joined us, Travis," Mr. Washington said. "The Panthers crushed the other team."

Travis shook his head. "I really don't care for football," he said. Actually, he thought it was a stupid, pointless game. Boys putting on pads and then smashing into each other. What was to be proven? What was there really to lose? Now on the streets, there was where the real stakes were. That's where the real men kept score.

"Well, I like football," Reba said boldly. "It's good, clean fun."

Willie laughed. "Didn't look too clean to me," he said with a giggle.

Reba was just about ready to respond when the squeal of tires could be heard. Travis looked up in time to see a black Dodge van screech around the corner and head straight for them. Even from where he was, he could see who it was.

"*Get down!*" he yelled and threw himself on top of Willie as the van door slid open and a spray of gunfire riddled the sidewalk and fencing around them. Travis could feel the heat of the bullets as they ricocheted off the pavement and whizzed through the cyclone fencing. Two seconds later, the van was around the next corner, and Travis released a sigh of relief and chuckled in satisfaction.

The buffoons missed, he thought smugly as he and the others picked themselves up. Then he heard a piercing, unearthly scream like he had never heard before and turned to find Reba, her hands shaking in front of her face as she stared at the pavement. Travis looked down and felt his whole world drop out from under him.

There, silent and still, lay little four-year-old Jocelyn in a puddle of her own blood.

Chapter 31

All Travis could do was stand and stare. He felt his stomach rebel as a nauseous wave crashed over him, and he knew he was going to be sick to his stomach. Reba continued to scream in horror, and a crowd, mostly spectators from the football game, had begun to gather. Only Mr. and Mrs. Washington seemed to keep their composure.

"Call an ambulance," Mr. Washington said calmly to his wife as he took off his coat and ripped off his shirt. He bent over the still figure, found the wound, and then pressed hard with his shirt to stop the bleeding. He knelt over and placed his ear near to his little daughter's mouth, trying to feel a small breath. It was too difficult, too many people around. Reba stood by gasping for her own breath, still in shock. The other children just stared.

"What's happened?" Amanda asked as she neared the crowd. She had stayed in the stands till the last player had left the field, hoping that if Alex looked her way, he would see her still there, supportive.

"Drive-by," one of the bystanders answered. "Hit a little girl."

"Oh my," Amanda said, feeling faint. *Why did these things*

happen? she thought. *Can people be so heartless and cruel as to shoot down innocent children?*

She was ready to move on, knowing that having too many people around could complicate the situation when the paramedics arrived, but as she tried to get through, she stopped with the next sound.

"*Noooo,*" came the sob. "*Please God, noooo.*"

The voice had a strange familiarity in it. "Excuse me," she said and pushed her way through. "Please, excuse me." She broke through the last group of people who formed a ring around the family, gasped when she saw the very small figure lying in the pool of blood, and then heard the soft plea.

"Oh, God, nooo. Please don't let her die."

Amanda looked up and saw Reba, her face tear-streaked and overwrought. In the background she could hear the loud wail of the sirens as they neared. She moved forward to help.

"Come on," she said and put her arm around Reba and backed her away. "Let's get the little ones out of the way."

Amanda's soothing voice and practical advice had an immediate effect on Reba, and she looked up into those deep green eyes that were filled with sympathy and determination. Reba locked onto those eyes for a minute, gaining strength. Then she reached up and wiped the tears away with the back of her hand.

"Willie, Jake, Chris. Come back here," she said with shaky authority. The boys backed up slightly but never took their eyes off of their sister. Amanda helped Reba herd them back against the fence.

Mrs. Washington reappeared about the same time that the screaming sirens rounded the corner and came to a screeching stop. The crowd opened up, allowing Mrs. Washington through first. Her face was torn up with worry, but she said nothing, only exchanging eye contact with her husband.

The paramedics came through a second later with a gurney, medical kit, and IV set up and ready. Mr. Washington moved away from his daughter, relinquishing care to the authorities. The little figure was lost beneath all the commotion.

"Blood pressure's low."

"Try and get her stabilized. We need to get her to the hospital, stat."

"I think we're set."

Amid all the activity, all Amanda and the others could do was watch. She wrapped her arms around Reba and Willie, while Reba held Jake and Chris close to her body.

"We're ready to transport," the lead paramedic said, and the gurney was raised and pushed toward the ambulance. The medic turned to the parents. "You want to ride along?" he asked. Both instinctively moved toward the ambulance and then Mrs. Washington stopped and turned toward the other children.

"Go ahead," Amanda spoke up. "I'm a friend of Reba's. I'll go home with her and call my mother. She'll come over."

Relief flooded Mrs. Washington's face, and she smiled gratefully at Amanda. "We'll call as soon as we know anything," she said and then hurried with her husband toward the ambulance.

The little group, huddled together, watched as the siren warmed up and then the ambulance squealed away. Two policemen stayed behind to ask questions and take a report from those in the crowd who might have seen anything. Though no one knew it at the time, there was one person missing who might have helped solve the mystery of the shooting––Travis Johnson.

"Do you mind if I say a prayer for your sister, Reba?"

Reba looked up at Mrs. Donahoe from where she sat on the couch, her arms wrapped around her three brothers. Pray? She had forgotten all about praying. Somehow God had just vanished from the picture. She felt a lump rise in her throat, and she swallowed hard to keep it down.

What kind of a Christian was she? Though many would have probably thought her life one of poverty and despair, Reba could never remember want of any kind: food, love, even money. Except for a little burp with her play disappointment, her life to this point had been very calm and uneventful, full of pleasant memories. And all of this she had chalked up to God's love.

But now, with the impact of one bullet, suddenly the tent of God's protection had come crashing down. Now he seemed miles, light-years away. *How* could he let this happen? *Why* had he let this happen? If he were really there at all … Her faith was badly shaken. She, herself, wasn't sure it would do any good to pray, but it might help the boys. She nodded.

Mrs. Donahoe reached out and grasped Reba and Willie's hands and bowed her head. The children followed suit.

"Dear God," she began. "We don't know why you let this happen. Why you would let a beautiful little girl be hit by a bullet intended for someone else or no one at all—just shot in anger. But we know you love the little children, and that you know every hair on our head, and that you see each sparrow that falls, and so we claim your promise to watch over us, and we ask that you take care of this little sparrow.

"Lord, you know the desires of our heart, but we know that you have an ultimate plan. Should our desires not meet with your plan, please give us the peace and strength we need. Amen."

"Amen," echoed Reba. She looked up into the solemn green eyes of Mrs. Donahoe, and the two held each other's gaze. Though the boys didn't understand, she knew what Mrs. Donahoe meant about God's ultimate plan. It meant that Jocelyn might die.

Once her mother arrived, Amanda did little more than sit back and watch and take it all in. First, she was taken aback by the stark poverty surrounding her, the squalid filth she had passed through just to reach this tiny apartment, and then the small oasis of cleanliness in such a meager setting. Though her family could barely be considered middle class, she had never thought anyone could survive with so little, but this tiny apartment, sparsely furnished, had proven her wrong. Yet there was a warmth, a closeness, and a spirit of God living here.

With moist eyes, she watched her mother comfort and console. *Lord, may I be a woman like that,* she prayed as her mother fixed each a cup of the hot chocolate she had brought with her and then hugged each boy and held him on her lap and talked to him. Then she sat next to Reba and put her arm around her and said nothing, as though she knew what the young girl was thinking.

Mrs. Donahoe had relinquished her spot on the couch for the boys who sought refuge next to their big sister, and when she prayed, Amanda bowed her head and listened intently, but added her own prayer at the end: *Please, God,* she wept, *don't let Jocelyn die.*

The hospital emergency room was strangely quiet for a Saturday afternoon. Doctors and nurses passed by in ghostly silence, exchanging information in guarded whispers. To an outsider it would hold an eerie quality, but to Mr. and Mrs. Washington, who sat with hands clasped tightly together and heads bent, it provided an atmosphere of worship, and both, though bound together by hands and hearts, were deep in their own thoughts and prayers.

My Lord, Mrs. Washington prayed for the hundredth time. *I know you love us and know what's best for us, but please restore my baby to health. Please bring back my little girl. I've lived without a lot, and been blessed by your presence through thin times, but I really don't know if I could make it without my little girl. Oh, Lord, please have mercy.*

Mr. Washington felt his wife's hand tremble, and he clasped it harder with his left hand while he pulled her tightly next to him with his right.

Oh, God," he prayed. *Give me strength, Lord, to hold my family together in the face of this tragedy. You know I want my little girl back, Lord. You know how badly I want that. But, Lord, should you decide to take her home, please, Lord, build me up and make me strong so that I can bring my loved ones through this time of grief.* He closed his eyes tighter, trying to control the emotions welling up inside him, but it was of no use. He felt the tears splatter on their clasped hands.

The phone rang again and again before going to voice mail again.

"Where could she be?" Alex wondered. He had seen her at the game, even after the game. But then she had just seemed to vanish. She hadn't waited for him, and she wasn't answering her phone.

He felt a bit miffed. And here he thought their relationship had just moved to another level. Well, maybe it had, but not the level he thought.

"Mr. Washington? Mrs. Washington?"

The two looked up in expectation, hoping to see a doctor standing before them with some news. Instead, they saw a middle-aged man, slightly balding, standing there, nervously crushing the brim of an old felt hat.

"Yes?" Mr. Washington said.

The man swallowed and smiled weakly. "You don't know me. My name is John Donahoe. My wife and daughter are with your children right now. I heard what happened, and I wondered if you would mind if I prayed with you. You know the Lord said, 'Where two or three are gathered in my name, there I am also.'"

Mr. Washington released the hand of his wife and stood to his full six-three height, towering over the man before him.

"Brother," he said, his eyes filling afresh with new tears. "We'd be mighty happy to have you pray with us."

With Reba's help, Mrs. Donahoe put the younger children to bed, reading them a story to take their minds off the situation. Amanda, left with nothing really to do, went to the kitchen to get a glass of water. Not until she saw the phone did she think of Alex. Reba came out of the bedroom and startled her.

"Sorry," Reba said and pulled down three more glasses.

"Reba, do you mind if I call Alex?" she asked. "He would really like to know what's happened."

Reba thought about it for a moment. She would rather no one know too much right now; it was all so uncertain. But she nodded, filled the glasses, and left. Amanda grabbed her purse and pulled out her phone.

Alex grabbed the phone on the second ring.

"Alex?"

"I wondered where you've been," he said. "Thought you'd given up on me since I only played all of two downs," he added teasingly.

"Alex," she began again, and he could sense the tension in her voice. "I can't talk long. I'm at Reba's. There was a shooting outside the stadium. Reba's little sister, Jocelyn, was shot."

Alex's heart froze in fear. "Oh, God, no," was all he could say.

"Alex." Amanda's voice brought him back. "Alex, you've got to pray."

Alex didn't know what to pray, so he just kept saying the same thing over and over. *Please, God, no,* he pleaded. *Please, no.* Everything had suddenly been going so well. The last three days had been wonderful. Didn't God want *anyone* to be happy? *Please, God, no,* he pleaded again, his heart heavy in his chest.

Chapter 32

"Graydon, please calm down. There must be an explanation," Martha pleaded. "Just sit down and think for a minute."

Graydon Richards wouldn't listen. As soon as the front door was opened, he headed straight for Danny's room, threw the door open, and started rifling through his belongings. He pulled every book off the shelf, opened every drawer, and took every piece of clothing out until the floor was strewn with clothes.

"Graydon, pleeease. What will Danny think? What will he say?"

"I really don't care what he thinks or says," Graydon replied and started for the desk.

"But what if you don't find anything?" she asked, distraught.

"I will," he said with a cold finality. "Whether it's in this room or not, I will."

The clock on the wall ticked incredibly loud, thought Martha. How long had they been sitting there in silence just waiting. She glanced at the offending object. A quarter to six. They had been waiting only about half an hour, but it seemed like an eternity. She could feel and hear her own heartbeat competing with the clock. What was going to happen? Her whole world was falling apart. Was Danny really doing drugs? Graydon seemed to think so.

"It all makes sense now," he had said after he had finished demolishing the room and had come up empty-handed. "The money. The lies."

"But you found nothing," Martha protested.

"Because I waited too long," he answered. "Didn't want to believe it, just like you don't want to believe it now." She couldn't think of anything more to say and so had stood there quietly and then started to clean up the room.

"Leave it," he said. "I did it. I'll clean it up later."

"It won't take lo—"

"Leave it!" he demanded. "I said I'd take care of it." And she knew that his words were laced with more meaning than just the room.

So they sat and waited. *We could be waiting for hours,* Martha thought. *Sometimes he doesn't come home till after ten.* She could feel the tension in the room growing with every tick of the clock. Then … another noise … footsteps on the porch. She stiffened. Graydon became instantly alert.

The doorknob turned. Her heart stopped. Graydon sat up … waiting. Danny entered the room.

"Hi," he said cheerfully, and when they didn't answer, he took a closer look, at his mother's pensive face and his father's cold, blistering stare. He licked his lips. "What's up?"

Graydon stood up and moved deliberately toward Danny, his icy eyes boring holes through his son.

"What's the matter, Dad?" he asked lightly, but felt himself shaking.

Graydon grabbed Danny's face in his right hand and squeezed tight, causing the boy's lips to pucker as he pulled Danny's face toward him. He looked hard, first in his left eye and then his right. Too scared to move, Danny didn't protest.

"You're as high as a kite," Graydon said and released his face with a push.

Danny tried to laugh it off. "I don't know what you're talking about," he said, shrugging his shoulders in an effort to straighten out his clothes.

"What is it? Marijuana? Or something stronger?"

Danny let out a jerky little laugh and glanced over at his mother for help, but all Martha could do was watch.

"Pull up your sleeves," Graydon demanded.

"What for?" Danny asked and took a step backward.

"Pull up your sleeves, I said."

"*No!* This is ridiculous!"

Graydon grabbed his arm before he could move any further and ripped the button off the cuff as he pulled Danny's sleeve up past his elbow. Danny tried to cover the bareness of his flesh with his other hand, but Graydon just pushed it aside. The needle marks were fully exposed. Martha gasped. Danny looked up at his father in fear. All Graydon could do was stare hard into his son's eyes. Now what was he supposed to do?

"Why?" Martha asked.

"Oh, why not?" Danny said, suddenly angry. "You and Dad had such high dreams for me, med school and all, and here I am a freshman and can't even pass the basic courses. I just couldn't handle it anymore. *You hear? I just can't take it!*"

The fear gone, he looked back up at his father with tired eyes. He had been caught, and he had confessed. The worst was over.

Graydon, too, seemed to have relaxed a bit. Somehow, finally knowing, finally having his suspicions confirmed, made it a lot easier to deal with. They could move on from here.

"Who sold you this stuff?" he asked calmly.

Danny looked up in horror. "I can't tell you that."

"Why not?"

"He'll kill me."

"He's killing you now. Who sold it to you?"

Danny shook his head. "I don't know his full name. All I know is his first name is Travis. He goes to Mom's school."

Martha gasped. "Travis Johnson?"

Danny shrugged. "I don't know—I told you. I don't know his full name."

"Is he black? About five ten, wears sunglasses all the time …" She went on to describe him in more detail.

Danny nodded. "Yeah, yeah. That sounds like him."

"Where does he live?" Graydon asked.

Danny stared in disbelief. "I don't know. I don't just go knocking on his door. We always met somewhere at the university." Graydon was not to be deterred.

"Martha, is he one of your students?" She nodded. "Then you have his home address don't you?"

She nodded again. "In my gradebook."

"Then get it please."

"But Graydon," she protested. "This could be dangerous."

He turned to her and his eyes were on fire. "This," he said and grabbed Danny's arm and pointed to the line of purple needle marks, "is dangerous! Now, please, get that address."

Travis sat in the empty house, shivering in the corner chair, the huge Bible lying shut in his lap. *She can't be dead,* he thought, rocking back and forth. *She just can't be dead.*

What was he going to do? He didn't mean to run away, not completely. He had first backed up because he had felt sick to his stomach. Funny, he had seen blood plenty of times before, but this was different.

Then, when he was outside the circle, he had just started to run. There was nothing he could do there. Too many people, especially the police, might be looking for him. The Washingtons were only in more danger if he stayed, right? he asked himself, trying to justify his actions. But the answers only brought more misery.

Who was he fooling? Here he had thought he was saving them, protecting them. What an arrogant idiot he had been. It was because of *him* that Jocelyn was hurt, maybe even dead. Did they know it was his fault? Did they blame him? Were the police looking for him now?

He felt that dull wrenching in his gut. He wanted to go back, to find out how she was, yet he was afraid to know. Afraid to be found out. But he had to do something. What?

He looked down at the Bible in his hands. He had no idea why he had picked it up. Perhaps just for something to hold on to, to grasp. He flicked it open and stared at the hundred-dollar bill that looked back at him.

That's it! he thought, his heart beating faster. *That's it! The money. I'll pay for the hospital costs.* "That is, if she's still alive," a tiny voice whispered back, but he tried to shake it out of his mind. "Please, God," he said as he scrambled through pages looking for money. "Please keep her alive."

He had no idea that he was praying. In his own mind it was only a subconscious thought. All he knew was for him to have a chance to save her life, she had to still be alive. In order for him to help, to be back in control, she had to be waiting for him in the hospital.

Travis felt a sense of renewed hope as he pulled out bill after bill, trying hard not to look at the words on the pages, those words that had started haunting him. But there they were, every now and then rearing their ugly head to plant new uncertainties in him.

"And the deeds of a man's hands will return to him."

"Wealth obtained by fraud dwindles."

"For what does it profit a man to gain the whole world and forfeit his soul."

"Their soul melted away in their misery. They reeled and staggered like a drunken man, And were at their wits' end."

"Ahhhhh," he screamed and pushed his hands clasped full of money against his ears. "Stop! Please, stop!"

He heard a pounding, and he shook his head harder, trying to get rid of the incessant throbbing, but soon realized that the noise was not coming from his head but from the door. He froze, and his heart stopped abruptly, and he felt a chill sweep over him. Was it the police? Reba? Were they here to tell him she was dead?

He didn't want to move, but the pounding continued more incessantly.

"Open up in there!" a man's voice yelled.

Somehow the idea of a confrontation comforted Travis. It was something he was familiar with. It would take his mind off of those verses and those voices. He stuffed the money back into the Bible, stood up, and moved to the door. He could even handle the police if he had to. After all, how many times had he played games with them before.

He opened the door, telling himself that all was well, that he could handle it. His eyes widened in surprise when he saw a man in his forties, dressed not in uniform but in jeans and a jacket.

"Travis Johnson?" the man asked. Travis forgot himself and nodded. "My name is Graydon Richards, Danny's father." He pushed the door further open and stepped inside and looked around briefly. "We need to talk."

Chapter 33

"Have you been selling drugs to my son?"

Graydon Richards had wasted no time in getting down to business. He had set himself down on the couch, and Travis had plopped back in the corner chair where he had been all evening. He was tired. Too tired to deny anything anymore. He just wanted it all to be over, to get out from under it all, but still he wasn't going to take the fall for Danny Richards. That was his own doing.

"Yeah, I sold him the drugs," he said. "But I didn't make him take them," he lashed out.

Graydon pulled his lips into a tight line. That was true enough.

"I agree," he said and sat forward on the edge of the couch, his hands clasped and his elbows resting on his knees. This confrontation was not what he had expected, at all. To be honest, despite how angry he was, he had been more than a little scared about coming over here. Besides the roughness of the neighborhood, he had no idea how a drug dealer would react to his questions, and he really hadn't expected a confession. There was more going on here, but what?

"Can you tell me what he was on?" he asked.

Travis let out a long sigh. "Marijuana mostly, to calm his nerves.

He was a real worrier that one. Then a couple of weeks ago, he moved on to heroin. They all do."

Graydon licked his lips. The kid was being honest with him. "Is it tough to break?"

Travis let out a little laugh. "It's all tough to break," he said, and Graydon felt that Travis's mind was on more than just the subject at hand. Graydon continued.

"I want you to stop selling to my son," he said flatly.

Travis released a little snort. "No problem," he said. "He wasn't coming up with the money anyway. But that doesn't mean he won't try and get it somewhere else." He paused. "Besides, I've got more important things to worry about."

Graydon looked at the boy carefully. He had lowered his shield, just a bit, and let him in. Was that on purpose or by accident? Should he push a bit more? The boy was obviously hurting in a deep way. Oh, what did he have to lose?

"Like what?" he asked.

Neither Graydon Richards nor Travis Johnson had expected the outpouring of guilt and fear that followed. Through shameless tears, Travis spilled it all and felt purged but not cured.

"But I can help," he said lifting the Bible in his hands. "If she's still alive, I can help."

Graydon stared at the Bible. What was this young punk drug dealer saying? That he was a Christian? That his prayers would be answered?

"See?" Travis said, flipping through the Bible and pulling out crumpled bills. "I have lots of money. I can pay for the doctors. I can pay for anything."

Graydon suddenly understood. "Is that all drug money?" he asked softly. Travis looked at the bills in his hands.

"Yeah, so?"

"So you think that after all the lives your drugs might have ruined, you can redeem yourself by buying a life back?"

Travis stared at him a moment and then grew angry. "*No!* That's not it at all!" he shouted. "I just want to help. I want to do something!"

Graydon thought for a moment. Maybe he was being too hard. Maybe this was what God meant by "all things work together for good," but it was tough to tell. There was way too much bad wrapped up in all of this. Yet, he was here, the Bible was here, Travis's heart was open …

Thumping footsteps and coarse laughter in the hallway caused both to cease talking. Graydon saw Travis immediately stuff the bills back in the Bible and then just freeze and stare at the door.

Instinctively, he turned, too, as the door of the apartment was flung open and a woman somewhere in her late thirties and looking like she had seen the harder side of life entered. She was wobbling and held up by a man twice her age but just as drunk. The two were all over each other, and at first neither seemed to notice Graydon or Travis.

When they finally rose for air, she caught sight of them and broke away, then smiled sweetly, trying to maintain her balance. "Well, well, well," she slurred. "What have we here?"

"Hello, Mother," Travis stated blandly.

Martha sat on the edge of the couch, twisting her wedding ring nervously, then wringing her hands, completely at a loss as to what to do. *Where did we fail?* she wondered. *What did we do wrong? We had to do something wrong for our son to turn to drugs. And we never even knew.* She felt a sense of pervasive guilt. *Well, Graydon suspected long ago,* she conceded. *It was I who stood in his way of a confrontation. Perhaps if I had let him …*

"How are your classes going?" she asked, trying to strike up some kind of conversation and sound casual.

Danny rolled his eyes. "How do you think they're going?" he asked sarcastically.

Martha felt a stab of pain. A semester lost as well. Had she been too wrapped up with the kids at school and their problems that she had blinded herself from her own family's problems? Had she thought her family immune from the temptations of the world? Or had she just naturally thought God would watch over them without any input from her?

The questions and the blame kept flying through her head for what seemed like an interminable time, and the silence grew heavier. For a woman who had her days organized to the hour, loved to have her class activities scheduled to the minute, and thrived on that feeling of control, this situation threw her. This situation forced her to look inside and admit her portion of the blame. Sure it was Danny's ultimate decision, but he had decided to turn to chemicals rather than his family. And that meant there was an inherent problem somewhere.

"I'm sorry, Danny," she said quietly. "Forgive me."

"And who are you? The police?" Mrs. Johnson asked, staggering to the nearest kitchen chair. The combination of alcohol and tight skirt made maneuvering tough. She pulled a drag on her cigarette and then looked for an ashtray. When she found none, she flicked the ashes on the kitchen table before collapsing in the chair.

Between the smell of stale alcohol and fresh cigarette smoke, Graydon found breathing difficult, but he tried not to cough or wave the stench away from his nose. The tension in the room was palpable, and he didn't want to set her off.

"No," he replied politely.

She took another prolonged drag and then lifted her head toward the lamp and exhaled long and slow. "Well, I know you're not from the school," and she laughed coarsely. "They could care less." She gave him the once-over. "So you must be a buyer. Though I have to admit you don't look much like one of his usual junkie friends."

Graydon felt Travis tense up even more. *What should I say?* he thought. It was more than obvious that there was no love here, but how bad might it get for the boy if he were to tell the truth. He glanced over at Travis, who now looked rather young and vulnerable. Heck, this lady even scared *him*.

"I'm a youth pastor from a neighboring church," he lied and immediately prayed for forgiveness. "I was just making cold calls in the area, trying to drum up a little business, you know," and he gave a little laugh, "and Travis let me in. I was just showing him a couple of interesting things in the Bible."

The cigarette stopped midair, and Travis's mother seemed to sober quickly. For a long minute, she just stared at Graydon and then finally crushed out her cigarette on the table, shook her head in complete disbelief, and laughed.

"You have *got* to be kidding," she said and then tried to stand up but had to grab onto both the back of the chair and the table to maintain her balance. She swallowed a belch and then pointed first at Graydon and then at Travis.

"Well, I can save you some time, Reverend," she slurred, and Graydon felt the sting of embarrassment from the delusion. "There's no hope for this punk. He's going to burn in hell longer than Satan himself."

Graydon felt Travis stiffen again, and his own anger kindled. How was that for a mother to talk about her own son? He refrained from what he wanted to say and let out a little casual laugh.

"Well, don't underestimate the power of God," he quipped and then proceeded quickly. "How about if Travis and I just finish our conversation outside? Do you need him for anything at the moment?"

She had walked over to the kitchen counter, followed by her silent and stumbling partner, but looked over at Travis with disdain. "He's good for nothing," she said scornfully. "I've never needed him for anything."

With that answer, Graydon was up on his feet, clapping his hands against his pant legs. "Well, then, we'll just be on our way. Do you mind if we take the Bible with us?"

Another coughing, cynical laugh. "Didn't even know we had one."

"Well, then," and he almost pulled Travis up from his seat and herded him toward the door, trying to figure out at just what point he had moved from Travis's accuser to his defender.

Danny stared in disbelief at his mother. This was not quite the response he had expected. Where was the righteous indignation about wasting his life, the lecture about turning to his family for help, the speech about ruining a perfectly good future? He had heard each of those before in miniature when he had felt his parents out about maybe taking some time off from school or changing majors. So where were they now when everything had hit the fan with a flying leap?

He dropped his eyes for a moment and then glanced furtively back at his mother. She was wrestling with herself, he could tell. There was torture written all over her face. What was she thinking? He didn't have to wait long.

"Do you like drugs?" she asked almost painfully.

For a second time, Danny's mouth dropped open, and he could only stare. He had *never* expected *that* question. But it got him thinking. Did he like drugs? Really? He chewed on his lower lip in thought.

Yeah. Sort of. The initial complete release from reality was heaven, but the return was far from it. As the drug wore off, the guilt and the need came surging back. Then there was the lying, and the pain he suffered as his conscience cut into his flesh, from the inside. And what about the alienation? If he thought about it, he really had no one he could share it with. In fact, he had to hide if from everyone, except those others who did drugs.

But they didn't care a thing about him—drugs was their only tie. No, it had been a very lonely life. And the money. He always had to have more money because the need always returned. The need *never* went away. It was never satisfied; it only grew and grew, like a cancer. It kept eating more and more of him until he had to have more and more. He must have been silent too long because she asked the question again.

"Do you, Danny?" she asked, and he could hear her pain. "Do you like drugs?"

His head came up and he looked straight into her eyes for the first time in more than two months and bared his soul.

"No," he said, shaking his head, but never letting his eyes leave hers. "No, Mom, I don't."

Chapter 34

As the evening wore on, the activity in the emergency ward grew. Sirens blared constantly; paramedic crews, with stoic efficiency, whisked in victims of gunshots and stabbings, automobile accidents, and multiple other crises. Nurses and doctors hustled back and forth through swinging doors.

Mr. and Mrs. Washington watched the constant activity with weary eyes. They had been sitting, praying, waiting for almost four hours for some news. John Donahoe, who had gone to get some coffee for them all, was carefully working his way back toward their seats, trying to balance the three brimming paper cups. Mr. Washington saw him and stood to help him out just as the surgery doors opened and a doctor, green surgical shirt drenched in sweat, walked tiredly through, pulling his surgical mask and cap off his head. Mr. Washington stopped.

The doctor saw them, smiled weakly, and walked slowly toward them. All three hearts ceased beating when he stopped in front of them and looked down at his hands.

"The bullet is out," he said, first looking at Mrs. Washington and then focusing on Mr. Washington. "But it tore her up inside pretty good, and she had lost a lot of blood by the time we got her. The bullet passed very close to the heart. Wouldn't be quite so serious for an adult, but she's so little."

Neither said anything. Both waited. The final word had not been given.

"She's not out of the woods yet, still critical," the doctor warned, "and she hasn't regained consciousness, but she is resting, and the vital signs are fluctuating around normal now."

Mrs. Washington released a small sigh. The first news at least was positive. Her daughter was still alive. The doctor smiled warmly at her and then turned back to Mr. Washington.

"Why don't you and your wife go home and get a few hours rest," he suggested. "If she regains consciousness, we'll call you immediately. But I really don't see anything happening right away. She's out of immediate danger. We'll just have to wait and see if anything else might crop up."

Mr. Washington turned toward his wife, but she shook her head. "I'd rather stay," she said. "I'll be okay, but why don't you go. I'd feel more comfortable if one of us were here."

He knew no amount of arguing would change her mind, and he would rather one of them be here, too. And if one of them had to walk the streets at night, he wanted it to be him, not her.

"I'll go home and check on the kids and then relieve you in the morning," he said and bent over to kiss her. "God is watching over her," he whispered, and he felt moisture against his cheek when she nodded.

"It's up here."

Graydon followed Travis through the front door of yet another dilapidated apartment building and up the narrow stairs. He still hadn't figured out when he had turned into Travis's helper—protector almost—but he wasn't going to fight it. Though a Christian since his late teens, and one who believed in God's guidance and providence, he had never actually seen it in process, never seen the overall picture from God's point of view while still in the midst of the chaos. Normally, it was only in retrospect that he could see God's guiding hand.

That was not the case now. Though he wasn't exactly sure what his role was to be, he knew God had placed him here, in this situation, at this time, for this young man in trouble. It was the most exciting thing he had ever experienced, and he wasn't going to miss it. Sure, he still had trouble at home, but even in that circumstance he could see God working.

He and Martha and Danny had been three ships crossing in the day and then shoring up at the same dock at night. They had grown distant, and suddenly God allowed a situation that brought them back together in a very stark and intimate way. But that would have to come later. Right now …

"This is it."

Travis had stopped in front of apartment 324 and just stood there. Gone was the cool, almost flippant, demeanor, and Graydon swore he could feel the boy shaking inside.

Travis stared at the door a long time, wanting yet not wanting to knock. What was the news? Did they blame him for running away? For Jocelyn getting shot? Did they hate him? This home was his one, his only refuge on earth. Had he sacrificed it? His whole body trembled in slight convulsions.

Never in his life had he felt so scared, so hopeless, so desperate. He clung even harder to the big Bible in his hands to calm himself and then knocked on the door.

Reba jumped at the sound of the knock and was at the door before the others actually realized what had happened. She flung it open in expectation, and when she saw Travis and Mr. Richards standing there, her face and heart dropped in disappointment. Travis noticed and felt his body drain of life. Reba then caught herself and corrected her social error.

"Hi," she said, trying to sound congenial. "I'm sorry. I just thought you were someone with some news."

"Wouldn't they call?" Travis asked.

"Oh, yeah, probably. Well, I guess I wasn't thinking."

"So you haven't heard anything yet?" he asked tentatively. At this point, no news was good news. She was possibly still alive.

Reba shook her head. "Not yet." For a second time she remembered her manners. "Would you like to come in?" she asked and then looked at Graydon curiously. Graydon reached his hand around Travis.

"I'm Graydon Richards," he said. "Mrs. Richards's husband. I ran into Travis, and he told me what happened. He was pretty shook up. I hope you don't mind my coming with him."

Reba shook her head, amazed at how fast the news traveled, and she stepped aside to let them in. Everyone else in the room stood and introductions were quickly made.

"The younger ones are already in bed," Mrs. Donahoe explained to Mr. Richards. "The rest of us were just praying silently."

Graydon nodded in understanding and then glanced at Travis out of the corner of his eye. "Would anyone mind if I said a quick prayer as well?" he asked. Looks were exchanged. No one objected.

"Have a seat," Mrs. Donahoe said and pulled out two kitchen chairs. Graydon sat down, followed by Travis, who still clutched the Bible. No one asked about it.

Graydon bowed his head, and Reba, Amanda, and Mrs. Donahoe followed suit. Travis watched, bewildered, and then not really knowing why, bowed his head.

"Father," Graydon began. "First of all, we know that you are watching over us right at this very minute. We know that you love the little children and Jocelyn especially, and, Lord, we know in the Bible that David reminds us that when they 'cried to the Lord in their trouble, … He brought them out of their distresses." Well, Lord, you know that each of us is crying out to you in his or her own way. Please hear us and walk us through this hour of need."

While the others were probably taking comfort in Graydon's words and the words of King David, Travis felt a chill sweep through his body at the mention of the Bible. His brief experience with it had brought nothing but fear. Those verses, those haunting verses about being dust, and about God breaking a person down forever, then snatching him up, and tearing him away from his tent, and uprooting him, and all that kind of stuff because the person loved evil—that's what he remembered about the Bible, and that's why he was scared spitless. He was one who had devised a lot of evil in his short life.

Or that verse that said something about their soul melting away in misery, and they were at their wits' end. That described him perfectly. At his wit's end.

But this verse—this verse he didn't recall. And this one had a different ring to it. One of hope. Unconsciously, he clutched the Bible a little tighter.

Mr. Washington stepped off the bus and walked the last couple of blocks home. He was tired, there was no doubt about that, but he was also feeling very much revived. Prayer—true prayer, not the three-minute duty session some people held in the morning, but true, heart-cleansing prayer—does that to a person. It brings you so close to God that some of his glory stays with you, an afterglow.

He breathed a long, tired sigh. Jocelyn was not out of the woods yet, and she may not make it, but he still felt a peace in his heart, and … what else was it? … a sense of anticipation? Yes, that might describe it. That God was going to show his glory through this. How, he wasn't sure, but he was willing to wait, for right now all he wanted to do was get home and go to bed.

The door opened, and five heads turned in unison. Mr. Washington stopped and looked as surprised as those who stared back.

"Dad," Reba said, but this time she didn't jump up. She watched him carefully, looking for some clue. "How's Jocelyn?" she finally asked.

Mr. Washington smiled tiredly. "Better," he answered quietly. "Your mother and God are still watching over her, and I'm not sure which is the more tenacious," he said with a wan grin.

Graydon stood and introduced himself. "Graydon Richards. My wife is Reba's teacher. I hooked up with Travis here and stopped by."

The look he gave Mr. Washington told volumes about what was going through the mind and heart of the young man sitting before him. Mr. Washington was no fool. He had lived in the ghettos of Detroit long enough to know exactly what Travis's occupation was and that his youngest daughter's condition could be directly related to it. He had also been a Christian long enough to recognize a young man hurting deeply and searching.

"Reba," he said quietly. "Your sister's resting easy now. Why don't you try to get some rest, too. I'll take you all to the hospital tomorrow."

Reba didn't argue, but rose to leave. Amanda put a hand out to stop her. "Call me?" she asked, and her eyes transmitted the sympathy she could not verbalize. Reba nodded and left the room.

"We'll be going now, too," Mrs. Donahoe said. "Amanda, get your things."

"Thank you," Mr. Washington said to her, reaching for her

hand and holding it in both of his. "For everything. And thank your husband again for his support."

Mrs. Donahoe smiled. "We're not through yet," she said.

From the warmth of her bed, Reba heard the close of the door and the deep voices of the men out in the living room. Travis had looked awful tonight, she thought. Almost pale—if a black boy could be pale—and weak. Had he been shot, too? She dismissed the idea almost immediately.

No, he'd be at the hospital, not here, if he had. Maybe it was just concern over Jocelyn, but if it was, she had never seen that much concern from him ever. Maybe it was ... She was too tired to keep thinking, and in another minute, she was fast asleep.

Chapter 35

Travis woke up to the sun streaming through the one narrow window of the Washingtons' apartment. For a moment he forgot where he was and then it all came flooding back to him. Mr. Richards, Mr. Washington, Jesus. He smiled self-consciously and felt kind of weird. Most of his life he had used the word *Jesus* as a cuss word. Now, however …

He rolled over on the narrow couch and laid there contentedly. He could never remember feeling like this in the morning, where he was at peace with himself and actually looking forward to the day. He breathed in deeply and then remembered Jocelyn, and a heaviness swept over him. Mr. Washington said that might happen. He said that just because he accepted Jesus as his Savior and all his past sins were forgiven that that didn't mean he could skirt the consequences or that he didn't still have to deal with the feelings of guilt.

"And remember," he had warned, "life doesn't automatically get better or easier for you. If anything, you might find things a bit stickier. After all, Satan's not going to be too thrilled about you switching teams."

Travis pulled the blanket up around him, and his eyes fell on the big Bible on the coffee table. "No more hidden treasure in you, is there?" he said to it hoarsely. Mr. Washington had not hesitated to accept the money for his daughter's expenses.

"That's one thing too many pious people don't understand," he had said. "That God can use the unjust to fulfill his plans for the just." He took all the money Travis handed him and gave it a quick count. "Oh, I bet ya this isn't going to set well with Satan at all," he added with a grin.

Travis suddenly realized the irony of his words and sat up. *Actually, now that the money's gone, all that's left is the hidden treasure.* He lifted the Bible off the table and grinned again to himself, remembering how frightened he was of even looking in it last night when Mr. Washington had opened it up.

"You should be scared," Mr. Washington had said, and Mr. Richards had agreed. "Solomon himself said that 'the fear of the LORD is the beginning of knowledge.' If you ask me, there aren't *enough* people out there afraid of him. But you have to know both sides of him. He's just, which means when the day of reckonin' comes, you'll be held accountable for all you've done. But he's also loving. Here, let me show you a few verses."

Travis now opened the Bible to one of the markers: "Cease striving and know that I am God."

He turned to another: "Bread obtained by falsehood is sweet to a man, but afterward his mouth will be filled with gravel."

Boy, did he know the truth behind that or what? And then there were the promises: "The LORD sustains all who fall, and raises up all who are bowed down," and "the LORD will accomplish what concerns me."

And then his favorite: "For God so loved the world that He gave his one and only Son, that whoever believes in Him shall not perish but have eternal life."

He closed the Bible and then closed his eyes. There was still a strong possibility that Jocelyn would not recover, and he would have to live with that the rest of his life, and yet because of his decision last night, he could still feel a peace in his soul, a peace that said God had rescued him early enough in his life so that he might make a difference, a peace that he had felt so often in this house and now felt within himself.

Reba sat stiffly in the pew and listened to the singing around her. She felt tired and years older. Had it only been last week that she had sung similar hymns and worship songs with empty and free abandon? With her mother and father at one end and she at the other, with all the little ones in between?

She looked down the pew. Willie was singing in his own self-conscious fashion. Jake, his clear, rich soprano, was belting out the lyrics with true gusto, while little three-year-old Chris just lifted his voice and sang any words that seemed to fit the music and the moment.

Reba felt a firm wrenching in her heart. Three people were conspicuously missing: her mother, her father—and Jocelyn. She swallowed hard.

Her father had left early that morning to relieve her mother at the hospital. When she had arrived home, she gathered the children together.

"There's been no change," she had said softly. "I need to get some sleep, but I'd like you children to go to church. Reba, will you get them all ready and take them?"

She had agreed and went through the motions of getting the boys set to go. Like the day before, Travis had disappeared. She thought little of it, but when they left their apartment building, he had been waiting for them, with a clean shirt and pants on and wearing what she guessed were his best shoes.

Like always, he fell into step with them, saying nothing. She sensed something different about him but couldn't lay her finger on it. Was it the way he walked? The way he carried himself? Just the air about him was different somehow. And then she had received the shock of her life. Instead of depositing them at the steps of First Neighborhood Church, he followed them in and sat himself down at the end of the pew.

She had looked at him furtively all service. His face was noncommittal as it always was, but there was a softness around the edges. And his eyes (minus their ever present Ray-Bans), what was it about his eyes? The hardness, the penetrating stare—they were gone as well, replaced by pain and sorrow.

But there was something else. It was the aura about him. The cockiness was gone, and in its place a sense of peace about him that she had never witnessed before. Something had happened yesterday, and at the present she was not privy to it. But she vaguely realized that her weekly, glib prayer for Travis might be getting answered, and at a price more costly than she had ever imagined.

She turned back toward the pulpit and stared at the sea of heads before her, but her mind was not on the singing or the message today. Last week she had sat in this pew as an innocent child, happy as only a child can be, oblivious to the pain of the world, confident in a God who took perfect care of her.

But her peaceful little world had been shattered. All year it had been rattled a bit, just a bit, just a little at a time, but yesterday it had been wrenched from her. How silly losing a part in a play seemed now when the loss of a life was so precariously close.

And yet, although Reba couldn't really say she was happy today, she could say she felt a sense of peace, a peace and joy deeper than she had ever felt before. She had been angry with God earlier this year with the play, and had worked her way through that, seeing more of God's overall plan with Alex. So now, even though Jocelyn's life hung in the balance, and her own life seemed twisted out of shape, she was willing to wait a little longer to see.

She glanced back down to the end of the pew to where Travis sat listening to the pastor's words. He was a part of God's plan, she knew that. Yesterday had changed his life probably more so than hers, she thought. But still, what a terrible price for a little four-year-old girl to have to pay.

But to God, all lives were sacred. All lives were valuable. She turned her attention back to the pastor as he asked them to open their hymnbooks to page 316 for the final hymn of the morning. Reba looked at the words. How many times had she sung this hymn without ever really thinking about the words? Well, today, she understood their full impact.

All to Jesus I surrender, All to Him I freely give;
I will ever love and trust Him, In His presence daily live.
I surrender all, I surrender all.
All to Thee, my blessed Saviour, I surrender all.

Alex waited in front of the Donahoe house for them to return from church. He had called earlier that morning under the guise of finding out how Reba's little sister was. He really did want to know. He had prayed what felt like all night that she might be better. But he had known deep down that Amanda probably wouldn't know too much. His real reason for calling was to see if she would meet him for lunch. Their first official date—kind of. After all, it was sort of spur of the moment. But he had learned some things over the past couple of weeks and then another last night. Now he needed to talk about them.

He had been right. She hadn't known much about Jocelyn, only that she was in critical condition and still unconscious. The news had sobered him. So sad; such a little girl. Reba had had her share of sorrows this year, that was for sure. But Amanda had agreed to meet him, and so here he stood—thirty minutes early for his first date.

Amanda had never experienced such a long church service in her life. The pastor's running joke that he could speak until three might just become a reality today. He was only on point two of a four-pointer and according to her calculations, if they were to be excused on time, he had about ten minutes for the last two points, five for the last hymn and invitation, and then a brief—and she repeated—*brief* prayer.

She hadn't heard any of the sermon. Her mind was in three different directions at once. First, Reba and her little sister. How tragic. She sent up another prayer for her recovery. And then there was the appearance of Travis Johnson—drug lord of Montgomery High—at the Washington home, with Mr. Richards no less. She had yet to figure that one out.

And then there was Alex. Her heart raced just at the thought of him. She couldn't believe how much she cared for him, and she had only known him for over a month. Her parents would chalk that up to immaturity, yet she knew it was much more. And most of that had to do with the last two weeks.

She had been more than pleased when he had called this morning. Just hearing his voice made her feel good. Then his genuine concern for Jocelyn. He was so sensitive. And then the date. It was perfect timing. She had wanted to see him, to talk to him, to tell him all that was on her mind, to define their relationship.

Amanda stopped herself. Maybe she shouldn't do that. She had heard from some of her friends that talking about a relationship was often the death of it. And what was it her Sunday school teacher had said a while back, when it meant absolutely nothing to her? That girls tend to be body modest and soul free, and boys, soul modest and body free?

At the time she hadn't been sure what he meant, but now it was beginning to dawn on her. She wanted to bare her soul to Alex, share everything she felt, lay it all out there for him to scoop up. But maybe that would make him uneasy. Guys didn't like to talk about their feelings much. That's what was meant by "soul modest." Well, then, she would just have to be content with his company, and as Mary, Jesus's mother did, "hide all these things in her heart."

"Is your pizza okay?" Alex asked for the umpteenth time.

"Perfect," Amanda answered again. This was getting a little annoying. What had happened? Yesterday, it didn't seem like they could be any closer. That their hearts and souls were in synch. But today. Man, they were miles apart. There was an awkwardness in the air. Was Alex having second thoughts about their budding relationship? He really seemed on edge.

"Not too spicy?" he asked, and she let out an exasperated sigh. She had had enough.

"What's wrong, Alex?" she asked. "You've been more concerned over my pizza than you would be over the outcome of the Super Bowl. What gives? What's bothering you?"

Alex swallowed. Despite the burden on his heart that he wished to share, he just couldn't get up the nerve to spill it. In the security of his room last night, the speech had sounded wonderful, but now when he sat across from Amanda, facing her eye to eye, and her no more than just a little irritated, suddenly his courage seemed to abandon him. If he told her, she would think him silly, sentimental, sissy. If he didn't, he would burst.

Best not to burst, he decided. He smiled wanly. "Sorry," he said. "It's just that I'm having a hard time getting up my nerve to say what I want to say."

Amanda stared at him for a minute. The only time she had ever seen guys this nervous was on TV when they were going to ask someone to marry them. Surely *that* couldn't be his intention. This was their first date!

"Well, find it fast," she urged. "We're running out of pizza for you to dote over."

He grinned at her, his nervousness abating a little. That's one of the things he liked about her. She pulled no punches. All right then; he could do the same. He grabbed his Coke glass, took a big gulp and then a deep breath, and dove in, keeping his eyes on his hands.

"I've learned something during the last two weeks, and I wanted to share it with you," he began and glanced up at her. Her expression hadn't changed. She just waited expectantly, and he had no idea that her heart was racing as fast as his.

"When I first ran into you—" he said. "Correction. When I first almost ran into the post and, consequently, met you," he said with a grin, "I thought I was in love."

Amanda felt her heart drop. *Thought he was?*

"You were the most beautiful girl in the world. You still are," he corrected himself again. "You've got a great figure and you're smart and you're funny and you're—"

Amanda held up her hand. "I get the picture," she said with a slight smile. "I'm God's perfect female, right?" She gave him her best "get real" look. Alex grinned.

"To me, yes," he answered. "And then when you seemed to like me, took an interest in me. Well, I didn't think life could get any better."

He stopped for a breath and to regather his thoughts. Amanda said nothing.

"But, you know," he continued, "as much as I liked you and as good as it felt to be around you, it wasn't until I shared my disability with you, my dyslexia, that I realized we hadn't really been *that* close. I mean, we had only been sharing the physical parts of ourselves with each other: our looks, our personalities …"

Amanda felt her heart speed up again. This was what she had been thinking. Could he really be about to say what she had longed to say?

"By sharing in that knowledge and knowing my frustrations and then my dreams, well, I felt like we were drawn even closer." He looked at her and spoke softly. "Though quite a few now know I have dyslexia, I haven't shared those frustrations and dreams with many people."

She nodded, her eyes speaking the volumes she longed to say.

"And then last night," he said, "when you called and asked me to pray for Jocelyn." He shook his head. "Amanda, I have never prayed with anyone before. As I was praying last night, and knew you were praying too, I felt that I was sharing the very core of myself with you. Do you know what I mean?"

Alex looked at her, almost pleading. He had said it all. He had laid himself out on the pizzeria table for her to see, and if she wanted, she could do some real damage.

Amanda smiled at him and their eyes locked. "I know exactly what you mean," she said softly. "I'm not trying to rush things at all, but it makes you understand what Jesus meant when he said, 'Do not be yoked together with unbelievers.' There would be something so vital missing, wouldn't there? That spiritual element."

Alex felt his whole body relax. She understood. And then he chided himself. Of course, she understood. She was God's perfect female, wasn't she?

Martha pulled a stack of papers out of her briefcase and then curled her legs up under her on the couch and let out a sigh. On the other side of the lamp from her, Graydon read the paper in his La-Z-Boy, and across the room, Danny sat at the dining room table, his books spread out before him in a concerted effort to get some studying done. From all outward appearances, the scene looked about as normal as ever. But as Martha took it all in, she reminded herself, "But by the grace of God."

The papers lay abandoned in her lap. Her eyes had been opened. Obsessed with controlling all within her grasp, and actually thinking she could, she had come precariously close to losing most of it. She hadn't been overly domineering, but then maybe that was the insidiousness of it all. Like the frog placed in cool water, which is gradually warmed until he is boiled without a whimper, so had those she loved or been given charge over succumbed to her demands until they too might have lost their lives.

She glanced at Danny. She had had such dreams and ambitions for him. Therein lay the problem. Those dreams were hers. She watched him working. Late last night, a compromise had been reached. He was to try and salvage what he could of the semester, and then he could choose his own options next semester.

Martha felt her heart twist a little. She had seen his hands shaking this morning as he was sitting in church. Had he wanted a fix? He had sat on them to hide the twitching, but she knew it wasn't going to be that easy. Yet he was trying.

She looked over at Graydon, still trying to get the hang of his bifocals, and smiled to herself. Martha had forgotten how insightful and sensitive this man she had married over twenty years ago was, but last night brought all of that back into sharp focus. After a long evening with Travis, Graydon had come home to begin mending the fabric of their fragile relationship with their son. He had dealt firmly yet lovingly with Danny, setting down the rules, then giving of himself to help Danny keep them.

Just like you, Lord, she thought. *You had to deal sharply, justly with me to wake me up, didn't you? But you are still all-loving. The problem was really just a matter of who was in control, wasn't it?*

CPSIA information can be obtained at www.ICGtesting.com
Printed in the USA
BVOW07s0859200215

388520BV00002B/2/P